UNTIL THE STARS DON'T SHINE

SILVER SCREEN SECRETS: BOOK 1

JOANNE HO

*For anyone who has ever needed a hero in their life.
This one goes out to mine.*

*My thanks go to BETA readers Mary Cline, Candy Robosky
and Tonya Gillon for their keen eyes and knowledge.*

SIGN UP TO JOANNE'S NEWSLETTER!

Don't miss another release!
Be the first to hear Joanne's news, book releases, and giveaways.
Apply for her ARC teams (she has one for ebooks AND one for audiobooks) to get free, advanced copies of her books to read/listen to and review.

Plus, you'll get a free book as a thank you for signing up! What's not to like?

Sign up and join the rest of the romance fans and dog lovers at www.johoscribe.com

1

———

He pored over the grainy photographs that covered the length of one wall.

Rubbed his eyes that were stinging from hours of staring, hours of working in the airless, dark, and dank room.

Stuck in a haphazard fashion, the photographs overlapped one another, blocking out much of the shot though that was of no importance.

Whether it was the row of snooty shops on Rodeo Drive that he wasn't brave enough to go into, or the grounds of the luxury estate that she called home, he didn't care what was in the background.

Only the person who had been carefully framed in the center of each photograph mattered.

He waited in the near blackness, breath held as he slid the exposed sheet into the tray of developer solution. Picking up the end of the tray, he agitated it, letting the chemical wash over every inch of the sheet.

The acrid smell of the solution stung his nose and

often gave him a headache, but there was no other choice: he couldn't have these photographs developed at a store — not if he didn't want to raise alarm bells.

It was a small price to pay for the miracle at hand.

He waited, calmly watching the liquid squish back and forth, knowing that patience was a virtue. It had been a hard lesson to learn as a young boy, but he could see now that he had benefited from it, and while he didn't cherish the memories, he had begrudgingly learned from them.

A picture of himself came into his mind, of a skinny, starving, small-even-for-his-age four-year-old, sucking his thumb and sobbing into his mother's chest.

He hadn't eaten since the night before. When would food be coming? *Patience child,* had always been the answer. *We're all hungry. As soon as we have some money, we'll get food.*

He needed to study, but the lights wouldn't work, why weren't they turning on? *Patience child, we just need the electricity to switch back on... once we've paid the bill.*

After walking hours to get home from school in the pouring rain with shoes whose soles had eroded away, he'd pleaded for a new pair only to be told: *patience child, one day we'll have enough money that you won't ever have to worry about holes in your shoes.*

How well that patience was serving him now.

He stared at the print, his mind playing over those desperately unhappy periods of his childhood as again, he wondered how life could be so unfair to some yet overload others with so many blessings that they couldn't even count them.

He ruminated over his lot, until, after some time had passed, the magic began.

The outline of her hair appeared first.

Thin gray lines that would go on to form the darkest part of the image. Then the skimpy brown bikini she had worn on the day that only just covered her parts. Line by line, section by section, she appeared on the print.

He recalled the moment he had captured her in his lens as if it were yesterday.

It had been a stifling Californian summer's day. Throughout the city, its citizens had taken refuge from the sun's relentless heat however they could. She, of course, utilized her family's spectacular infinity pool that overlooked the ocean.

As usual, she had been on her own.

In all the time he had watched her, outside of her family and two failed short-lived relationships, she never seemed to have many friends. Then again, it wasn't *that* surprising: you only had to dig a little under the surface to uncover what lay beneath.

Despite how often he stared at her, the sight of her beautiful face with that wanton body still caused an unwelcome reaction in him. Feeling the heat surging through, he had to close his eyes and force himself to remember the truth.

Beneath that angelic face lay a monster.

He had studied her for hours as she'd first swam, then sunbathed while reading a screenplay beneath a wide-brimmed straw hat. He'd zoomed in with his camera, hoping to see what had captured her attention so fully. It would have been fortuitous if it was something he could use to expose just how two-faced she was, but the lens on his camera hadn't been up to the job.

The one he'd wanted to use was far too expensive for him to afford.

His stomach clenched at the thought, at how unfair it was that she had everything handed to her on a silver platter — not even silver... gold — while he'd had to struggle quite so much.

She had never starved or worried about what she could and couldn't afford. He doubted she'd ever even considered the price of a purchase, not with the kind of wealth her parents commanded. He didn't know the exact number that they were worth, but Entertainment Tonight had listed it in the region of nine figures.

And their *home*?

It was outrageously opulent, dripping in riches. There was even a two-story outbuilding that was bigger than the biggest dwelling in his neighborhood, a spare building that he knew the family never used.

It was especially heinous when you took into account that only three of them actually lived there. The state of California commanded one of the highest rates of homelessness, yet three people lived on a property that could have easily housed several hundred if not *thousands* on its grounds.

Life was terribly unfair, but made even worse with people like her.

Dragging himself out of his thoughts, he stared down at the fully developed image in the tray.

Using a pair of rubber-ended tongs, he lifted the print carefully, rinsed it under water, then submerged it into the stop bath. This step would stop the image from developing any further. Then it went into a tray of fixer. One more much longer rinse and it was done.

Squeegeeing off the remaining water on the surface of the print, he hung it up to dry beside the dozen of other prints he'd already developed that day. They moved gently in the breeze caused by the fan he had brought in to speed up the process.

Wiping his hands on his pants until they were dry, he sat on the stool by the bench he'd crudely made using pieces of driftwood he'd found and bound together.

A large brown envelope waited for his attention in front of a line of wooden figures that he'd painstakingly carved by hand. He liked that they seemed to be watching him as he worked, his little silent friends. *They* never had a bad word to say about him.

They never said a word at all.

Carefully opening the mouth of the envelope, he shook its contents onto the bench. Black alphabetical letters that he'd pre-cut from magazines and newspapers floated out, stockpiled for just this purpose.

This would be the third note he was sending to them. With each one, he was becoming better and better at making them.

A jolt of excitement shot through him as he thought of how his plan was coming together.

Using his whittling knife, he arranged the letters onto a sheet of white paper, gluing them down until the two sentences were formed. Leaning back from the bench, he held up the sheet of paper to the red light that was suspended from the ceiling and read over his work.

You act like you're so nice, but I know the truth. And I'm going to make you sorry. I'm going to make you ALL sorry.

His mouth curled into a sneer.

Turning back to the wall of photographs, he glared at her many oblivious faces, from all the times he had watched her without her knowing.

Soon...

Soon he would make her pay.

2

———

He had just come off a trying assignment and was looking forward to some R&R when the call had come, smack in the middle of what constituted packing.

A few shorts, his trusty camo shirts, briefs, and cargo pants as beat up and put through the ringer as he was, were being shoved into a canvas backpack when his phone had buzzed.

The melodic rap by D'angelo that had been blasting from the old school sound deck that provided his one luxury in life stopped playing, replaced by that annoying ringtone that seemed to reverberate around the tin walls of the Airstream Travel Trailer he called home.

Though it was only thirty feet long, the trailer had everything he needed for full-time living: a bedroom with a double bed that connected to a small but serviceable living room that also doubled as his kitchen and office, with a shower room and laundry at the other end of the trailer. And it came with one of the most glorious views of the Malibu ocean that he would never be able to afford in his lifetime if he wasn't living in a mobile home.

Truly, it offered the best of both worlds. And the icing on the cake? When he inevitably felt that siren call to move, he could simply shift his home and his life by attaching it to his truck and hauling it off to the next place.

The ringing continued its insistent call, interrupting his thoughts. Lips turning down with disapproval, he looked for the phone but couldn't locate it anywhere near him.

"Bud," he called out. "Fetch my phone."

The German Shepherd who had been snoozing by the bed sprang up and raced into the lounge, letting the rings guide him. When he padded back, the phone was gripped carefully between those two strong jaws of his. Intelligence shone from his brown eyes as he looked up at his owner for approval.

"Thanks, Boy."

He took the phone from him and ran a hand over his dog's smooth head in the way that he liked. Bud chuffed happily, lifting first one paw, then the other before returning to his position by the foot of the bed, circling round in the way that dogs do before lying back down.

The man stared down at his phone, at the name of the lowlife who dared to interrupt this most holy of times — that of vacation.

He'd worked long and hard, and this downtime was due him. People knew better than to bother him when he could almost taste the grit in his teeth and feel the desert air whistling through his hair.

It was going to be him, his bike, his trusty dog and the unforgiving outback of the desert.

Which was just how he liked it.

His eyes slid over a shelf of framed photographs and knick-knacks collected from a lifetime of experiences. Landed on the only picture he had kept from high school, back when he hadn't been half as tough or rugged as he was now.

The two teens in the picture were skinny things, all arms and legs with glasses and unfortunate zits that were the cause of many a beating from the jocks that'd had their run of the school.

After a pretty miserable childhood being bullied and living under the roof with a drunk for a father, and a drug addict for a mom, when Kane Turner suddenly grew two feet — seemingly each way — he'd fled to the marines as soon as was feasibly possible.

Disciplined, driven, and relieved to be getting out of his crummy home situation, he advanced up the ranks quickly due to formidable physical skills and an almost sixth sense for danger.

Didn't matter if he was in the sketchier parts of downtown or conducting a dawn patrol in Afghanistan, Kane always knew moments before contact with a hostile was initiated. It was this uncanny ability that had kept him alive throughout each of his tours when so many of his brothers had fallen by the wayside.

Despite being so good at his job, he never enjoyed it.

It was in his blood to protect and serve, but he didn't like fighting people, didn't like hurting them, however misguided they were. Still, he would have stayed a marine if it wasn't for the devastating loss that occurred in Operation Condor.

It was supposed to have been a routine expedition.

A simple patrol in a small town in the middle of nowhere where only a handful of people lived. They were to show their faces, let the locals see that the US controlled the region when an IED went off as they neared.

The car ahead had flipped over, though luckily, Kane had felt that tingle in the back of his neck, that flutter in his stomach that had warned him something was amiss.

Slowing down his vehicle as he scouted the area, he had been far enough back that the bomb only did surface damage. The wounds he sustained would leave a few wicked scars, though they were nothing compared to the devastation his marine brothers faced.

Suffering through weeks of agony, their injuries finally proved too great as a number of them died one after the other. Those who clung to survival did so by a thread: tormented by PTSD, they only made it through the day by medicating themselves with whatever was available.

And those were the lucky ones.

Unable to work or return to normal civilian life, a few became homeless, sleeping on the streets before vanishing off the face of the earth completely.

Kane hadn't wanted that for himself.

He hadn't survived his childhood to let that be the end of his story. He knew he had to quit before his number came up.

After he returned to civilian life, Kane flitted around

from city to city, working various manual jobs from construction to bartender to a stint as an Uber driver, until his high school buddy Wilson had called, offering to employ him.

The class nerd, Wilson had gone on to make a major success of himself and now ran one of the most sought-after VIP security services. Having heard that Kane was struggling, he wanted to help the one person who hadn't made his life a misery at school.

The money was decent, and it was fun to mix with the Hollywood elite who were as eccentric, as out of control as a person would expect. From well-organized "sleep-overs" featuring some of the country's best-known faces to basement S&M dungeons, Kane had seen it all.

Despite some of the crazy things he'd witnessed and how he could likely fund the rest of his life if he would only pen a book detailing the madness he'd been privy to, Kane was a consummate professional and would never betray his employer's trust.

This kind of integrity was a quality often missing in LA, and so he found his services in constant demand, particularly when the employer happened to be a bored and lonely housewife.

Many fell for his brooding good looks, while others simply loved the challenge.

Kane frequently found himself in uncomfortable situations where he would catch his client walking around in nothing more than a thong and a smile.

He never took advantage of the moment.

The women who threw themselves at him? He never found them attractive. He didn't like their too-tight facial features so often caused by surgery, or the voluminous breasts that never moved. The fake tans made him think of overcooked frankfurters on a grill. In fact, he hated fakeness in general, which was why, although he was seen as a catch, he still hadn't found The One.

Not that he believed in that kind of thing.

Having seen what a loveless marriage could do to two people, he had sworn off the idea. This was just as well, as none of his previous relationships had been at all successful with an average lifespan of only a few months — if that.

He knew he was far from perfect, but he'd considered himself above average in many respects and most of the women he came across tended to agree... until they came home with him for the first time.

Apparently, his tiny tin home didn't hold quite the same appeal for them as it did him.

After the first night, many didn't bother returning while the ones who hung in there he would inevitably find fault with.

What was it about the women in this town that made them all so focused on fame and money?

He'd lost count of how many celebrity parties he'd worked at where women initiated conversations with potential "love" interests by asking them what job they had or how much square footage their house contained.

It all left a bad taste in his mouth.

Having finished a trying job with a diva pop star who'd acted very badly when Kane had rejected her drunken advances, he had packed a bag and was ready to take off on his Harley for a week in the mountains. Now, the one person in the world he couldn't ignore was calling.

"Wilson," Kane answered his phone. "I'm literally walking out the door so this had better be good..."

"I know, but this just came through," Wilson responded with uncustomary excitement.

Mack "Stonewall" Rockefeller, the well-known movie mogul who owned Pinnacle studios, was receiving death threats. This wasn't unusual in and of itself — the rich and famous were always being targeted by money grabbers and weirdos. However Wilson was particularly concerned as the threats were coming from the same source...

And they seemed to be escalating.

The Rockefellers had a daughter who they had managed to keep out of the limelight for most of her life. Not much was publicly known about her other than she was about to turn twenty-five and an enormous yet "private" party was being thrown to celebrate the occasion.

Wilson explained how bad an idea that would be: Stonewall would essentially be opening his home to thousands of strangers. If anyone wanted to do something to them, there wouldn't be a more perfect opportunity.

Stonewall and his movie star wife Mandy were resisting, however, and were in the process of finalizing the firm they would go with for the job. In particular, they were looking for a bodyguard for their daughter. The literal King and Queen of Hollywood, Wilson had fought for their business for years. If he was able to win this contract, it would set up the company for life.

"So what's the problem?" Having had all this explained to him, Kane wasn't sure the point of his call.

"I'm stuck on this detail in DC right now and none of my usual men are cutting it. I need someone different, someone who might shake things up."

Kane ran through what he'd been told about the family in his head. "They sound high maintenance and I just got done with a job like that."

"Just meet them. Talk to them like you would any other client. If they don't go for you, fair enough. But I'm telling you, every firm I know is fighting to land this gig. It would mean a tremendous amount if we could win the account."

Kane glanced over at Bud. His ears were pricked high as he listened keenly, picking up on his reluctance.

"I already told Bud we were going. You know I hate disappointing him."

As if he understood, Bud sighed, staring at him with sad, accusatory eyes designed to pull at his heart. He tossed a rubber bone at him that Bud snatched out of the air with his jaws.

"Tell him there's a giant marrow bone in it for him if he'll wait just a little longer." Wilson sounded hopeful, knowing his pleas were working.

"Tell him yourself," Kane grumbled, shaking his head. He looked longingly out of a window at the faint outline of the mountains that seemed to be moving further away into the distance.

"Thanks man. Appreciate it. Get the job and you can have a long break after. As long as you want."

"Don't forget the marrow bones," Kane reminded him, determined that Bud would not lose out.

"I'll have a box shipped over," Wilson laughed. "You'll need to get there this afternoon. Go flash them some of the Kane charm. Clara will collate a file and send it over to you ASAP."

Clara was Wilson's assistant. She'd worked with him for close to five years now. She wasn't the quickest, but Wilson swore she was loyal and could be trusted with anything.

Kane hung up the call and sent Bud an apologetic look.

"So... it looks like we're going to have to put a pin on that vacation I promised you..."

Bud responded by groaning and covering his eyes with a paw.

"Don't be such a drama queen. At least you've got bones coming."

At that, Bud perked right up. His tail thumped against the laminate floor tiles.

"Let's grab a walk before we head over there. I've got a feeling this job is going to be rough."

Barking with the kind of excitement that would make a person think he had never been out on a walk before *in his life*, Bud raced to the door, jumped up to the handle and tugged on it with his mouth. The door swung open. Light and sea air flooded into the trailer that had his mouth opening to capture it all, but he stopped short of going outside.

He was too well trained for that.

Kane nodded, giving a hand signal. "You can go."

At that, Bud bounded outside, yapping and barking like he was a puppy again and not the grown-up three-year-old that he was.

Rolling his eyes at his dog's antics, Kane joined him outside.

3

The Rockefellers' palatial property was an eight bedroom, ten bathroom mansion with panoramic views of the Pacific Ocean and the famous Griffith Observatory.

Having led a simple and pretty frugal life, this kind of abundant living was so out of this world that even Kane found himself admiring the impeccably landscaped grounds.

He was parked in his truck at the end of the Rockefellers' two miles long drive, Bud snoring quietly by his side. Their walk had turned into a swim fest and play session that had tired his mutt out but served as an invigorating impromptu workout for him. Pumped and primed for action, he was *almost* ready to deal with the nightmare ahead.

He checked his laptop for the file Wilson had promised, but there was nothing in his inbox other than the Rockefellers' address. Clara was likely still putting it all together.

Never one to wait — waiting made him antsy — Kane decided to take matters into his own hands. Paws too, counting Bud. They did all of his jobs together, had done since that fateful morning when he had saved him.

Bud had been found chained in the backyard of a drug dealer who had kept the dog in squalid conditions his entire life. He'd only been a year old then, but having suffered nothing but abuse, he had been as feral as they came. His matted fur coat had been criss-crossed with what looked to be lashes that had left him covered with welts. And he was skin-and-bones, having existed on one tiny meal a day.

After police raided the house and arrested his owner, Bud was finally rescued, though he fought with them the entire time, not realizing that they were trying to help. He had earned the respect of the shelter volunteers, though that hadn't helped his chances at being re-homed.

No one wanted a dog who needed time and careful training. They wanted puppies or cute dogs, not ones riddled with scars and issues.

Nobody had wanted to give him a chance.

Kane had been working at the shelter as a builder at the time, among a crew of four others there to repair the roof that had been damaged after an overlong drought.

While working, he had heard a dog barking ferociously each time one of the shelter's helpers came to feed him. Yet, as soon as they left him alone, he would cower at the back of his cage, trembling with fear.

The ferociousness was all for show.

There was something about him that caused Kane to

take stock, and it wasn't only the matching scars that they bore.

He wasn't called Bud then, didn't actually have a name. Someone at the shelter had dubbed him Rover just so they could call him something, though Kane knew the name didn't suit him. He wasn't a Rover kind of dog.

After each day of work, Kane would sit outside his cage — hunching over to be as small as possible to signal that he wasn't a threat — tossing him treats. Bud would act out his usual performance, but when Kane showed no resistance or aggression, he would simmer down, though he never stopped keeping a wary eye on him, even when he snatched up the treats.

Kane would talk to the dog about his time in the marines and of the crimes he'd witnessed — all in the name of war. His voice would grow hard with emotion, but he wouldn't stop, needing to exorcise his demons while hoping to help the dog with his.

The odd thing of it all was, he hadn't even wanted a dog.

He'd grown up without contact with animals other than the odd playdate at a neighbor's house, so he certainly wasn't experienced with them. But seeing how the dog was suffering so like a human would, something had compelled him to try.

For weeks he'd sat outside talking to the dog, but nothing seemed to work. He was resisting and time was fast running out.

When the overrun shelter informed him that they needed his kennel, that if no progress was made, they would be forced to euthanize him, Kane risked his life by going inside the cage. Bud had snarled and yelped as usual, but Kane's trusty sixth sense hadn't gone off.

He truly believed that the dog would not hurt him.

He sat down, keeping his eyes on the ground, knowing that the dog would feel safer if he didn't make eye contact.

Speaking in a calming voice, he continued feeding treats while explaining why he needed to trust him. When all the treats were gone but one, Kane offered it up to him in the palm of his hand.

"We've both been through the wars," Kane had said, nice and relaxed and without any of the strain he had felt. "So I'd like to keep my fingers. If you take this treat from me, I promise you'll have many more in your future, but you've got to trust me. I won't let anyone hurt you ever again."

Bud had whined at him, scared and unsure what was happening. He retreated further into his kennel, but when Kane didn't move, he lowered his snout to his hand and took up the treat delicately.

In that tiny but momentous moment — and for the first time in his life — Kane had felt the beginnings of real love.

He adopted him, naming him Bud, and proceeded to win his trust.

Within a year, Bud had blossomed, but Kane had felt there was more to his dog than had been utilized. He was smart — almost human smart — and nothing made him happier than to please his owner.

He took them both to a specialist training school

where Bud had aced the classes, head and shoulders above the rest of his classmates.

After that, Kane had read every book, watched every video on YouTube. He'd trained Bud in his own unique way, the two of them forming a kind of shorthand with signals and verbal commands until Kane couldn't imagine life without the mutt now.

Even if he did have bad breath.

Bud snorted in his sleep, paws paddling the air as he dreamed of chasing after critters. Kane turned away from his dog to study the house through professional eyes.

The double-height front door was imposing with sturdy locks that wouldn't be easy for a criminal to crack, though they didn't often opt to enter in such an obvious manner. A line of twelve-foot-tall windows flanked the door, leading all the way around to the back of the house — where there would be more of those windows, no doubt.

Windows were a problem, though not so much from the fear of being smashed. Houses like this didn't scrimp on materials so he was ninety-nine percent sure that they would have smash-proof glass. But that didn't stop a wide-zoom lens or binoculars from invading a property, particularly if curtains and blinds weren't drawn at night — something he knew the wealthy seemed never to do, as if their fame and fortune made them untouchable.

Clearly the Rockefellers were learning differently now.

The second floor was a good deal above ground, but with several balconies and terraces potentially providing weak points, security cameras would need to be erected to cover every possible point of entry.

He noted down where they were in the dictaphone he carried around for such things. The digital file would be sent to Clara later who would use software to transcribe his findings as Kane wasn't much for computers.

Preliminary survey done, he leaned over and stroked Bud's stomach. The dog's eyes flew open.

"Time to work, fella."

"*Woof!*" Bud answered, yawning and blowing out a mouthful of doggy breath.

"We've gotta do something about that breath of yours though."

Bud made a sound that was suspiciously like a "no."

They got out of his truck. Several cars were parked in front of the Rockefellers' house, though judging by the companies, they most likely belonged to the visiting security firms, trolling for business as Wilson had warned.

He walked briskly up the drive, Bud padding alongside. His eyes swept the area, noting down every detail. Even Bud had his work face on, head high, nose sniffing the air in all directions.

Gravel crunched underfoot, causing Kane to wince.

He didn't want to announce their presence. Much of what he was doing now relied on not being detected until he was ready for it. He watched Bud for signs that his paws were bothered by the gravel but the dog was fine, happy to be working if the tail wagging from side to side was any indication.

When they were twenty or so feet from the house, a man came out wearing a designer suit and carrying a briefcase. Kane ducked behind a stone statue, signaling for Bud to do the same. They waited, hiding in place as the man cursed under his breath, but loud enough that Kane could hear him. He got into one of the parked cars, making a call. The car roared off, wheels churning as Kane overheard the man complaining that the family were a nightmare to please.

Great. Another difficult client. Just what he needed.

Wilson would owe him big time for this.

A security guard emerged, doing a lap around the property, but he was easy enough to evade. The man was yammering away on his hands-free phone on what was obviously a personal call.

Kane noted that down, too.

The man would need to be replaced, STAT.

He waited for the guard to disappear around the corner, then sprinted over to a metal side gate that was maybe eight feet tall. He scaled it easily, using a nearby modern granite art piece for leverage — that would have to be moved — and unlocked the gate to let Bud through before locking it back behind them.

He had broken into the Rockefellers' property, yet it had been worryingly easy for him to do so.

Lush landscaped grounds on staggered levels greeted him as the scent of exotic flowers filled his nostrils. An infinity pool looked out across the ocean, seemingly without end. To the East he could see a pair of tennis courts, beyond that a basketball court. There was even a golf course, complete with hills and a pond.

Walking past several of those large windows, he spied an office, then a library filled with volumes of leather-bound books that looked as if they had never been opened, much less read. There was a bar and a home theater complete with rows of leather recliners, discreet dimmable lighting, and a popcorn maker.

The entire place was an adult wonderland.

Bud's tail whipped from side to side, enjoying the parklike grounds.

They stole past a room that looked to be where the interviews were being held, Kane hunkering down to Bud's level. The dog found this amusing, taking the moment to sneak a lick of his face. Kane hissed, "Stop that!" But Bud didn't seem too bothered by his response.

Bud chuffed, his mouth forming a loopy grin before moving ahead to scout the way. Suddenly, he stopped dead, dropping his stomach to the ground, moving out of sight. Instantly, Kane followed suit, rolling behind a hedge as the guard came into view.

The two of them froze, the guard's voice chattering a mile a minute as he gossiped to whoever was on the other end about the troubles the Rockefellers were having.

Not only was he making personal calls on the job, but he was betraying his employers' confidences by talking about their private business.

The man would need to be replaced for sure.

And sooner rather than later.

When the coast was clear they took off, walking around the perimeter of the house, ducking out of sight whenever someone might see them. It was all too easy to do with Kane barely having to try. While the Rockefellers might be richer than God, their security was worse than those small villages in Afghanistan he had come across. At least there, the people were watchful.

He came upon a wing of the house that was at odds with the rest of the mansion. It had beautiful craftsmanship, but the modern style of the extension was a recent addition. A dog barked nearby causing Bud's ears to swivel round, though he kept his cool when others would have torn off to investigate. Instead, he moved closer to Kane's side, protecting him in case the unknown dog attacked.

A movement in one of the rooms caught his eye.

A figure had walked past but hadn't seen him. Plastering himself to a window, he took a look inside...

And almost swallowed his tongue for his efforts.

The woman inside must have just come out of the shower as there was the tiniest of towels wrapped around her glistening body. The curves it barely hid did something feral, pulling at the very core of him. Her dripping long dark hair was slung carelessly over one shoulder as she went to a vanity table and sat down.

She was in her mid-twenties, likely the daughter whose birthday was coming up. Though why hadn't Wilson mentioned that she was possibly the most glorious looking female to have ever walked the Earth? For the first time since they'd known each other, Kane cursed his friend, then Clara. If she'd been faster with the file, at least he would have been given a heads up.

Instead, here he was, standing outside their potential client's bedroom like a creep.

He should notify her of his presence he knew, but

when he went to move, his body refused to cooperate, his feet cemented to the ground.

Three military tours and several years working security for Hollywood VIPs, both of which had thrown up plenty of sticky situations before.

Surely he could think of a way out of this one?

4

———

Lexi had it all.

The only child and the beloved daughter of two of Hollywood's greatest talents, Alexia Gray-Rockefeller had the kind of life that most only ever dreamed of.

Her mother was none other than mega movie star Mandy Gray. Herself the daughter of Hollywood royalty, Mandy began acting when she was a toddler playing her father's adorable on-screen child. Her sweet smile and cute nature had turned her into the nation's sweetheart, a love affair which only continued as she grew up in the public eye.

When she turned twenty-three, Mandy — now a huge star herself — fell in love with the sexy studio exec, Stonewall Rockefeller. With a strong jaw, soulful eyes, and built like a tank in all sense of the word, he was the only man among many to sweep her off her feet.

Within weeks of knowing each other, the two began a passionate affair on the set of Mandy's breakout movie,

Woman In Red, that ended in a marriage and an Academy Award. Though infidelity was rife in this town and both had an equal amount of ardent fans throwing themselves at them, Stonewall and Mandy's union was rock solid.

They were the real deal, and neither had nor would ever cheat on each other.

Lexi had come along two years after they were married and she was even more beautiful than her mother, if that were possible. She had inherited her mom's creamy skin, pouty lips and to-die-for hourglass figure, while her father passed on his intelligence and love of reading.

Although Lexi had been a happy girl, she grew up without many friends. Her peers, she didn't have much in common with, while regular kids her own age either found her lineage too intimidating, or they cared about it a little too much...

It was always the same story.

Someone would befriend her but after only a few hangout sessions, Lexi would discover she was paying for much more than the restaurant bill.

The sob stories would come out, sick fathers and siblings which Lexi would later discover sometimes never existed at all. Then there were the wannabe actors who thought a friendship with her would somehow develop into a role for them.

She was a compassionate girl who couldn't help but buy into their stories, wanting to help her new friends as much as possible.

Having lived a sheltered life despite her parents' fame

(or maybe because of it), it never crossed her mind that people could be so duplicitous.

She'd been lucky enough to make some great friends when she went to college to study literature, but after graduation, some moved to the East Coast while others became too busy with their new boyfriends.

Whenever Lexi suggested they could meet up — and she would invite their boyfriends too, knowing that her friends seemed reluctant to part with them even for a short while — her offer was always declined. It wasn't until her mom discovered her crying in her room that Mandy had explained a sad fact of life: as ridiculous as it was, her friends were scared Lexi, with her looks and great personality, would steal their boyfriends away.

Apparently, she was a threat to her girlfriends even if she wasn't remotely interested in their guys.

Annoyed that her mother might be right, she signed up to a local writing group under a pseudonym, but that had been a bust too; it wasn't long before her true identity had been revealed.

After her last group of friends sold the family stories she had told them to ET, she decided she would be better off without them and cut them out of her life.

So far, she hadn't regretted her decision to do so, but with her birthday looming, it was becoming increasingly clear that something was missing from her life.

Lexi was turning twenty-five in a few days and it was going to be celebrated with a luxury charity event/birthday party on the grounds of their home.

Located around their swimming pool, with a buffet catered by celebrated television chef, Jean-Louis, fresh lobster was being flown in from Maine. A French pastry chef who had designed the cake for the King of Monaco's recent (and fifth) wedding, had promised that Lexi's centerpiece would overshadow that. A stage was also on its way, to be set up by the rose garden for singing sensation Stella Speed to perform a private concert for the guests.

There was even talk that Logan Steel — THE — movie star would swing by to say hi. He had broken out in one of Stonewall's movies a few years ago. Now that he was dating popular sitcom actress Ellie Godwin, the entire world worshipped at their feet. With his smoldering good looks and Ellie's girl-next-door lovability, they were the most admired — and desired — couple on planet Earth. Even Time magazine had declared them so.

Anyone who was anyone would be there. The wealthiest, most famous people in Hollywood.

It all filled her with tremendous anxiety.

All Lexi really wanted was a quiet dinner alone with her parents, but one thing had stopped her from planning one: there wouldn't be a better opportunity to raise money for PAWS, the animal shelter that she volunteered at on the weekends.

PAWS was a no-kill shelter that was constantly overwhelmed with animals that needed help. They tried their best, but the recent raging wildfires had pushed not just PAWS but all local animal shelters to their limits. While the State diverted all emergency funds to assist families who had lost their homes and businesses, there wasn't much left over for the animals and pets that were affected. Many family pets were currently lost.

Frightened by the fires, they had escaped their homes only to find themselves on the streets scared, alone, and hungry. Other luckier pets were saved, but with their families displaced, they were forced into temporary accommodation, many of which didn't allow pets. Lexi had witnessed firsthand many devastated families who had lost everything only then to have to relinquish their beloved pets too.

She couldn't close her eyes at night without reliving the agonized cries of the little kids whose best friends were torn away...

Some of them, forever.

Short of giving away her parents' money (and she had done so to such an extent that Stonewall's accountant had called in alarm), Lexi wanted to exploit this opportunity to help as many as possible. The need was urgent, and this was one way she could bypass the government red-tape and get help to those who needed it — fast.

Much as she'd like everyone to believe that her motives were entirely selfless, there was also a personal one for the party too.

Originally expected to be a tent-pole affair to rival that of the latest superhero offerings, Mandy's latest movie production had been plagued with issues as first one-leading A-list man, then another, dropped out.

They were for unrelated reasons, but the tabloids hadn't seen it that way, with headlines screaming that America's sweetheart had turned into a raging, aging diva who was running her co-stars off the set.

Truth was, Mandy needed some good publicity.

A few years shy of turning fifty, she was starting to feel cinema's waning love affair. She would always be one of the most beautiful women in the world and could still hold a candle next to most, though no amount of moisturizer or hot yoga could hide the lines that had seemingly appeared on her face overnight.

Oh, she tried to hide her sadness away, but beneath her brilliant smile, lurking in her eyes, Lexi could see her mother's confidence fading like a blazing comet coming to its end. Having built her entire career around them, her fading looks and the subsequent decline in quality roles were a bitter pill to swallow.

Instead of the sexy love interest, recent offers were for a depressed divorcee and an angry single mom set to take on her son's elitist school.

As if one parent's issues weren't enough, her dad's job as CEO of Pinnacle Studios seemed to be taking a toll on him, if the increasing gray hairs that peppered his usually dark head of hair was anything to go by.

Stonewall had been doing the job for close to three decades now, rising through the ranks from lowly development exec to VP of production and beyond. Promoted some five or six times, he knew the business like the back of his giant hand.

A smooth operator, he conducted work and pleasure with the ease of one who had never worried for anything — what then could be troubling her father enough that it caused endless late-night phone calls?

Her gaze slid over to the pile of manuscripts that were stacked beside her desk. For the past year she had been working full time at her father's studio reading script submissions and writing coverage reports for them.

She — among a handful of others all doing the same job — formed the first line of defense, wading through the millions of screenplays that were sent through for consideration by agents, managers, producers, and actors. She would read the scripts then fill out a detailed form summarizing the story, if she thought the film would do well and whether it should be considered for the studio's upcoming development slate.

Right after college, Stonewall had offered her a job as an executive in his company bypassing the entry-level position, but Lexi had declined. She'd wanted to work her way up — just as he had — earning her own stripes. It was important to her that she worked, that she earned her own salary, especially when she still lived at home.

Truthfully, she didn't have to do either: on the day she turned twenty-one, she'd been given a trust fund that her parents had set up when she was born. As a matter of pride, however, she hadn't touched a penny of it other than to donate the interest it accrued to charity.

A knock on the door interrupted her thoughts.

"Come in," she called out.

Their housekeeper Ruth entered, carrying a tray with a chicken salad and some fruit she had arranged into a pretty platter.

In her sixties, she was a petite woman with salt and pepper hair that was tied up in a neat bun. She always had a warm smile on her face though presently, her brow was creased into a frown that she turned on Lexi.

"You need to eat something! All you do is work! You're as bad as your father."

Without waiting to hear whether Lexi wanted the food or not, she set the tray onto the desk, automatically starting to tidy the mess on it.

"I'm fine, Ruth. I don't need you to keep making me lunch—" Lexi began only to be cut off from a *look* Ruth shot her.

"Your excuses didn't work on me then and they won't work on me now. Either you promise you'll eat or I will sit here watching until you do."

Lexi knew she meant it too. With a laugh, she hugged her small shoulders, dropping a kiss onto her lined forehead. "I promise I will."

Patting her hand, Ruth nodded, appeased. "I want to see everything gone. An empty plate is a happy plate after all." She quoted the saying she often repeated to Lexi as a child, whenever she was left to look after her on Mandy and Stonewall's frequent absences.

Ruth still treated her like the child she had half-raised, but Lexi didn't mind: the woman was like family. She was the one who taught her how to tie her shoelaces properly, and they had spent many a happy afternoon baking chocolate chip cookies that they had eaten on the terrace. She was the one Lexi had run to, hiding herself in her apron when kids at school had been mean.

"I need to get back. So much to do today." Ruth was half out the door before Lexi could reply, but she didn't leave right away. There was a look on her face that Lexi couldn't discern, a wariness, no. Concern?

Before she could ask what was troubling the other

woman, the look was gone, replaced by a harried smile. "A happy plate, remember."

The door closed behind her.

At the smell of the food, her stomach rumbled. It probably was time for her to eat something. She started for the plate of salad when real-time footage of the wild-fires appeared on the giant plasma television that covered the width of one of her walls.

Smoke billowed, crowding out what would have been a Californian blue sky. The bright sun shining down onto Sonoma County was at complete odds to the dystopian scene being broadcast as firefighters, their figures shockingly small against the blazing landscape, fought bravely on.

Unable to hear any more of the tragedies taking place, Lexi muted the television. Appetite abruptly gone, she turned to study the rail of designer dresses in front of her.

It felt so wrong to be doing something so shallow, and dare she say it, privileged, that she felt no pleasure at the task ahead. All around the city, families were losing their lives and homes, yet here she was deciding which designer dress she should wear for her big event.

Her eyes roamed the room she had grown up in, at the oversized King bed she slept in with sheets that were imported from Paris — as they were known to be the best — with a price tag to match. Truthfully, she hadn't picked anything in her room: their interior designer had taken care of it when they had created this wing for her. It was only when a curious schoolfriend had asked about them that Lexi discovered her entire bedding had cost some five figures.

Or, as her short-lived relationship with the friend had put it, "more than my family spent on our car."

After that, she was careful not to ask about prices anymore, and certainly knew never to pass on that kind of information to anyone outside of the family.

Despite wanting to ditch this whole affair and head outside where she might be able to do some immediate good, she knew that looking the part was necessary. Whether she wanted it to or not, appearances mattered in this industry.

She pulled on a pretty wine-colored number with a skirt that hugged her curves and assessed her reflection in the mirror. The color made her complexion pop, and she liked how curvy yet classy she looked.

But, twisting to examine the dress from all sides, it also seemed too fussy, and she wasn't very comfortable in it. If it were up to her, she'd be in flats and jeans with the occasional maxi dress. Dressing up was Mandy's great love though she had been warned many a time, that the public expected more of her, and she couldn't let her parents down just because she couldn't be bothered to make an effort when she left the house.

Apparently, in the eventual event that she was recognized, even a short trip at Whole Foods required some effort.

She tried on a tight black dress next. The sophisticated lines felt better, but the plunging frontline was much too low cut and that was before she noticed the thigh-high slit. Her breasts were practically falling out of the dress which might suit the Kardashians but it wasn't something she wanted for herself.

Rifling through the rack, she came upon a white dress and slipped it on. It was an off-the-shoulder number, beautifully cut with an empire waist and flowing skirt that ended at her ankle. She looked like a Greek goddess — and more importantly — felt comfortable in it.

Lexi smiled at her reflection. This was the one.

Even if a party wasn't really her style, at least the dress would be.

She took it off and hung it back up. In her marble bathroom, she stripped out of her underwear and turned on the shower when her cell rang. Mandy's famous face flashed up on the screen, though it wasn't the usual publicity shot or even a still from one of her movies. It was a picture that Stonewall had taken of Mandy on a happy vacation when it had been just the three of them.

Face devoid of makeup, beaming up at her husband with Lexi between them, this was the mom Lexi knew and loved, the one the rest of the world didn't get to see.

It was her favorite picture of Mandy.

"Hey, Mom," Lexi answered.

"Have you decided on a dress?" Mandy sounded strangely subdued.

"I just found one I like."

"Good. I can't wait to see you in it. I pulled a few favors to get those to you so quickly, you know how designers are."

Her mother wasn't saying anything she didn't already know, having spent a lifetime watching how this all worked: celebs wore designer gowns at glamorous events giving the designers free advertisement, and in return, celebrities could request clothes from them for free. The bigger the event, the better the gowns.

Judging by the ones on the rack, her charity birthday party was considered big business. Noticing the time, a little after four in the afternoon, she frowned.

"I thought you were working until late?"

"I was, but something came up." Mandy's voice sounded hesitant over the line. She picked up on it immediately.

"Oh God, what's happened now? Have you lost another co-star?" Lexi asked, concerned for the spate of bad luck her mother seemed to be having.

"Nothing like that," Mandy was quick to reassure.

"Then what is it? You don't normally come home early and you know you're going to see whatever dress I pick later."

"I can't call to find out how my only child is doing?" Her mother's voice turned testy.

"Not in the last week of production, usually you'd leave that to Suki," Lexi replied. Suki was her mom's longtime assistant without who Mandy would be totally lost. Lexi never held it against her when work took over, understanding how difficult and all encompassing shooting a movie could be. Not wanting her to think she was complaining, she softened her tone.

"This is... unusual is all."

There was a pause over the line as Mandy gathered her thoughts.

"OK, you got me. I was calling to see if you were free right now?"

"I was just stepping into the shower."

"When you're done, can you meet your dad and me in the study? We have something we need to discuss with you."

It wasn't her imagination: her mother was definitely being cagey.

Lexi figured they had some other party surprise they wanted to spring on her, but, knowing that she hated surprises at the best of times, they would get her take on it first. "Sure. Give me ten minutes, I should be done by then."

"Perfect. See you in a bit."

Lexi hung up the phone and stepped into the shower. Steam fogged the air as powerful jets massaged her body. Pouring her favorite organic shower wash into her hand, she lathered herself, rubbing the creamy foam against her skin as the calming aroma relaxed her.

A short while later, she sat down at the vanity table wearing only a towel that she'd wrapped around her. Picking up a brush, she ran it through her hair, getting rid of any tangles her detangling spray might have missed when something caught her eye.

There was a man standing outside her room.

In their yard, frozen like a deer in the headlights. He stood on the stone terrace staring at her, eyes round with shock.

The next thing she noticed about him was his size.

He was big like her father but carried himself with an animal grace. Dressed in cargo pants and a sandy shirt the color of the desert, old scars played peekaboo beneath the collar of his shirt. He hadn't shaved that day, his face covered with a shadow that only made him more appealing.

His ruggedness stood out among the sea of perfectly presented Californians. Something terrible must have happened to him, but she didn't have a chance to think what that might be as she suddenly found herself pinned by his startling blue eyes.

They were as blue as the Pacific Ocean and clouded by a veil of mystery.

Her hand froze in mid-air.

She stared at his chiseled jaw beside a strong, firm mouth. His skin was bronze, like someone who had spent a lot of time in the sun and he had thick almost black hair that was shaved military style. A Celtic band was tattooed around one muscular bicep.

Lexi found herself unable to breathe at how incredibly handsome he was.

But then the truth also hit like a rock — however good-looking he was, he was also *spying on her*.

She noticed the dog by his side next, a German Shepherd who amazingly, having been caught by her, now seemed to be crawling toward a bush to hide.

Stunned by what she was seeing, Lexi dropped her brush and shot up to her feet.

5

____

A million thoughts ran through Kane's mind at the sight of Lexi — in that tiny towel, hair and skin still wet from her shower.

Unfortunately, none were very gentlemanly.

Bud had the right idea.

On being spotted he'd immediately gone into abort mode and was now making like a bush, albeit one with four paws and a tail. But him? His brain had gone into meltdown.

And all because of the sight of this near-naked girl.

He'd seen plenty — more than plenty — of beautiful women in this town, many in various stages of undress (he never pretended to be a saint), yet something about this one was causing all kinds of unnerving reactions in him.

Even if she was one of those spoiled, privileged girls that irritated him no end.

The job, Kane. Stop gawking at her body and think about the job.

From beneath the bush, Bud huffed like he agreed with his thought.

Forcing his mind to cooperate, he considered his options.

He could knock on her door and explain what he was doing there. Honesty being the best policy and all that jazz, though, he wasn't sure she'd give him enough time to talk.

Would he be able to say all of that before she started screaming?

Maybe he could call Wilson, get him to talk to her parents who would for sure be hearing about this in the very near future?

Nope, it seemed much smarter if he simply hunkered down and snuck off like the coward he was. He'd decided on this safest course of action when she had spotted him in the mirror of her vanity table.

Startled, she'd grabbed the knot on her towel securing it with her hand and jumped up, white as a sheet. Seeing the fear in her eyes, he'd instantly regretted not warning her of his presence earlier.

Really stupid, Kane!

He put both hands up to indicate that he meant no harm, but before he could react Lexi did the one thing he hadn't anticipated — she rushed at him, all the fury of the world flashing in her eyes.

She yanked open the door, her yells seemingly amplified by the endless grounds.

"If you think you're going to spy on me in my own house, you have another thing coming!"

Quick as a flash, despite having only a towel to conceal her modesty, she reached behind the door...

And pulled out a bottle of mace that she leveled at him.

The shrinking violet, terrified girl that he'd pegged her for only a moment ago was a figment of his overripe imagination. Kane could only gape at her, fire shooting from her eyes.

Behind him, Bud had sprung out from his hiding place. Seeing the threat to him, Bud bared sharp, sharp teeth, snarling a warning that only a fool would ignore.

"This isn't what it looks like," he began, hoping that he could calm the situation before things got worse. He wasn't so much concerned for himself — he could disarm her before she'd even know what had hit her — but there was a chance the spray could go off and get into Bud's eyes. And an even bigger one that tackling her would cause the knot in that tiny towel to unravel...

Which, all things considered, would not be a smart move.

Lexi's eyes narrowed. "It's funny how you all recycle the same excuses."

The "all" in her sentence bothered him.

"You get a lot of men sneaking around your room like this?"

"Every now and then. Though they don't usually get quite so close." She looked him up and down, mind racing. Assessing. "Where's your camera?"

"Camera?" Suddenly the fog that had been in his head since the moment he had seen her, lifted. "You think I'm paparazzi?"

"I'm the one asking the questions. You are trespassing and we can probably throw sexual harassment in too since you caught me half-naked. I'm sure your boss would love that."

Considering how vulnerable she should be feeling, it was miraculous she was so calm. Kane felt a grudging respect that almost overrode his flickering annoyance at being caught.

Wilson was going to give him hell for this.

"Miss. Rockefeller! Are you alright?!"

A man shouted close by. Footsteps thundered toward them, heavy and sluggish, as if the person wasn't used to this much exertion. When the security guard rounded the corner, out of breath and red in the face, Kane wasn't surprised to see he still had one hand on his cell. The display was lit up. Whoever he was talking to was still on the line. The imbecile wasn't prepared to deal with a potential situation even now.

A simmering heat bubbled inside Kane's chest.

As a marine, one of the first things he had been taught was that when you were on the job, it was your sole focus. Lives depended on him being able to stick to that simple order. While they weren't on tour now, and this man was clearly not a soldier, the rules of engagement were the same: he had been hired in a protective capacity, one which he clearly wasn't fit for.

The guard went for his weapon, fumbling with the holster as Kane saw a sudden vision of himself lying dead on the ground because the idiot had turned trigger happy.

"I'm not a reporter. I'm also not a threat to anyone.

I'm actually here about the job. This was just reconnaissance work to show you where your weak spots are."

Lexi blinked at him, confusion clouding her eyes. "What are you talking about? What job?"

"The new security detail."

Since they were conversing now, Kane signaled Bud that he could stop being aggressive. The dog relaxed his jaw, though he still stood protectively beside him, pressing into his leg to let Kane know he was there. He was trained to understand how dangerous weapons were, and while there was one pointed at him, his dog would stay frosty.

"You're bluffing, trying to buy time to get yourself out of this." Lexi didn't seem to have any idea what he was talking about. A sinking feeling gathered until it became a tornado that smashed into him harder than a speeding truck.

She didn't know.

Her parents hadn't told her about the threats. And man, there was no job worth being the one responsible for that.

While Kane had been thinking, the security guard radioed for help, finally putting that damned phone away. "Sir, we have a situation by Miss Rockefeller's room. There's a man here. He was spying on her."

Some of the color had returned to Lexi's face, though she looked less scared now, more angry and bewildered, yet still with enough distaste that showed she doubted his words. "Explain yourself."

"I think it's better if we wait for your parents."

His answer didn't have the desired effect of calming

her. Her brows shot up and her expression changed, those rose-bud lips tightening into a thin white line.

More footsteps crashed toward them, the sound of a heavy person, but this one was surprisingly light on his feet. The hairs on the back of Kane's neck lifted as his sixth sense kicked in.

Oh Hell.

The thought had barely entered his head when the door to Lexi's bedroom burst open as a giant of a man barreled in, sparks shooting from his eyes. He must've been six foot five of solid muscle, with hands the size of footballs and feet that could stomp a man to death, if the shoe size was anything to go by.

At a little over six two himself, Kane was no shrinking violet, but against this man — who he guessed instantly must be Lexi's father — even he took a wary step back.

Stonewall took in the situation, saw the gun pointed at Kane's chest and his jaw clenched.

"You son-of-a-bitch!"

He charged through the room at Kane, a tornado of rage and power. Furniture flew out of his way, flung from those giant hands as Lexi cried out. Seeing the hulking man coming for him, Kane's mind assessed the situation fast as a flash, all the years of training coming into play.

While Stonewall was big, he was also consumed by emotion, signaling his every intent. When the impact came, Kane sidestepped easily, bringing up a foot to trip the other man. He grabbed Stonewall's shirt with both hands, so that when he fell, he wouldn't be injured, as Kane took the brunt of the man's weight.

Stonewall found himself spun 180 degrees, with his nose pressed against the polished stone terrace floor.

Out of the corner of his eye, Kane saw the guard starting to level his own gun at him, and that was one more than he was comfortable with.

"Bud! Stop him!" he snapped, looking straight at the guard. Bud reacted immediately, flying at the hapless man who, faced with almost ninety pounds of snarling dog, looked instantly terrified.

"Ah!"

Bud snapped his jaws around the man's wrist, forcing the hand with the gun down, so that it was now pointing at the ground, away from Kane. Threatening growls rumbled deep in his throat, warning the man not to make another move or he risked having his throat ripped out. The guard believed him, standing still and gray as a statue.

"What on earth is happening in here?!" a female voice cried by the doorway. "Lexi!"

Kane looked over to see the spitting image of Lexi if she were twenty years older. Mandy Gray — as Kane knew her to be — had the same killer curves, creamy skin and good looks of her daughter, but where Lexi's hair was a rich chestnut, Mandy's was much darker. Beside her stood a man in a designer suit carrying a leather brief-case. He looked uneasy, out of place, like he wasn't part of whatever was happening.

"Did he hurt you?" Mandy rushed to her daughter. Lexi sagged against the terrace doors, the mace down by her side as her mom took her into her arms.

"I'm not here to hurt anyone," Kane snapped. "I'm

here for the job, Mr. Rockefeller. I'm with Diamond Security. Wilson sent me."

Stonewall stopped struggling. Kane loosened his grip. Twisting his face to him, Stonewall glared. "Then what the hell are you doing in here with my daughter? Why is she naked?!"

"I decided to see how far my dog and I could get, sneaking onto your property. I wanted to highlight where all the weak points are. I was just passing by your daughter's room when she saw me and mistook me for paparazzi. I was trying to explain my presence here when you appeared. As for your second question, my guess is that she had just stepped out of the shower when I turned up outside."

Stonewall's eyes turned flat as Mandy fell silent. A look passed between them with something unspoken.

Kane released his hold on him, offering his hand to him to help him up, but Stonewall didn't take it, shooting him another of those death stares as he got to his feet.

Kane wiped his hand on his thigh and whistled. Bud's ears twisted round to him as he let go of the guard and went back to Kane's side, though his eyes darted at the group, ready to attack at his command.

Seeing that her parents weren't alarmed by the sight of him anymore, Lexi's expression turned from shocked to confused. Grabbing a robe, she slipped into it quickly, securing the belt.

"Will someone please explain what's going on? Who is this man and why is he here?"

The security expert touting for business must have

sensed an opportunity, as he started to speak in a weedy, hesitant voice.

"This is highly irregular. You're reckless and have no regard for the privacy of our clients. Look what a fright you gave Miss Alexis! Our firm would never be so unprofessional."

He spoke fast, his words running into each other.

"Her name is Alexia," Kane replied in a voice that was quiet but deadly. "Alexia Gray-Rockefeller. If you're trying to get their business, at least learn the names of your clients." Turning to Stonewall, he continued. "And while my ways are unorthodox, I was able to uncover several weak points in the few minutes of my actions. Firstly, you—"

He pointed at the guard.

"You need to be fired. During his patrol around the property, he engaged on a personal call, and when trouble came, he was out-of-breath before he even got here. He fumbled with his weapon, failed to announce himself to me, and even let my dog disarm him. He's not fit for purpose, and the first change that needs to be made around here."

The guard's face turned red. He spluttered, outraged, but couldn't find the words to deny what was the simple truth. "Sir... Mr. Rockefeller... he is out of order!"

"But he's right, isn't he?" Stonewall agreed, to Kane's surprise. "I've seen you walking around talking on the phone myself, but I gave you the benefit of the doubt and assumed you'd be up to the job if push came to shove. Clearly, I was wrong."

Lexi sighed, the frustration in her voice impossible to miss.

"If someone doesn't tell me what's going on, I am going to lose it!"

Mandy rested a manicured hand on her daughter's arm, sharing a concerned look with her husband that Kane caught. Stonewall gave an almost imperceptible nod, agreeing with the unspoken question on Mandy's mind.

"Get dressed, sweetheart. We need to have a talk with you. We'll be in the study."

Mandy pinned her sapphire eyes on Kane, imploring him not to give the game away just yet.

"Why can't we just talk here?"

Stonewall closed his eyes, taking a breath. Despite his huge size, he looked suddenly weary, as if he could be knocked over with a feather.

"We'll explain everything in a moment. Just get dressed. It won't be a quick conversation."

His answer seemed to suck all the air out of the room.

"What's your name?" Stonewall turned to Kane.

"Kane. Kane Turner."

"Come with me." Stonewall led the way out. Kane hesitated, looking at Lexi and hating the concern that was growing there. For the first time since he'd seen her, she looked vulnerable and scared.

Lexi didn't react. Her mind was racing with questions that she had no answers to. It wasn't until a soft, warm tongue licked her hands that she looked down.

It was his dog. What had he called him?

Bud.

No longer the terrifying guard dog, he whined at her, tail wagging in what looked to be an apology.

Mandy had led the other two men away, but Stonewall stood waiting in the doorway, keeping a watchful eye on Turner.

He wouldn't leave her alone with him.

Kane half considered apologizing to her, but with her father glowering at him from the door, the inclination passed. Whistling for Bud, he then turned and followed Stonewall out as Bud bounded after him.

6

They kept him waiting in the well-stocked library.

After they left Lexi's room, Stonewall had promptly fired the security guard. The man had pleaded, talking about the five kids he had to put through college, but Stonewall had stayed as rock steady as his nickname.

No one toyed with his daughter's life, and certainly not when they were on his payroll.

Once he had gone, it was the other security firm's turn to be seen.

Worried that Kane might have already won the contract with his stunt, Todd Phillips of AAA Security had insisted upon finishing his pitch, the one that had been so rudely interrupted with Kane's unorthodox stunt.

Kane could have argued back and, in typical fashion would have — the guy was a jerk and needed to be taken down a peg or two. But he decided it might be wiser to pick his battles and forced his ego to take a backseat.

The armchair he sat on was about as comfortable as a

rock and must have been chosen for aesthetics more than anything else. The rest of the furniture seemed equally uninviting, which seemed strange given the environment. Weren't libraries meant to house people who wanted to read for long periods of time? Why would this be the furniture of choice?

Unless this was where they sent guests who displeased them.

He glanced over the spines of the leather-bound books on the shelves. If they weren't encyclopedias — and who used those when there was Wikipedia? — they had titles like The History of this, The Battle of that, all subjects you couldn't pay him to read, not unless he was suffering from a bout of insomnia. Then, the books might have come in handy.

By an antique mahogany table, screenplays, with their titles written in the spines in black marker, were stacked in neat piles. Unlike their book counterparts, they were well thumbed-through, having been read many times. Though he wasn't an ardent theater-goer, even he recognized a few of the titles, several of which were vehicles Mandy had starred in.

Bud sat beside him, still on high alert. He knew they were working and wouldn't properly relax until they arrived back home on the beach, which was why his sneaky lick of Lexi's hands had surprised him.

As affectionate as his dog was to him, that affection wasn't usually directed at others so his apparent affection for her was particularly unusual.

His canvas messenger bag pinged with notification of an email. Checking his iPad, he opened the message. It

was the file from Clara he'd been waiting half the day
for.

*Sorry for the delay, Kane. Here's the overview of the client I've
put together for you. If you need anything else, just call me.
I'm always around. xoxo*

She always signed off his emails with "xoxo" which he'd
thought was just a Clara thing. It wasn't until Wilson
explained that he received preferential treatment that
he'd realized Wilson's assistant had a crush on him.

*Maybe if she did her job better, he'd take her out for a
drink.*

Nothing irritated him more than people who didn't
do their jobs properly.

Tapping on the attachment icon, he waited for the file
to download. A window opened with a full-screen image
of Lexi confronting him with her startling beauty yet
again.

Thick chestnut hair fell to her waist in waves. Her big
blue eyes, a shade or two lighter than her mom's,
sparkled with warmth, yet seemed to keep all at arm's
distance at the same time. Her beauty was effortlessly
timeless, with the gamine quality of Audrey Hepburn
mixed with the dangerous body of a Victoria Secret's
model.

He dragged his eyes away from her face and started
on her written file.

Lexi grew up in the shadow of her parents' fame.
Although her childhood had been one glamorous

Hollywood event after another, she'd held good grades and healthy hobbies. She loved to read though her greatest joy was riding her thoroughbred horse, Spirit, until he passed away a few years ago. For whatever reason or another, she never replaced him.

Graduating with a degree in English Literature, Lexi surprised everyone when she didn't move ahead with a career as an author, a direction in which it seemed she'd been heading. Instead, she'd taken a low-level job at her father's studio, writing coverage for screenplays that were submitted.

He raised a brow at how little the job paid, having expected her to have been made an exception to the rule, considering Stonewall's role in the company. Having said that, it wasn't as if she was lacking financially, not from what he could see of her trust fund.

There was more money there than he'd ever see in his lifetime.

He found a handwritten note scribbled in Wilson's untidy scrawl that had been scanned and added to the file. He had to squint to make out the words.

Wilson had noted that Lexi had recently started fundraising for several local charities. She used the contacts she'd made through her parents to raise financing for Apples, a charity that specialized in saving ex-racehorses from the butchers block, and PAWS, a no-kill shelter that was bursting at the seams. She also volunteered there on the weekends.

"That why you like her?"

In response to the question, Bud cocked his head and chuffed. His dog must have picked up on her love of animals. Dogs — animals in general — seemed to know when a good person was in their midst.

He wasn't swayed in his initial opinion of her: however nice she might be to animals, she could still be a nightmare as most Hollywood spawn were.

He carried on reading.

She had a few friends that she would hang out with, but their gatherings seemed infrequent. Clara had scoped out her friends' Instagram feeds and provided a small timeline of who was who. All the posts that featured her seemed to have been from years back. He couldn't find anything recent about her: there were no pictures of her online past the age of sixteen.

He turned to the section on her love life.

She'd only had two relationships: one that had lasted one semester at high school, and the other during the last year of college with Peter Jackson, a fellow student in her class.

Jackson's numerous social network posts consisted of his travels, where his sole aim seemed to be to party in every major city of the world. With barely any time between he and Lexi's break up, he took up with a model who was constantly featured in the press for her wild ways.

There was another note from Wilson mentioning that Jackson's model girlfriend had been a close friend of Lexi's, but since the two had gotten together, unsurprisingly, the girls had never spoken to each other again.

This was something else he kept coming across in this town: people leaving their partners for someone close to them. The place was such a cesspool of cheats and fakes that he was giving real thought to moving somewhere nice and honest. Canada maybe, where the air was clear and the people just as transparent.

He flipped back to the images of Lexi that had been taken from her family's photo albums, noting how natural she looked in all of them. Not for her were the posy "duck trout" faces most half-decent women struck whenever a camera was pointed their way, or the cheesy peace signs. She simply smiled a smile that caused an unfamiliar pull in his chest.

His forehead furrowed into a frown at this unexpected reaction.

He would have to ignore this initial physical attraction he was feeling, get the job done, and take off on that vacation he'd promised Bud.

The girl was bound to be an ordeal.

All he'd have to do was spend a little time with her to find his attraction fading.

He'd bet the house on it.

7

It was five or so minutes later when Ruth, a chatty woman in her sixties who had been with the family for years, poured Kane a scotch.

Despite having worked for most of the day, her uniform was spotless. She handed the scotch to him, her hands rough from the years of manual labor, yet nimble and graceful as a woman half her age. Kane took the drink, inclining his head in a nod of thanks.

"I can count the times I have poured this drink for guests on one hand," she informed him.

"Do the Rockefellers have a rule about alcohol?"

She shook her head. "On the contrary, they are connoisseurs, but this particular bottle is usually only brought out for special circumstances. You must be an important man, Mr. Turner."

He was hardly that to them. What possible reason could they have for bringing out the good stuff?

Were they trying to poison him?

Maybe this was punishment for seeing his daughter half-naked…

The heat from the scotch burned his throat as his imagination took over. Oblivious to the direction his thoughts had taken, Ruth continued.

"So many movies they've made… Mr. Rockefeller, he works very hard. It's terrible what is happening to them."

"They spoke to you about it?" Kane kept his voice deceptively soft, but Ruth caught the edge in it. Looking suddenly alarmed, she flushed and stammered over her next words.

"I overheard them speaking. It's just… I love Lexi like my own daughter."

She stopped talking, panic setting in. A sheen of sweat appeared on her brow that she wiped away with a shaking hand. She tossed a look at the door that separated them from the Rockefellers, worried that they might be able to hear them.

"It's probably best if you don't speak of this with anyone, Ruth. Not even your son, Hank," Kane replied quietly.

Ruth looked startled.

She had not mentioned anything of herself to him, yet Kane knew that Ruth had an adult son who she had raised single-handedly after her husband had died when her son was only six. Shortly after his death, she was hired by the Rockefellers, and had been looking after them for some twenty years. It was one of those facts Clara had noted in the file.

"Of course not," the housekeeper stammered. Kane gave her a small smile to soften his words, but kept his eyes hard. It was easier to do his job if people were slightly afraid of him.

Her head bobbed up and down as she spun and headed out of the room, moving as fast as her short legs could carry her. Kane had put the fear of God into her and she couldn't wait to get away. When the sliver of guilt rose up, he quashed it with a gulp of scotch.

The door in front of him opened, revealing the office beyond.

Mandy perched on an armchair, sipping from a glass of white wine as Stonewall greeted him by the door.

"Come in."

Kane walked inside, Bud close at his side, toenails clipping on the wood floor. There was no sign of the other security man, and looking at the Rockefellers' faces, he couldn't tell either way if they had come to a decision to hire him or not.

"Have a seat," Stonewall gestured at a bank of sofas on the other side of the room. Kane sat where he would get the best view of the entire room. It was another part of his training that had stuck: a smart man made sure there were no blind spots at all times.

"Why don't we skip the introductions and jump straight to what you discovered on your little recon trip?" Stonewall stood leaning against the wall, looking every inch the tough guy he was.

"Fine by me. You've already heard what I think about your security guard."

Stonewall's eyes went darker. "He's already been taken care of."

"Yes, but he's not the only one on your payroll, is he?

I'd like to speak with them all after this meeting, find out for myself what they are like."

Mandy crossed her arms, diamond bracelets jangling. "You haven't got the job yet. Don't you think you're being a little presumptuous?"

"No. I'm the best there is, and the sooner you realize that, the sooner we can start talking about the real threat here."

He'd no sooner said the words when a side door opened as Lexi came inside breathing heavily.

Her hair wasn't as wet now, having been run through a dryer briefly. The roots were dry, though the tips still clung to her damply. She'd pulled on a pink sweater that was thin enough for him to see the tank beneath, that she'd paired with a pair of jeans. On her feet, she wore flip flops. A pale peach polish gleamed on her toe nails.

It was a simple look, understated, carelessly thrown together even, but she could have just been styled for a shoot. Apparently, the girl could not look bad even if her nerves were frayed.

Her sudden appearance wasn't what drew their attention, however, but the manner of it.

Despite their altercation, Lexi barely spared him a glance, her gaze fixated on the phone she held in her shaking hand. Her eyes were wide with horror as her complexion went from tanned to porcelain.

"What is it, honey?" Stonewall strode the few feet to her side. She wasn't able to tear her eyes away from whatever it was that disturbed her on the screen. She lifted the phone so he could get a better view of it.

"What the..." Stonewall's neck began to flush an angry shade of Merlot. "Who the hell did this?!"

His voice was husky, heavy with regret, yet colored by a terrifying rage that even Kane could feel way across the room.

Uneasy by their reactions, Mandy hurried toward them. "What is it? Show me."

As soon as she took in the phone's display, her hand flew to her throat, and she gasped. "Oh no. Honey... I'm so sorry."

Kane couldn't keep silent any longer. If there was a new threat, then he needed to be made aware of it as soon as possible.

"Has something happened?"

Stonewall tried to contain himself in an effort not to upset his daughter further, though he had to spit out the words.

"Pictures of Lexi have just been released all over the gossip sites. Pictures where she is dressed in only a biki-ni.... Some of the positions look... suggestive."

As he said the words, Lexi became more shaken. Mandy threw an arm around her, steering her to one of the couches. They sat, Mandy taking hold of Lexi's ice-cold hands in hers.

"We deliberately kept her out of the limelight — by her request — to the point where there aren't even any photographs of her as an adult. We wanted her to be able to live her life free from the shackles of our fame," Stonewall explained, voice hoarse with feeling.

"But now the world has seen me practically naked,

and we'll never be able to get those pictures back," Lexi whispered, numb with shock.

"Do you mind if I see them?" Kane asked.

It seemed likely that this was done by the same person who had been sending the threats to the family. It could be that they were ramping up, making good on their promises to "make them pay." It was crucial to learn as much from the images as possible.

Stonewall handed the phone to him. Kane examined the images with a critical eye.

Lexi had been sunbathing by the pool, a pair of shades hiding most of her face. Her skin glistened from a recent swim, hair wet and twisted to one side much as she'd had it a few moments ago. It took only a few more moments to recognize the terrace behind the pool and the bank of bushes beside it. After all, it hadn't been that long ago that he'd considered hiding in them.

The photographs had been taken of Lexi while she had been at home.

And with that sudden realization, their reactions made even more sense.

Home was meant to be safe from prying eyes, yet it had now been invaded in the most terrifying of ways. If they could take pictures like these, what more did they have? Videos of the family or the famous actress in her most private moments?

And then there was the other very real concern: what if photographs and videos weren't all they were after...

What if they really wanted to hurt the family?

"How did they get them?" Lexi directed her question at him, finally coming out of her daze.

Studying the slightly grainy images, he mentally did the calculations.

"From the position of the sun in correspondence to your terrace, I'd say with a wide-zoom lens from a West-facing vantage point."

"So they weren't actually on our property?" Stonewall seemed eager for this to be the case and Kane couldn't blame the man: no one wanted to think their loved ones were at risk.

"Impossible to say without further investigation but it's highly unlikely someone would take the unnecessary risk of being discovered when you could do the same job — legally — from outside your fence."

Technically, this was true, though taking the previous threats into account, the ones Stonewall had forbidden their company to speak of, he was more inclined to believe otherwise.

His answer caused some of the tension to leave Lexi's face. She tucked a strand of loose hair behind an ear and licked her dry lips.

"If you hire my firm, the first thing I'll do is to take a nice, long walk around the property with my dog, Bud. It's amazing what traces people leave behind that a specially trained dog can pick up, traces that would otherwise be missed by a human."

"Are we hiring more security because of this? But it only just happened. How did you know?" Lexi was quick to put two and two together.

Stonewall didn't blink when he answered. "Your mother and I had already been discussing the possibility of changing our security, as we felt it wasn't up to scratch. I think today's events have proven our concerns right."

He paused, eyes sliding across the room to his wife. They shared a meaningful look before Mandy took over the conversation.

"With this new turn of events, I think it's best if we hire a personal bodyguard for you."

Lexi sat up straighter, looking even more startled. "No. I don't need a bodyguard."

"We'll feel much happier if you have one," Stonewall explained, spreading his hands wide. "Your mom already has her team, but I think we should both have our own now too."

"It's just some creep making a fast buck at my expense. How does this warrant my needing protection?"

The question hung heavy in the air. Kane waited for her parents to spill the entire story, but they stayed silent.

"We've given this a lot of thought, Lexi. I know it's not what you want, but it's better to be safe, don't you think?" Mandy attempted to soften the blow.

Lexi's shoulders fell, the wind knocked out of her. "But I'm no one. The only interesting thing about me is the two of you. No one would want to threaten me."

The fact she thought this about herself spoke volumes, and cut Mandy to the quick. The movie star visibly flinched, though Lexi — staring blindly at the floor now — missed it. Mandy's fingers interlaced on her lap, knuckles clenched in a death grip.

"That's not true," Mandy started, only for Lexi to shut her down with a look.

"Mom, please. I don't need fake platitudes. I'm a

grown woman and I don't need a bodyguard. I can handle myself."

"The matter has already been decided. I'm sorry you're not comfortable with it, but now that the world knows your face, it's a necessary step. We can discuss this again at a later date, but for now, this is happening." Stonewall's voice brokered no argument, and Lexi must have known it, as all the fight suddenly left her.

Stonewall forced himself to stand taller, assuming an air of control even if he didn't quite feel it himself. While he was used to the odd catastrophe at work, trouble at home was something he'd not dealt with before. This was an entirely new and most unwelcome development.

"What do you suggest we do?" he asked Kane, turning from his daughter to avoid seeing the devastation in her eyes.

"I'd start with a detailed search of your property. I'd find where those photographs were taken from, and see if my dog can pick up anything they left behind that could lead us to them. Then, I'd get my team to set up a new security system around the property. Just on my short inspection alone, I discovered several blind spots. We need to eradicate those, have eyes on every corner of your home."

"You mentioned interviewing my staff?" Stonewall's tone had become resigned, knowing that his family was about to undergo intense upheaval.

Kane felt some sympathy for him. His own home — though small — was a haven to him, a private and necessary sanctuary where no one could intrude. The ocean helped to calm, while the peacefulness kept some of the terrors of war away.

He of all people knew how important it was to feel safe in your own home.

"Yes, I'd need to speak to all of them, not only your current security, but the maids, gardeners, everyone who works here. I'd also want details of any regular suppliers that are used."

"Ruth has been with us for years, she'll have that information for you."

Kane nodded his thanks. "From now on, each of you will have to have your own security detail. You can't step foot out of this house without a bodyguard. For the time being, you'll also use our trained drivers instead of your usual ones."

At this, Mandy balked. Uncrossing her legs, she moved to the edge of her seat. "Is that really necessary? Jose has been with me for a long time. I'm positive he wouldn't have anything to do with this."

"He might not, but he isn't trained to deal with an emergency. You need drivers who know how to react if you are suddenly attacked."

His words must have conjured up a vivid image in their minds as, other than Lexi's eyes growing impossibly wider, there was no other kickback to his suggestion.

"What else?" Stonewall had moved to his wife and put his arm around her. She leaned into him, taking his strength as her own.

In that split second, Kane saw how connected the two were. Even after all these years together, they loved each other with a passion he wondered if he would ever feel.

"That'll get us going for now."

Stonewall looked at Mandy. Their gaze held for several beats, an unspoken dialogue going between them. Finally, Mandy nodded her approval. Turning his gaze to his daughter, he waited for her opinion. "What do you think?"

"I guess, if we have to do this, then he's as good as any."

Her response deflated Kane's ego some. He hadn't expected cheers and a parade, but some kind of recognition for his good work would have been nice.

"Then you have the job."

"Good. I do have one thing I'd like to raise now, since all three of you are here." He went on without waiting for their consent. "Wilson mentioned something about a party taking place in a few days' time. Given the circumstances, I think it's best if you postpone it. A party with the kind of numbers you are planning on will open up your home to hundreds, if not thousands, of people, each of those a potential opportunity for threat."

"No," Lexi answered, looking suddenly alarmed. "Absolutely not. It's important that we go ahead with it. We've already spent months planning. It's too late to cancel now."

Kane was shocked by how willfully strong she was about this. Annoyance took hold of him. Given all that had occurred, how could she care so much about a party? That didn't take long for her to show her true colors.

Mandy looked torn, wanting to please her daughter,

yet needing to keep her safe. "Maybe we could postpone? Everyone will understand."

"You think all those people who have lost everything will understand why we can't inconvenience ourselves for them? What about their pets? You think they will understand?"

Her voice had turned sharp with feeling.

"Lexi… you know that's not what she means." Stonewall's tone held a note of reprimand. No one lay into his wife, not even his own daughter.

"Am I missing something here? I thought this was just a birthday party?" Kane didn't bother to hide how little he thought of the idea. Hollywood people had such strange notions about what constituted a life-and-death emergency.

"That's just an excuse," Lexi explained, pushing up her sleeves that were a little too long at the cuff. "It's really to raise money for those who have been displaced by the wildfires and help fund the local animal shelters. They've been swamped recently."

She went on to explain.

"Whatever families have been saved, haven't been able to keep their pets with them in their new lodgings."

Kane hadn't read much about it in the news, but it made unfortunate sense. He stole a glance at Bud, sitting quietly beside him. His intelligent brown eyes met his.

He imagined his trailer being burned by the wildfires, and Bud being taken away and forced back into a cage. The vision made his hands become fists. Bud sighed as if he too could see it only too well, though Kane questioned her motives for doing such a thing.

Most celebrities did "charity" work, though they generally weren't in it to help those in need. It was performed as an act of publicity, another way in which to play the fame game and find favor with the masses.

Animals and children were the go-to charities of choice, in particular sick children. It was why, whenever some scandal was about to implode an A-Lister's career, you would suddenly find them doing a "low-key" visit to a children's cancer ward, that would somehow still find itself plastered all over social media.

YouTube was full of these visits.

"The shelters are struggling, especially the no-kill ones. Help is needed now, and this is the best way I can do the most good. As soon as the money is pledged to me, I can start giving it to the ones who need it the most."

She spoke earnestly, as if she truly meant it, but Kane wasn't quite ready to drink the Kool-Aid just yet. It was entirely possible that Mandy wasn't the only actress in the family. Even so, he had to respond.

"In that case, this will be a bigger operation than usual. My men will have to search every guest and staff member who arrives, even at the party. It won't be popular."

"I don't care if you have to strip search every single one of them," Stonewall glowered from across the room, his eyes narrowing into slits.

"If it'll keep my family safe, you do whatever is necessary."

8

With a gentleman's handshake agreement and a confirmation sent from Stonewall's email to Wilson, the contract was granted much to Todd Philips' disgust, who, it turned out had waited anxiously outside, expecting his company to have won the job.

The women retreated to digest what had been discussed, leaving Kane to address the elephant in the room.

"Your daughter needs to be told about the threat to your lives. Not only is it negligent not to inform her of the dangers, it will also make my job that much harder. If she is unaware that someone potentially means you harm, she won't take any of this seriously."

Stonewall considered his comment before brushing it away with the blink of an eye.

"No. You just need to do your job and keep her safe. She doesn't need to know about that."

Kane couldn't understand why he was so dead set

against the idea. Lexi was as she had pointed out already — a grown woman. As far as he was concerned, she didn't need to be coddled like this.

"I think that is a grave mistake."

He knew the moment he had crossed the line. Stonewall crossed his thick arms over his chest, pinning him in place with eyes that had turned icy.

"Lucky then that you're not hired to think. If you don't like my opinion, there are plenty of other firms desperate for our business. Philips probably hasn't even left the property."

He left the threat dangling between them.

Normally, Kane wouldn't have balked at quitting. If it were up to him, he'd walk away and leave the Rockefellers to their fates. One less job working for demanding celebrities was no skin off his nose.

But this meant a lot to Wilson, his buddy who had thrown him a lifeline right when he'd needed one, when no one else had given a damn. He owed him, and this was the first time he had asked to collect.

This wasn't a job he could walk away from.

"I'll do as you request for now. That's all I can give you."

Stonewall wasn't the only one who could play this game. Kane knew he was the best, and the man wasn't a fool: he'd already seen what he could do.

After several moments, the other man nodded. "Fine. I need to return to work, but you have free rein to do as required. If you need help with logistics, speak to Ruth."

Kane nodded that he would do exactly that.

Business handled, Stonewall bent suddenly and patted Bud on the head. "He's a great dog."

The unexpected compliment took Kane by surprise. "I might be biased, but you'll get no argument from me."

"Lexi's always wanted pets but Mandy's allergic."

"Will Bud's presence bother her then?"

Stonewall shook his head. "If she doesn't touch him, she'll be OK. It's cats that are the biggest problem."

A phone started ringing from inside Stonewall's linen pants. He nodded that he was done with the conversation, and answered the phone on his way out. "What is it?"

Kane glanced down at Bud. "It's just you and me again. Ready to get back to work?"

"Woof!" Bud agreed, happy to follow him to the ends of the earth.

———

The grass was springy beneath his feet as he took a walk around the imposing property. Bud walked beside him, tail swishing from side to side, nose twitching, taking in all the splendor.

They were far enough away from the raging wildfires that their smoke was only a distant blip in the sky. The air quality here was as fresh and clean as new-fallen snow.

Spicy floral scents tickled his nose. Despite feeling as if he were in another world, the familiar sight of the ocean, that sang him to sleep each night, filled him with reassurance.

They passed an organic vegetable garden with a dizzying array of crops, some of which even he had never seen before.

As a marine, nutrition was just as important as physical training, since what he ate affected not only his health and weight, but also his physical and mental performance. It even affected his ability to maintain control on the field and how he might heal from an injury. As such, their diet had consisted of low-fat, nutrient-rich foods designed to give optimal performance. Subsequently, foods were consumed rather than enjoyed.

When he'd left his last assignment, the first thing he had done was to splurge on all the foods he hadn't been able to eat on the job: In and Out burgers, milkshakes, prime rib steaks the size of his head, Korean barbeques, pasta dripping in cream and cheese, and pizza.

So much pizza.

After a month-long bender that left him with the beginnings of a gut and carb-induced lethargy, he had reined it back in, kicking up his daily kettlebell work-outs and beachside jogs until he had whipped his body back into shape.

As disciplined as he was now, the one thing he couldn't control was his wicked appetite for good food. Seeing the lush vegetables all around him, he couldn't help picturing how they would taste sauteed in a garlic butter sauce.

He picked up his pace, leaving the vegetable garden and thoughts of food behind. He walked the perimeter, checking both the six-foot tall metal fence and the area around for signs of interference.

He recorded voice memos into his dictaphone, which would be transcribed at the end of the day. While he was out on rounds like this, he liked to keep moving: having to stop and type everything up would only distract him from his work.

They'd been walking for an hour when Bud suddenly alerted, nose to the air. He'd picked up a scent of some kind. Barking, he padded up to the fence, pawing at the ground by the metal stakes as his nose went to town.

Kane went to his side, and got down to his level to see what had captured his attention.

The grass continued on the other side of the fence. Beyond that, a hedge of evergreen Ficus trees provided privacy and sound proofing from the road bordering the property.

He could see nothing out of the ordinary.

The fence was undisturbed, there were no footprints on the grass, though that didn't mean no one had been here.

He knelt onto the grass with all of his weight, crushing it as much as he could before rocking back onto his feet in a low crouch. Already, the flattened grass was beginning to bounce back up.

The constant sun, combined with whatever regular treatment was given to the lawn, made it strong and healthy.

Bud continued pawing at the spot until Kane had to move him aside. "Let me see."

Bud whined, but stepped aside for him.

Something glinted in the sun on the ground, but it was too far for him to reach through the fence to get it.

He'd have to go *over* the fence if he wanted to see what it was.

He approached the nearest support post. This part of the fence was the thickest and, as luck would have it, the top of it was flat even though the rest of the fence was spiked — this flat edge was exactly what he needed.

"Be right back," he told Bud, who whined again, turning in a circle, already anxious at their imminent separation.

Resting the flat of his left hand — and his stronger arm — on the flat surface of the support post, he jumped up, simultaneously pulling on his left arm to give himself more height. When his hips were about level with the top of the spikes, it was a simple matter to swing himself over the fence, twisting his wrist in the process so that it wouldn't break.

He'd learned this neat trick from a short stint training with some local parkour enthusiasts. Having spotted a group of them in his regular park while out on a walk with Bud, he'd befriended them, noticing how they were some of the fittest people he'd ever seen, prone to performing insanely agile feats with their bodies. While he couldn't do the flips they could, or run up vertical walls, this trick had come in handy many times over.

He moved toward the metal object lying on the ground.

Half buried in the grass, he wouldn't have noticed it if not for Bud's amazing sense of smell. Taking out a plastic bag that he kept for such occasions, he slid his hand into it, using it as a glove as he carefully retrieved a soda can that had been crushed in such a way that he couldn't see what brand it was.

All he could tell was the can was red with white lettering — which didn't narrow it down much. Turning to examine it from all angles, he noticed that the metal hadn't corroded at all, which meant only one thing.

It had been left very recently.

Rising to full height, he glanced at his watch before peering into the sky until his eyes found the sun. Where they were standing right now was due west of the house, right about where the shots of Lexi could have been taken from. The angle of the pictures had been low, which meant the photographer hadn't been standing on anything other than the ground.

"Good find, Boy."

Bud woofed, pleased with himself, as Kane slipped his hand through the fence and rewarded him with a few of his favorite treats.

He studied the hedge, which reached several feet above his head. Unlike the fence, there was no way anyone could have jumped it. How had they gotten around this hurdle?

He found his answer further down, where light seeped through a gap in a section of the hedge. It wasn't wide, maybe a foot and a half, enough for an average person to slip through. He examined the edges of the hedge to find they had been sawn through.

Being above average size himself, Kane had to suck in his stomach to slip through the gap. He made it — just — though the effort might have cost him some skin.

Through to the other side, he saw a line of tall oak trees that all but hid the hedge.

The photographer had been smart, choosing a spot that was hidden from any cars that might have passed by on the road by a thick tree trunk. There wasn't any sign of the shorn off hedge itself: he assumed they had taken it away to draw less attention to this site.

All of that premeditated thinking caused a tightness in his chest.

This wasn't some silly prank at all.

Whoever was doing this was deliberate and careful.

Pocketing the crushed can, he jumped back over the fence to resume the rest of his search.

exi was having a tough time focusing on her volunteer work.

Since that explosive meeting in the library, all she could think about, all she could see in her head were those pictures.

She felt unclean and exposed, but the worst of it was the shame that had overtaken her body. It didn't matter that someone had done this to her: in the court of public opinion she was going to be found guilty.

It was happening already.

She knew she shouldn't look — it was the first rule of having famous parents — but she hadn't been able to stop herself. The comments section of the articles featuring the photographs were filling up with vitriol. There was name-calling and slut-shaming with some even theorizing that she had been kept out of the public eye just for this big pay day.

There were people who actually thought this was a stunt for money, and while there were many fame-hungry seekers who did exactly that, Lexi wasn't one of them.

And the thing that burned most of all: while she knew the photographs had been of *her*, she wasn't stupid enough to believe it was *about* her.

It never was.

Whenever something happened, it always had to do her parents, more usually her mom, but her father too had seen his fair share of drama.

Growing up, it almost seemed as if no one had been very interested in her. At times, that even applied to her own parents.

Even when she was a child, Lexi had been unusually sensitive to the wants and needs of her mother, and perhaps that was the way she had engineered it: Mandy had chosen a man who worshipped her above all else, then raised a daughter who did the same. Like the rest of the world, Lexi had lived off her mother's smile and approval.

Yet, despite how she adored her, Lexi wasn't blind to her mother's faults.

In this line of work, self-absorption came with the territory, coupled with long spells of absence. Much of which couldn't be helped, as it was part of Mandy's job not only to disappear off to far-flung locations to shoot the movies, but also to promote them. And the occasions when she'd brought Lexi with her were few and far between.

Her childhood had been a juggling act of nannies, assistants, and private flights in jets, the latter of which had lost its sheen by the time she'd hit double digits.

After all, no amount of flying in private jets could replace an absent mother. In the end, it was decided Lexi was better off under the care of Ruth, since the woman doted on her as much as she did her own son.

And her father?

As much as he loved her, Mandy was the center of his world. She lit up his life. Having witnessed the many nights he raised her alone, and how, as strong and capable as he was, he always seemed lost in those moments without his love by his side, Lexi had never expected anything else.

Now that she was an adult, their small unit had fallen into a nice rhythm. Mandy was around much more than she had been previously, her last three movies having been shot in and around the state.

Feeling that things had been going well, Lexi had secretly started looking for a place to call her own.

Wanting to take her mind off her current troubles, she pulled up the images she'd saved on Gold Realty, the realtors most used by the rich and famous.

The moment the weathered blue door with the white shuttered windows of the beach house came up, her heart swelled. It was a small, cottage style home, just three bedrooms and two bathrooms, and its back yard wasn't more than a patch of grass, but it was surrounded by mature lemon trees with the ocean right on its doorstep.

A white porch wrapped around two sides of the property, leaving her with visions of herself in a swing sipping lemonade as she watched the sun go down, a pair of rescue dogs and cats by her feet.

The entire vision made her heart sing.

Though the property wasn't big, the price tag was not reflected by the lack of square footage. The location and proximity to the water pushed it into an eye-watering bracket. At least, for the average person. She would have to use a sizeable chunk of her trust fund to secure it, and had been prepared to do just that when the fires had started.

She'd called an immediate halt to her plans, not willing to use up her resources when the landscape was in such upheaval. It seemed her decision had been fortuitous given the day's events. Much as she didn't want to admit it, the safest place for her right now was at home.

A blur streaked past on the lawn outside, a dog sprinting across the grounds. She tensed, a chill gathering in the pit of her stomach. It was that security man's dog, Bud. Had he found something?

All thoughts of her dream home faded away as the man himself appeared in view. He seemed in no hurry to go after his dog. It wasn't until Bud raced back to him that Lexi saw the red ball in his mouth.

They were playing.

She watched them, her curiosity over the man piqued. He wasn't like anyone she had known before. Most people reacted in a certain way in front of her parents. There was the usual awe and shock followed by the strange compulsion to be noticed by them.

This man had been different.

He hadn't seemed to care what they thought of him other than how good he was at his job. He didn't need their attention, wasn't hungry for it. Didn't care for their validation or time.

Which made for an intriguing cocktail.

Kane took the ball from Bud, snapped his arm back far behind and hurled it with a strength that made her take note. Biceps rippled, his excellent form seemingly highlighted by the setting sun.

The sight of him was magnificent, causing a tremor to go through her body. She couldn't stop staring, which was ridiculous. While he might be nice to look at, he seemed lacking in the personality department — the man hadn't even apologized after bursting in on her today.

Bud bolted for the ball and started running back to him, when he suddenly swerved and headed straight for her. Startled, unable to react fast enough, she froze by the door.

Kane turned and caught her staring.

The hot heat of embarrassment washed over her, and she jumped away from the door, hiding behind a long white curtain, although that was probably the worst thing she could have done. She should have styled it out, pretended that she hadn't seen him, instead of making it patently clear to all that she had.

Her hope that he would ignore her ridiculous behavior was gone the second a knock sounded on the door. When she didn't immediately react, the dog woofed as if he was asking her why she was being so silly.

No idea, Bud.

No idea at all.

Breathing out a deep sigh, she stepped away from the

curtain and opened the door. Kane cocked his head at her, an expression of mock concern on his face. He held up both hands.

"Can we talk, or are you going to threaten me with your mace again?"

"Don't flatter yourself. I only get that out on special occasions."

The corners of his mouth twitched as if he were slightly amused, but he seemed unable to crack a grin.

"So I'm special?"

"That's not what I meant..." She trailed off, irritated at the sight of him. He would be a constant reminder now that the normal life she'd tried so hard to cultivate would soon be destroyed.

It wasn't entirely fair to blame it on him, she knew, but it was just how she felt. Hunky or not, something about him rubbed her the wrong way.

"Is there something I can help you with, or were you just hoping to cop a look at me half-naked again?" For some unfathomable reason, his very nearness was causing her to feel jumpy. Goose pimples ran up and down her arms. She rubbed at them, hoping they would go away.

His face turned hard.

"Don't worry, that will never happen again. I don't need to spy on women, Miss. Rockefeller. That's not how I get my kicks."

Shame made her take a moment. She felt bad for her sudden reaction to him. However cocky he was, he had already proven good at his job. Maybe she should take him at his word too. She couldn't quite make herself apologize though some form of explanation was in order.

"I didn't mean to sound so hostile. I'm not quite myself."

His eyes weren't exactly soft now, but they weren't brittle as glass either.

"Well, that's why I'm here, to reassure you that we have it under control."

"We?"

"My dog and I."

Hearing himself be mentioned, Bud lifted up a paw, as if to make her acquaintance. It was impossible to stay angry with that face staring back at her. Her coldness heated up several notches.

"Thanks for the effort, Bud."

She reached down and shook his paw, much to the dog's delight. He nudged at her hand, demanding that she now stroke his head. She obliged, enjoying the uncomplicated joy of his silky fur against her fingers as a smile came upon her lips.

"Did you train him yourself?"

Her smile unnerved him. She seemed almost nice flashing it at his dog. The simple question she'd asked suddenly seemed loaded with danger.

"We trained each other."

His tone wasn't exactly rude, but it wasn't welcoming either. Lexi wasn't sure what his deal was, but it was almost as if he had a problem with her. Yet why would that be when they'd only just met?

"My team will be on site first thing in the morning to install the new security system," he continued briskly, apparently all done with the small talk. "I wanted you to know that there will be a camera outside your room on the terrace right here." He moved into position, gesturing at a section on the corner of the terrace.

"It won't point into your room so you'll have privacy. But if anyone tries to go through these doors, they will be caught on camera and an alarm will be triggered."

"Is that really necessary? I'm not sure why my folks are overreacting like this. Those pictures..." Her voice trailed off as their images flew into her mind. "They're unpleasant, but I really doubt other paparazzi will attempt more of the same. Now that we know it's happened, we're obviously going to be more prepared for it."

"If you have a problem with it, you'll have to speak to your parents." It was the only explanation he could offer without giving the game away.

She stared at him, wondering why he was being so cold, when he was clearly capable of being nice — she'd witnessed that in each of his interactions with his dog.

She turned to the corner where the camera would go, pushing his attitude from her mind. "Will they know if it's been triggered?"

"The alarm? No. You won't hear it from here, but we will. We're setting up our base of operations in one of your outbuildings so there will always be a team of us on site. If the perp doesn't know they've tripped it, it gives us the advantage and more time to catch them."

What he said made sense, and though it should reassure her, a shadow of apprehension crept along her spine. As unlikely as it was, in the event of an attack, would a camera be enough?

Maybe he read her mind, as he answered, "We won't ever be far: someone will always be within a few steps of you. If you're concerned, all you have to do is call or press the panic button that's arriving tomorrow."

She nodded, wrapping her arms around herself. "I'm going to be out most of the day, so I guess my guard will have to come with me. When will I meet them?"

"You already have."

"It's you?"

He nodded, looking about as pleased by this as she felt. At least there was the dog, she consoled herself. That was one friendly face.

Kane was thinking a similar thought, sending a prayer of thanks for Bud, who would make this job at least somewhat tolerable.

As much as he didn't want to be on her detail, she was the main target. He'd have to keep close to her at all times.

Oh, what joy that was sure to bring.

10

Against the rising sun, Kane took off on his morning jog along the beach.

With the near silence of the world and nothing but the waves lapping on the shore, breaking dawn was his favorite time of the day.

Out here, he could release whatever stress the day ahead might bring.

After he'd left Lexi, he'd spent the rest of the night crewing up. Wilson had a database of men he'd previously vetted, a handful of whom Kane knew from working the same events with them. He'd called up a dozen or so of them, explaining the job until he'd sourced the ten men he needed.

Despite the lateness of the hour and the lack of notice, it hadn't been as much of a hard sell as he'd expected — turned out, there were a lot of Mandy Gray fans in the world — many of whom, couldn't wait to help her. A few were curious about the daughter too, possibly wondering if she would be half as gorgeous as her mother though of course, they knew better than to ask.

He'd gone over his security plans then packaged up the soda can he would be sending for analysis. He'd wanted to unflatten the can to examine it further, but not at the risk of rubbing off any potential prints. That was best left to the experts.

Wilson had a forensic lab he contracted for moments like this, though Kane wasn't sure how helpful it would really be. Even if they managed to pull prints off the thing, they would only be useful if a matching pair were already in the system. Still, it gave them something to work on and bigger cases had been broken on lesser evidence than this.

With his team sorted and security plans revised, he had finally fallen asleep. At some point in the night, he had woken up as he usually did. Sleep was something that didn't come easily anymore. As soon as he closed his eyes, the memories would inevitably come and with them, the emotions he'd managed to bury during his waking hours raised their ugly heads.

Maybe one day he'd sleep through the night. Until then, he took each day as they came, one breath at a time.

His feet pounded the cool sand. He ran until his chest heaved and sweat dripped down his face. Part of his obsession with working out came from a need to keep his body in its prime. After all, a man was only as capable as his body.

When the sun was over the horizon, he called it quits and took a short swim in the sea to wash off. The shower was one of the worst things about living in the trailer, and he much preferred the refreshing coldness of the ocean to wake him fully.

He guzzled down a protein shake while Bud demolished a dish of raw food he'd prepared the night before. Less than an hour later, they were at the Rockefellers' home with his team already at work patrolling the property and laying the groundwork for the new cameras and alarms.

At precisely eight AM Lexi appeared at the security base.

Her hair had been pulled back into a pony, her face scrubbed free of makeup. She wore a pair of old jeans, a faded T-shirt with Converse sneakers yet somehow she still managed to look like the prettiest girl alive — if not a pretty grumpy one. She didn't seem too happy to see him, though she managed a smile for Bud.

"Morning."

She seemed to have directed the greeting to his dog, who apparently wasn't picking up on the negative vibes. His tail thumped on the floor with abandon.

"Are you ready to leave?" Possibly he should make more of an effort, though where would he start? Small talk was never his forte.

"Yes, though I'd prefer to go alone, without all this fanfare."

I'd prefer that, too.

Wisely, he kept the thought to himself. He nodded at one of the members of his team, a wiry Asian man in a chauffeur outfit pulling up in a black Mercedes.

"This is Johnny. He's going to be our driver from now on."

"Nice to meet you, Miss Alexia." Johnny's voice held a twinge of an accent that he hadn't quite shaken off. She guessed he must have moved to the US in his teens.

"Call me, Lexi. I'm only Alexia on my passport."

"Yes, ma'am."

"Please don't 'Ma'am' me — we're literally the same age."

Johnny flashed a grin that lit up his whole face. He had an easy-going manner that seemed to charm most people, and it seemed it was already working. "Sure thing."

"Better," Lexi smiled back at him, climbing into the backseat of the car.

"You mind if Bud sits with you?" Kane asked, gesturing at the dog who was his shadow. Bud jumped up, placing two paws on the seat beside her, tongue hanging out in welcome.

"Of course not. Come on, Bud. Sit here with me," Lexi patted the seat next to her. Bud waited for Kane to give him the signal before climbing inside. Once again, Lexi admired how well-trained he was. He didn't do a thing unless Kane told him it was OK.

Lexi threw an arm behind him, holding the dog close. He relaxed into her embrace, a goofy look coming over him.

"You better be careful or he'll start thinking you're his girlfriend," Johnny warned.

Lexi laughed. "I would be so honored."

"You say that now but wait until you smell his breath," Kane responded without thinking, caught up in the easy-going banter Johnny always inspired.

Lexi shot a look at him, unable to hide her surprise that what — he had a personality? Her expression made him wish he hadn't said anything. Closing her door, he made his way to the passenger seat as Johnny twisted round to ask, "Where are we headed?"

Normally, Kane would have his client's schedule at least a day if not more in advance — the more notice he had, the more chance he had of making preparations, but as this was his first official day on the job, they were going to have to roll with it.

"The PAWS shelter on West Olympic Boulevard. Here's the address." She showed Johnny the full address she had pulled up on her phone. He set the course on the Sat Nav and started the car. Trees flashed past as they drove down the winding drive.

"How many stops do we have today?" Kane asked.

"Just the one. I'll be there for most of the day, sorting out the party while getting a few walks in."

"Walks?"

"For the dogs. I like to take them out whenever I can, they spend far too long cramped up in those cages as it is."

Kane agreed with her but stayed silent. She said all the right things regarding the volunteer work, but he knew that most celebrities were coached on their responses: some even had speech writers.

"Bud was a rescue," Johnny volunteered.

"He was?" Lexi looked at Kane, unable to hide her surprise. "I thought you'd gotten him from a breeder."

A twinge of annoyance flashed in his chest. Why would she think that of him? Now he was forced to explain himself.

"He'd suffered a lot of abuse and wouldn't let anyone near him, even after he was rescued."

Johnny smiled at her through the rear-view mirror. "He wouldn't let anyone near him for *months*, but Kane was patient and spent time with him every day until he caved. And the rest is history."

Lexi's eyes softened as she turned to smile at the dog. She scratched him under the chin, causing his tail to thump against the door and a big sigh to leave his lips.

"What made you decide to adopt him?"

Kane considered her question but didn't know how to respond without getting personal. Luckily — or unluckily as the case might be — they had Johnny with them, who had apparently turned into Chatty Cathy this morning.

"Didn't you say you saw something in him that reminded you of yourself?"

Kane was starting to regret his decision to bring him onto the job. "I don't recall—"

But Johnny was on a roll, somehow oblivious to the looks Kane was giving him.

"And after all the tours you'd been deployed to, you felt like a canine companion wouldn't be such a bad thing."

Lexi looked at him, comprehension dawning on her

face. His disciplined manner, the stiff way he sometimes
held himself.

"You were in the army?"

"The Marine Corp."

"Must have been tough."

His didn't answer, but a veil had come down over his
eyes. It wasn't a subject that was easy for him to talk
about, and she wished she hadn't pried.

The rest of the ride went by in silence. She wondered
what life must have been like deployed to another
country so far from home and his loved ones. What
horrors he must have seen and maybe even had a hand
in. She felt a desperate sadness at what he and others
like him must have gone through.

When they arrived at the shelter, Johnny parked the
car in one of the staff parking spaces and prepared to
settle in for the wait with the latest audiobook from
James Patterson.

Kane handed what looked to be a small keyring
to her.

"Before I forget... here's your panic button."

Her doubtful expression conveyed all the reluctance
she was feeling. Weren't they going too far with all this?

"Giving my parents peace of mind is one thing but
what with you and Bud's presence already, surely we can
forgo that? I hardly think anyone's going to come at me
with the two of you standing around."

"This isn't up for discussion." He understood her
plight, but his tone held no compromise. "In all likeli-
hood, you'll never have a need for it, but you don't ever

want to be in a situation where you do only to find that it's not there. Let's not make you a precautionary tale."

His words painted a striking picture that caused her mouth to go dry. She took it from him. It was cool to touch and nothing more than a small fob that contained a single large button. She wasn't sure what it was about the innocuous item, but holding it in her hand had her stomach recoiling in waves.

"Some like to attach it to their keys. So long as it is on your person or within unobstructed reach at all times I'm not too particular about where you keep it."

She went to slide it into a pocket on her jeans, then stopped. "How do I know it won't accidentally go off?"

"It needs a pretty decent amount of pressure to be activated so that's not a concern."

From the way he spoke, it was clear the subject was over for him and Lexi wasn't sure how she felt about that. She did have one pressing thing on her mind that she needed to flag up with him before they went inside.

"Other than my boss, I don't want the people here to know you're my bodyguard."

"That might not be possible—"

"I've spent a long time trying to convince them all that I'm one of them. It's taken months for them to let me in, but if they see me walking around with my own security detail, it'll just remind them again of how different we are and I don't want that. Please. It's important to me."

Her eyes were luminous as she stared up at him, causing something to shift in his stomach. She looked so concerned that he felt he could cave on this one issue.

"If I'm not your bodyguard, then who am I? I'm going to be with you every step of the way."

"Every step?" Her brow raised high.

"Well, maybe not inside a toilet stall but I'll certainly be outside the restroom."

She didn't look very pleased, and while he couldn't blame her, this was a necessary step. Her eyes leveled on his as she stared at him silently. He imagined that a lesser person might find her directness nerve-racking after all, ignoring her beauty, wealth, and pedigree, this was the girl who had shoved a can of mace right at him without breaking a sweat. But Kane met her gaze full on. When he didn't back down, she sighed.

"Fine. Then I guess you're my friend."

"Friend it is," he responded, though he wondered how they would pull that off given the tension between them.

The shelter was two floors of solid concrete, barely disguised by the cheerful mural of happy animals someone had painted on the walls. A brightly colored sign did its best to welcome visitors, but nothing could hide the fact that this was a place where animals waited to be homed.

That suffocating desperation was in all of them. That sense of a clock ticking down. No matter which one you went to, whether they had a no-kill policy or not, they all felt the same.

Inside, she greeted every staff member with a smile and by name. From the looks of things, she was adored and cared equally as much about the people working here as she did the animals. She took a moment to ask each how their sons were doing at school, or if they had managed to perfect their gluten-free baking yet.

As she made her way to the main office, Lexi couldn't help but notice how the women were behaving around Kane. Eyes went wide. Some blushed while others whispered to their female colleagues. Even women she knew who were happily married were responding to his presence.

Kane himself seemed oblivious to all the attention.

He would notice every small thing about his dog and surroundings, yet nothing about the women vying for a glance his way. Historically, her gaydar had always been pretty on point, but she was getting no vibes from him which made the man all the more intriguing.

Why wasn't he interested in any of these women?

She stole a glance at his ring finger — empty. So he wasn't married. He could still have a girlfriend or fiancee at home though. Possibly even a wife. Not wearing a ring wasn't a surefire sign of anything, especially in his line of work where any personal information could be used against him.

Edward, the manager of PAWS was sitting at his desk on a call when the two of them came into the room. In his sixties, he carried more pounds than his small frame warranted due to a fondness for his wife's pies, and his gray hair was thinning on top, but he had the energy of someone half his age. He smiled and waved, pointing them both to a chair as he finished his call.

Lexi went to a water cooler and filled two paper cups, one which she handed to Kane, the other she poured into a steel bowl that sat on the floor.

"Here Bud, in case you're thirsty."

Bud's giant pink tongue lapped up the water even though Kane was pretty sure his dog was fine. It was almost a rule of thumb that if you offered a dog a drink in a new bowl or location, they had to try it out, just for fun.

Edward hung up the phone, turned to face them.

"So who do we have here today?" His question was directed solely at Bud, who he was leaning forward in his chair to fuss. "Look at that coat and those bright eyes. You are a gorgeous thing aren't you?"

"Now you've done it," Kane replied. "He was already big-headed but now we'll never fit him in the car again."

Lexi found herself momentarily taken about by his instant friendliness to Edward. Where was this coming from?

Edward laughed. "Was he one of ours?"

"No. But he was a rescue." Kane answered.

Edward's smile grew bigger, if that were possible. He was a kind soul, full of love and goodness despite the worst of humanity he'd been privy to. He was the perfect person to run this place, and it had flourished under his care for the last twenty years.

"Good on you. We need more people to adopt rather than purchasing from puppy mills. Let's not fund these criminals! Anyway, good to meet you. What brings you here today, has Lexi managed to persuade you to adopt another dog? Or perhaps you're here to volunteer?"

Kane saw immediately why Edward was so good at this job. Within the space of seconds he had managed to ask the top two things of him that they needed without missing a beat or sounding rude.

"Not exactly."

He let Lexi explain. She filled him in on the whole ordeal. As Edward heard the story, his face fell until no hint of his smile remained.

"Why, that's simply awful. How terrible for you."

"It might be nothing but dad wanted to make sure I was protected and that it wouldn't happen again so Kane and Bud are my bodyguards. I wanted you to know the situation so you wouldn't be startled or concerned if you came across either of them."

"Thank you for trusting me with this. I will keep it confidential. Meanwhile, mi casa es su casa. If you need my assistance with anything, let me know. I take my staff's safety very seriously, but particularly in the case of this lovely young lady here. Lexi has helped us so much and continues to do so with each passing day. No more harm must come to her!"

His compliment caused a blush to appear on her cheeks.

"That's good to know," Kane said and meaning it. He didn't need the man's permission, but it was kind of him to offer.

"Now, we had a date to discuss this party you are throwing didn't we?"

"Yes. Are you good to talk now?"

Edward took out a pad and pen, giving Kane a sheepish look. "I'm old school, I'm afraid. Just can't get a handle on computers. Can't even send a text message without hitting all the wrong keys. It like I have asbestos thumbs."

For the next two hours, while Edward made notes, the

two discussed various aspects of the party. In addition to raising funds, Lexi was hoping to find homes for some of the longest residents of the shelter, both cats and dogs. A few were already showing signs of trauma, having been locked inside a cage for too long. Away from the noise and fanfare, Lexi planned on showcasing a few of these animals by setting up a meet and greet area in their home theater, which was soundproofed.

She hoped that as people interacted with them, they would fall in love and go home with a new and deserving pet, but they needed to make sure they had the best candidates for the job: it would be pointless trying to set up a home for a dog who was skittish around children when so many of the celebs who were attending had families of their own.

They ran through the database, noting down possible candidates. Lexi wanted around twenty possibilities. Any more than that and it would be hard to control, plus the animals might become too stressed being in such close vicinity of each other. It was very much a game of balance that they worked hard to get right.

When they had a final shortlist, Lexi decided to spend a bit of time getting to know each of the animals: if she was going to have them potentially adopted, she needed to be able to say she had firsthand experience with each pet and that they were safe to handle.

Kane only half listened to their meeting. Lexi was surprising him with her passion and genuine interest for the work she did here. Whenever he glanced over, she was deep in focus, having forgotten his presence altogether.

Most of his attention was on the window that over-looked the entrance to the shelter. In his mind, he was keeping a running log of the people that came and went. Although he didn't believe she would be attacked here, he sure as hell wasn't going to slack off.

Although it meant being in the line of fire, he would risk his own life if it meant saving the client.

11

When the meeting wrapped up, it was time to make the rounds. Bud yawned and stretched, gave Edward a quick nudge goodbye, then followed the two of them to the back of the building where the animals were housed.

"He seems like a good man," Kane commented.

"Edward? He's the best. He's spent most of his whole life dedicated to helping animals. He even gave up a high-paying job once."

"What was that for?"

"Some cooperate thing. They saw how well he was running this place and tried to steal him away. They offered three times the salary he has now but Edward turned them down. Said they didn't need him, but there were plenty of animals who did."

Their conversation was coming a little easier now, the few hours spent with Edward having seemed to have relaxed them both. The definite edge that had been there this morning had faded somewhat.

They arrived at the kennels where Kane was immediately hit by the overwhelming smell of dog. The room was of average height, but it stretched out like a barn. Kennels flanked either side of the room housing all breeds of dogs, though every other one seemed to be of the same type.

Catching him staring, Lexi explained.

"Pit Bulls are still the number one breed that end up unwanted. A lot of people get them to fight with, but when many prove they have no aptitude for it, they get dumped on the streets or people assume their personality will reflect their 'tough' look. The public are still pretty uneducated about their nature as they tend to make great family dogs. You'll get the occasional aggressive one, of course, but that's true of all breeds. At the end of the day, their upbringing has a lot to do with it."

Kane stared into the kennel of a particularly sad Pit Bull. His ribs protruded from his body while the white of his eyes seemed far too bright. His chest heaved too quickly, panting and highly distressed. Kane clenched his fist, hating the dog's pain.

"Hey, Boy. It's OK. We're not going to hurt you."

He kept his voice low and friendly, attempting to soothe some of his distress but the dog just whimpered and turned his back on them, hoping they would go away.

"That one's been here for several months now. He was found in a junkyard, living in a totaled car. You can't see it now but his neck had been covered in rope burns. We're not sure of his entire backstory, but it seems likely that he'd been tied up for a long time but managed to escape. He was severely malnourished and dehydrated when he was rescued. We've tried to get close to him but he's too scared for human contact which makes him unadoptable."

"What happens to the ones who can't get along with humans?"

"This is a no-kill shelter so they won't be euthanized, but it does mean that potentially, he could spend the rest of his life in a cage. It's no life at all, really."

Sticking close to Kane's side, Bud wasn't his normal bouncy self. His body shook, plagued by his own memories of being in a place like this once. He shoved his nose into the back of Kane's hand, seeking comfort.

"You're good, Boy. This won't happen to you again."

They stopped by a brown Labrador Retriever next with only three legs. Where the fourth should be, there was a stump that was bandaged. Despite whatever had happened to her she seemed relatively happy. Tail wagging, she half hopped, half walked up to them.

"This one's Delilah. Someone had dumped her outside in the middle of the night. We think she'd been hit by a car. Her leg was amputated, but she's otherwise in good shape."

Kane slipped his hand through the wire fencing as Delilah shoved her head against it, craving his attention. Bud moved up close to the fence and whined. Delilah turned her attention to him. The dogs's noses touched as they introduced themselves in their own particular way.

"She's sweet. Won't she be easier to re-home?"

"Not necessary. People will be afraid of any ongoing medical costs for her but since she's such a sweetheart,

I'm hoping she's one of the ones I can get re-homed at the party since no one there should have an issue with the cost."

Kane looked out across the room, feeling a rage building in his heart. There were so many animals that needed help, far too many to even count.

When he adopted Bud, he knew it would be a lifelong commitment, but it hadn't phased him one bit. One look into his eyes, at the first lick of Bud's tongue when he wouldn't go near anyone else, Kane had been sold. From that moment on, he knew he'd do right by his friend. How then, was it possible for so many other people in the world to have tossed aside their own pets as if they were nothing more than garbage?

A skinny teenager came by pushing a cleaning cart. He tucked stringy shoulder length hair behind his ear as he shot Lexi a shy smile. Half of his face was covered with the kind of unfortunate acne that made Kane have a flashback of a time when he'd suffered the same. He wanted to tell the kid to hang in there, that there was hope for the future, but knew it would only embarrass him.

When Lexi smiled back at him, his cheeks turned red, which only made his acne stand out more. Poor guy had a crush on her though she acted like she didn't notice — however hard it was not to.

"Hey, Chris, how's it going?"

"Hi, Lexi. Not bad. Busy today, Emma didn't make her shift."

"Why, what happened?"

Chris shrugged thin shoulders, his eyes darting to the

ground by her feet. It was as if he couldn't look her directly in the face.

"She went to her sister's wedding yesterday. She feels bad but said the world won't stop spinning."

Lexi grinned. "That is what happens when you drink too much."

Chris tossed a look Kane's way, eyes widening when he took in the sight of him. He tried unsuccessfully not to sound intimidated.

"Are you a friend of Lexi's?" He sounded almost challenging when he asked it, clearly feeling threatened.

"Yes," Kane answered. "We've known each other for a while."

Chris stared at him, then back to Lexi, trying to figure out the exact nature of their relationship, which was none of his business. Kane stared him down. While he sympathized with Chris's issues, he wasn't going to make an exception for him, and if the kid decided to be rude, he would have no choice but to set him straight.

"Is anyone covering for Emma?"

Chris shook his head reluctantly, dragging his gaze from Kane. "No one else is available."

A frown creased Lexi's brow as she took in the length of the room and all the kennels inside.

"You'll never finish cleaning all of these by yourself." She hung her bag up on a hook on the wall and rolled up her sleeves.

"What are you doing?" The question slipped out of Kane.

She arched a brow at him. "What does it look like?"

"You're going to clean the kennels? I thought it's mostly fundraising that you do for them?"

"It is, but you heard him. No one else is coming to help today, and these cages still need to be cleaned out. No one wants them lying around in their own filth."

She crossed over to Chris's cart, removed the extra broom. "Of course, this will go a lot quicker if there were three of us doing it…"

She sent him an impish smile that caused dimples to appear on her cheeks. The impact was like a punch in the gut. She looked so damned adorable, but this wasn't what he was here to do and she knew it. He couldn't say anything without blowing his cover, so he chose to glower instead.

"Imagine if it was Bud in one of them…" she continued ruthlessly. Not playing fair at all.

Bud chuffed in what sounded suspiciously like laughter, earning a glare from him. His dog responded by issuing a long, loud yawn, letting him know just what he thought of that. Blowing air out of his nose, he circled the ground, then promptly laid down.

"Well, you can forget those marrow bones."

Kane's threat was met with a closing of his dog's eyes.

It was ridiculous.

He'd fought terrorists with his bare hands, but couldn't seem to win a battle against his own dog.

"Since I am here, I guess I could help." He growled the reply ungraciously, ignoring the triumphant smile on Lexi's lips.

"Start with the terrier closest to you. She's completely tame and won't be a problem, but leave the ones on the far end to us — they're a lot more nervous around strangers so they'll need someone experienced who can handle them," Chris informed.

There was a superior note in his voice that Kane chose to ignore, mentally reminding himself that he had trodden on the kid's ego.

He entered the kennel beside him. The kid had been right: the terrier was a gentle dog, playful and not the least scared of him. Overjoyed by the company, she danced around him yapping and bouncing with so much energy that he thought she would exhaust herself.

He stroked her head, causing her tiny body to tremble with excitement. She sank into him, sighing a big doggy sigh, tail whipping a mile a minute. He waited for her excitement to fade, but after several minutes had passed, realized it wouldn't be forthcoming. Gently, he eased her to the back of the cage and started to sweep.

He kept one eye on Chris while he worked, his ears pricked for any sign of trouble. While he might joke around, he never lost sight of his real purpose. Putting folks at ease was a smart move, too — people had a habit of revealing their true intentions when their guard was down. So while Chris might only be an awkward teenager with a crush, he was a person of interest and Kane would make sure to keep him in his sights.

Chris left his cart with Lexi and went off. He returned moments later with an additional cart and also a cheap radio that he plugged into a wall. Lexi was given the choice of a station and chose one that only played classic 90s pop songs, saying that era was fun and didn't take itself too seriously. She kept the volume low enough that it wouldn't bother any of the dogs but would provide entertainment for the humans.

They worked in companionable silence for hours cleaning, when Chris disappeared off with a dog on a walk.

Seeing Lexi heading off with the friendly terrier in the opposite direction, Kane set his broom aside and followed a few feet behind, causing Bud to wake from his slumber. Shaking himself, he got in line behind Kane.

Lexi stopped after a few moments, looking over her shoulder with a bemused expression when she noticed the procession behind her.

"What are you doing?"

"I told you that I can't let you out of my sight. Did you think that was a joke?"

She blinked. "No, but I thought... I'm just going around the block."

"Which means I'm also going around the block."

Behind him, Bud woofed, as if to say "Me too!"

"I can't believe this. Who's going to take pictures of me here, doing this?"

"No one, not while I'm standing right next to you," Kane confirmed, not moving an inch on this.

The man was infuriating!

Across from them, Lexi caught a glimpse of two women openly staring at them. As luck would have it, they were the two who had taken her the longest to win around. They couldn't have this conversation here, not without the women hearing — and if they knew what Kane's real purpose was, the gossip would be flying around the place before the end of the day.

"Fine. I won't walk them today then. Come on."

Seeing how nervous she had become in front of their audience, Kane followed her back inside as they took up the cleaning again.

He tossed a bag of waste into Lexi's cart. "Your dad mentioned your mom is allergic to animals."

Lexi looked over the top of the head of a Corgi mix whose head she was stroking and nodded.

"She goes into anaphylactic shock if a cat even goes near her and dogs make her sneeze but they're only a problem if she touches them."

"So you've never had a pet?"

"No."

A look of such naked longing came over her that Kane felt awkward for witnessing it. Bud had been there for him through thick and thin. The two shared an unbreakable bond unlike any other. It was something everyone should be able to experience.

"Maybe I'll be able to have some pets of my own in the future. When I get my own place."

"Is that in the cards?"

The question wasn't idle curiosity. If Lexi intended to move out, he needed to know and allow for it in their security plans.

"Not with everything that's going on." Her eyes flicked over to Chris who, although working, his stiff body language showed he was very clearly eavesdropping on their conversation.

For a moment, she seemed as if she might have confided more, but then a wall came down over her eyes.

"Whenever you're ready to, I'm sure these guys will be thrilled."

He inclined his head at the row of dogs.

They felt rather than saw Chris's eyes burning into them. The corner of Kane's mouth pulled down with annoyance, but Lexi shot him a silent plea that asked for his patience. She knew exactly what was going on with the kid, but didn't want to make a thing of it.

Work continued. Kane's mind wandered when he noticed that Bud had moved. No longer sleeping, he had moved across to the section with the more nervous dogs. His tail wagged in a friendly manner as he tried to engage the young black and brown collie inside.

Lexi crouched by his side, murmuring at the collie, but he bared sharp teeth at Bud, threatened by the other dog's nearness. Kane pursed his lips, preparing to whistle for him to retreat when Bud backed up anyway, tail sinking between his legs.

His head was hanging low, saddened that he wasn't able to befriend the collie, but he knew enough to understand that his presence was only making the other dog more edgy.

He padded to Kane's side, tossing a look at him that asked why the collie didn't want to be friends.

"Some dogs need more time. He'll get there."

Bud chuffed in answer and pressed against him when the hackles on Kane's neck stiffened like icy pins. The collie's growling hadn't lessened, instead it seemed to have become more insistent.

And it was all directed at Lexi, who was now inside his kennel with him.

She froze just inside, talking in her calm, reassuring voice. The door to the kennel opened inward in order to make it harder for dogs to escape — but it also meant that Lexi would have to move a foot or two *closer* to the collie before she could open the door wide enough to leave.

She continued talking as she inched back, though there was a slight tremble in her voice now that he picked up on.

Which wasn't good.

If he heard it so would the dog and the worst thing a person could do when up against one who felt threatened was to show any weakness.

Kane swore and looked around for Chris, but the kid was outside somewhere walking another of the dogs.

There would be no help coming.

Moving slowly so as not to alarm the collie further, Kane pulled a clean towel from the cart and started for the cage, gesturing silently at Bud to stay. The collie was nervous enough without adding him to the mix.

Bud plopped his butt down but whined, not liking the command but having to obey.

Lexi moved another foot back, feeling blindly behind her for the door, but it was still a few feet away. She kept her eyes on the dog, knowing that turning her back on him would only make her more vulnerable.

"Keep coming back slowly. I'm almost there. I'll open the door for you. All you have to do is keep moving back just as you are."

She nodded stiffly, her shoulders so tense that any movement seemed as if it would crack her body in two.

A blanket of tension covered the air. Though the radio still played, its bubbly pop music seemed suddenly distorted, as if being played from far away.

But the dog's growling was broadcasting loud and terrifyingly clear.

She moved another step back when her ankle twisted to the side. She flung out her arms for balance but fell, careening into the kennel.

Startling the already frayed nerves of the dog.

Opening his jaws, the collie lunged.

12

___

The world slowed to a crawl as Kane watched Lexi falling backward.

The dog had hunkered down onto his haunches, muscles rippling in his legs, preparing to attack.

Relying on those blazing fast instincts that had kept him alive, Kane wrapped the towel around his left arm, bolting the last few steps to the kennel. There was no time for stealthiness now. His only hope of getting her out unharmed was to reach her as soon as possible.

Even if that meant alarming the dog further.

Throwing the door open, he thrust his hastily padded arm in front of Lexi as a last line of defense just as the dog's jaws clamped down around it.

A scream shot out of Lexi, but Kane didn't have time to see if she was hurt. Snagging hold of the back of her shirt with his other hand, he yanked her from the kennel.

She tumbled out, stumbling on unsteady feet as he

turned his focus on securing the loose end of the towel, making sure the dog's teeth didn't sink into his flesh. The collie held his arm in a forceful grip, the white of his eyes large and alarmed.

Unable to obey his command now that he could see that Kane was in danger, Bud sprinted to the side of the kennel. Morphing from his sweet companion to fearful defender, Bud snapped at the collie while Kane blocked the open path with his body.

Lexi was outside now but he needed to make sure the dog wouldn't get past and attack either of them.

"Get out of here, Lexi!"

Fear was an irrational beast driving all logic from the brain, and that applied to animals as well as humans. Whatever this dog had been through had made him a quivering wreck, and right now, the dog thought he was fighting for his life.

"What?" She sounded alarmed. "I can't leave you in there with him!"

"My job is to protect you. I can't risk the dog slipping past and attacking you again. Get to safety. Take Bud with you and get some help."

He felt rather than saw her hesitation.

"I'm not leaving you."

She was as stubborn as his dog, who was equally refusing to do as he had commanded for once.

"This isn't up for discussion! I mean it, Lexi. Get out of here!"

The towel slipped an inch from the pressure of the dog, swinging his head from side to side. He wouldn't be able to hold on for much longer.

A door clanged shut a little way behind him: Lexi had retreated into the kennel of the friendly terrier... and she had taken Bud with her.

It was a smart move, if not exactly what he'd ordered. Once they were done here, it was clear that a conversation was needed, one where the rules of engagement — and his authority — were explained in crystal detail.

Chris's startled voice cut through the mayhem.

"What's with all the noise—"

He didn't get any further with his question. Rounding the bend, he slid to a halt in the doorway, taking in the scene before him with unblinking eyes.

"Get help!" Kane barked.

And for the first time since he'd met him, Chris didn't argue, sprinting off in search of assistance, though Kane knew it wouldn't arrive in time.

Strong as he was, his arms were screaming, tiring from keeping the wall of ferocious dog at bay.

He needed a change of tactic, but what could he do?

Kane studied the dog, mentally noting his movements. When he shook his head again, Kane dropped his grip on the towel at the greatest moment of the dog's tugging. Not expecting this, the collie tugged too hard and fell crashing into the side of the kennel.

It was now or never.

Kane dove out of the cage, slamming the door behind even as the collie scrambled up onto his paws and started for him again. Kane bolted the door, securing it as the collie snapped his jaws harmlessly against him.

Adrenaline pumping through his veins, he glanced

over at Lexi and Bud. Other than fright, both were uninjured.

He drew in a deep, relieved breath.

"You can come out now."

Lexi emerged from the terrier's kennel. Wisps of hair had escaped her ponytail, framing her face against the pale pallor of her skin.

Bud bolted to Kane's side, paws skidding over the recently mopped concrete, sniffing him all over as he performed his own check. Kane could feel his wet nose on various parts of his body and was reassured by it.

Lexi took hold of his arm, her blue eyes running over the length of it. Vivid red scratches and teeth marks covered the skin, though miraculously there was no punctures or blood: he had escaped unscathed.

"He didn't do any real damage." She confirmed what he'd already surmised.

"Good to know," he answered. "I like doctors about as much as Bud likes vets."

She didn't know what to make of his joke, unable to gather her thoughts together yet, then decided it must be a coping mechanism for stressful situations, and probably one of the reasons he'd managed to last so long as a marine.

Kane reached down and pulled up the hem of her jeans to calf level. His fingers were cool and rough, yet they scorched her skin. Her heart — already beating fast — hammered inside her chest.

His fingers probed her ankle gently, examining it for injury. She knew what he was doing. Understood that he was only making sure she hadn't twisted it. Why then was his touch causing shivers to race up and down her spine?

"Does it hurt at all when I move it?"

He slipped off her sneaker then cupped her bare foot (she wasn't a sock girl) in one large hand, the other wrapped around her ankle to stabilize it. Her hand reflexively rested on his shoulder for balance.

Tight muscles rippled beneath her fingers. She had a sudden flash of his naked torso in her mind — at least, what she imagined it would look like — and her mouth went as dry as the desert.

Forget pain, what was all this heat she was suddenly feeling?

"I'm fine."

Please let go of my foot before I embarrass myself.

He set her foot back down, releasing it from his grasp. The immediate emptiness she felt took her aback. Her foot felt cold even after he put her sneaker back on.

Edward hurried in, a fresh coffee stain on his shirt as if he had set a cup down too fast. The dark brown liquid was still blossoming against the white of his shirt, soaking into his chest and turning the material translucent enough that Kane could see the outline of the small silver cross he wore around his neck.

Chris followed closely behind, bringing two people with him. A tall woman with a pristine cut bob who looked to be in her forties carried a first aid kit with her while the other staffer — a security guard with a limp and a worried expression — gripped onto a tranquilizer gun.

"Are you all OK? Is anyone hurt?" Edward's sharp,

dark eyes swept the room, darting between them. The earlier jovial character Kane had met had disappeared, replaced with a concerned boss and friend.

"We're all fine," Kane responded.

"He has some scratches on his arm," Lexi supplied, unwilling to dismiss any possible injuries the collie might have caused. "He had Kane's arm in his mouth for a while but he managed to keep him from damaging it too much."

The woman hurried to Kane and opened her first aid kit. "Let me have a look."

"It's nothing, really," Kane started to object, but the woman fixed him with eyes that were as sharp as her haircut.

"It's procedure. We need to inspect both the incident and the people involved."

Her no-nonsense tone brokered no disagreement. Reluctantly and despite feeling that it was overkill, he let her clean the scratches though he drew the line at bandages.

"It was the collie who attacked you?" Edward gestured at the cage where the collie had retreated to the back of his kennel, still growling, hackles still raised as his eyes darted between them all.

"Yes."

The guard moved toward the dog, lifting the tranquilizer gun.

"No, don't shoot him!" Lexi cried. "He was just upset because of all the changes today. He only came in a few days ago. I think he was under Emma's care but she's not here today and I think we were a few surprises too many for him to take."

A flicker of doubt crossed Edward's face.

"You know an attack on one of our volunteers is not something we take likely."

"I do, but it was resolved and he really wouldn't have attacked us if we hadn't scared him. He doesn't need more trauma. He needs kindness and understanding, and if you see the magic Emma has worked with him, I know you'll agree."

She was so earnest even Kane felt swayed by her argument. He was also somewhat impressed that she was putting the dog's welfare above her own.

"Alright. But when he calms down, we'll move him into a quieter section."

Kane could feel her relief and was suddenly, unexpectantly moved.

Why would the rich daughter of Hollywood royalty care so much for the welfare of a stray who had tried to attack her?

He studied her from the corner of his eyes, realizing that there were many more layers to her than he had first thought.

And rather disturbingly, he was interested in finding out more.

13

The LA traffic stretched on as far as the eye
could see.

After all the excitement, Edward had
moved them to the simpler, uneventful duty of unpacking
and sorting through the boxes of donated food that the
shelter received on a weekly basis — all of which had
taken much longer than Kane had anticipated.

Now, with the traffic to Lexi's home barely moving
and the day advancing rapidly, he was acutely aware that
Bud needed to be fed.

Right on cue, as if he could read his thoughts, Bud
complained with a snort that ended with a paw on the
back of his shoulder.

"I know. In fairness, I didn't know we'd be out this
long. I'll be better prepared from now on."

Bud blew out a long sigh that revealed how unimpressed he was with his answer. Lexi observed their
conversation with one brow raised quizzically. "What am
I missing?"

"He's hungry but I forgot his food at home."

"We can stop at a store?" she volunteered surprisingly. Kane wasn't used to his clients being so accommodating, not when the world usually revolved around them.

"Bud eats a raw diet with special supplements that I mix up for him. Commercial dog food gives him the runs, so it's best to stick to what I have at home."

"Is it far?"

"What?"

"Your home?"

"No. We're in Malibu, right on the beach."

"Will we get there faster than us going home then you going all the way back to Malibu?"

Johnny answered from the driving seat. "Oh, for sure."

"If he's hungry now, it's not fair to make him wait. After all, I know how life and death meal times are to a dog."

He couldn't argue with her logic given the bumper-to-bumper traffic clogging up the roads. She smiled at his dog, rolling her eyes at him and earning a lick on the face for her troubles.

"Clearly you've been around many an animal before."

"I certainly know what drama queens they can be, yes." Bud stared through his lashes at her as if hurt that she could think such a thing about him.

"That sounds like a good idea," Johnny said. "It could be awhile before I get you back through this. There must be an accident up ahead."

Lexi stared out at the cars, thoughts ticking inside her

head. A rumble began in her own stomach, reminding her that Bud wasn't the only one who needed sustenance. All she'd had was a green smoothie that Ruth had prepared for her and that must have been at least eight hours ago.

"Sounds like someone else needs a meal too," Johnny commented, having heard her stomach. Lexi's cheeks flushed pink.

"I could eat."

Kane wasn't sure how this was quite happening, but it seemed their plans had be decided without even his input. It was enough to make a man vexed, except... a thought came to him that brightened his eyes.

"We're going to pass by one of my favorite joints. We can pick up something there, eat back at my place?"

It was a matter-of-fact suggestion brought on by necessity and hunger, but somehow, it also sounded like a date — which it clearly wasn't — but tell that to the butterflies that had suddenly decided to dance around her stomach.

Had it been *that* long since she'd had attention from a man?

They stopped off at Geoffrey's Malibu, a stunning beachfront restaurant that commanded undisturbed sea views. Lexi was surprised that this was the 'joint' in question, not because of the location — you'd have to be a serious Grinch not to admire it — but due to the exclusivity.

While the close by and better known Nobu catered to celebrities who wanted to be seen, this was where they went to for privacy. It was a well-kept secret on the circuit, and not the kind of place she would have thought he'd have much experience with — if any.

But private or not, it wasn't a place you could swing by without a reservation. They certainly did not have an ordering out service.

A fact which didn't seem to bother Kane. When Johnny parked up outside, he waved off the valet. Lexi wasn't sure how she could point this out to him without causing embarrassment.

"Shouldn't we call first and see if they can accommodate us?"

"No need. Is there anything you don't like or can't eat?"

She answered the question automatically. "I'm good with everything but kiwi fruit. I'm allergic to those."

He turned to Johnny next. "How about you?"

Their driver looked pleased to be considered. "I eat anything, man. Thanks."

He was out of the car in a flash before she realized he hadn't checked with her to see what she had *wanted*. A flash of annoyance sparked in her chest. Had he mistaken her for a doormat just because she was *nice*?

And why the hell did she care what he thought of her, anyway? Fit as he was — and you'd have to be blind not to admire his amazing body — he was still only there in a work capacity. And she couldn't forget the way he'd treated her earlier: he'd had a definite problem with her that she wasn't convinced had completely evaporated.

She turned her attention to Johnny, quietly admiring the ocean view. "How long have you worked together?"

Johnny smiled at her through the rearview mirror.

"About a year. I was a private chauffeur before. Kane was working security for a high profile crime case involving a rich banker. We ran into some trouble, but I managed to get us out of it. After that, he recruited me and we've been a team ever since."

"What kind of trouble?"

Johnny's smile stayed on his lips, though a shutter came over his eyes. "Oh, you know, some exciting stuff. This line of work is never boring."

She wondered what he wasn't allowed to tell her but took comfort that Johnny didn't reveal their client's business no matter how chatty he might seem.

Bud leaned forward, resting his chin onto her shoulder, his breath tickling the back of her ear. Even though Kane had been gone only moments, she could sense the dog's anxiety. He wouldn't be happy until his owner returned. This sense of loyalty and love from an animal was truly miraculous. As usual, she felt that pang she always did, wishing she could have her own pets.

But maybe that time was coming sooner rather than later, once all of this — whatever it was — was over.

The picture of her perfect house with the blue shutters and cheerful walkup breezed into her mind. She was still imagining herself inside when Kane returned, arms laden with paper bags. She wasn't able to hide her surprise.

He placed the bags carefully into the trunk of the car and climbed in.

"Even I struggle to get a reservation unless I shamelessly drop my parents' names. How did you persuade them to do takeout?"

Kane shot a smug smile her way.

"I did a job for the owner once. When he realized how much I loved the food but hated eating out, he made an exception for me. I order out from them a couple of times a week."

A couple of times a week? The place wasn't cheap so unless he was also granted a large discount, he must earn a decent salary though she would never have known that judging by the clothes he wore. The guy gave military chic a new meaning.

"Why don't you like eating out?"

It was a simple question, but it seemed to have taken him aback momentarily. His eyes turned cagey.

"I'm not keen on loud places."

There was something in his tone that suggested there was more to this, but since he seemed reluctant to elaborate, she let the matter drop.

Johnny drove them down the Pacific Highway, the sea air pleasant to her nose. She could still see the smoke from the wildfires in the horizon, though they were distant enough not to bother them. Even with her concerns for its victims and the amount of work she still needed to organize for the party, some of the tension left her shoulders, eroded away by the peaceful waves lapping on the shore.

When they finally pulled up to the Airstream trailer, Lexi couldn't have been more surprised.

Barking excitedly, thrilled to be home, Bud dove out of the car the moment the door was opened, tearing along the beach.

"This is where you live?"

"I know it's not much compared to yours but it's home to us."

His reply was a little short.

"No," Lexi flushed, picking up on the miscommunication right away. "I love it. All the peace you must have here and that beach. I can only imagine how stunning it must be the first thing in the morning. I was just surprised that your home would be so low-key when you regularly eat at such an exclusive restaurant."

He saw himself from her eyes and the heat that had been rising at what he'd mistaken as a disparaging tone went down a notch. Truth was, he was protective of his home and barely invited anyone here anymore — particularly given what had happened the last few times he'd brought a woman back — so this was very out of the ordinary.

"I'm a simple man who lives a simple life. The only area I'm lavish with is my food. Living so close to one of the best restaurants in the country is a challenge."

"I can imagine." The food at Geoffrey's *was* to die for.

He went around to the driver's side of the Mercedes as Johnny moved his seat back, giving his legs extra space. Hooking his elbow out the window, he relaxed into his seat.

Kane looked surprised. "Aren't you coming in?

Johnny shot a look at Lexi, then Kane, a small smile appearing on his lips. "I'll be fine in the car just me, some good food, and Patterson's latest. We're about to discover who the bad guy is."

A sudden jolt of panic went through Kane. This entire time, he'd thought Johnny would be eating with them. Without him, that would leave just the two of them together.

He and Lexi.

He wasn't sure he was prepared for that.

"The car's no place to enjoy food like this," he said, trying again.

"Seriously, I really am fine here. Don't worry about me."

I'm not you fool. I'm worried about me. What the hell are the two of us going to talk about?

But Johnny couldn't be swayed. Annoyed and wishing he could just command him to obey like he did with Bud, Kane headed to the trailer and unlocked the door.

Bud bolted inside. Lexi thought he might be heading to some food but instead, the intrepid dog went up to a mini fridge beside the seating area which had a piece of what looked to be rope tied to the handle.

Gripping it in his mouth, he pulled the door open. Sticking his snout into the fridge, he grabbed a can from the top shelf and swung his rump at the door to close it. Padding happily as if he did this every day, he brought the can of Budweiser to Kane.

Kane took it from him, but shook his head. "Thanks, Bud, but I'm not drinking until later. We're still on the clock even if we have come home."

Bud cocked his head at him, barked as if to say "OK" then sat down on the floor to stare out at a seal swimming not fifty feet away in the ocean.

Lexi was busy admiring how smart Bud was when

something clicked into place. Her face turned incredulous. "Wait, did you name your dog after a *beer*?"

Kane tossed a surprised look at her as he took out a marrow bone and a packet of steak from the larger Smeg fridge in the kitchen: she caught on faster than most.

"Yes. Seemed as good a name as any."

"But... *why* would you do that?"

His answer came readily. "Because I Iove them both equally."

Bud made a noise that sounded like he was insulted. Lexi patted his head. "I wouldn't be too pleased by that comparison either."

Kane gave Bud the marrow bone to chew on while he unwrapped the meat and started to slice it into large chunks.

"Mind if I give myself a tour of your home?"

He nodded, but it seemed a little stiff, like he wanted her to do anything but. "Knock yourself out."

Squeezing past them, Lexi took in the smartly designed space, marveling at how there seemed room for all the usual sections one expected in a house though in miniature.

As expected for someone living in a tiny house, Kane didn't have many belongings, though what he did have was both comfortable and utilitarian.

The one shelving unit that she could see contained a few books — nonfiction from what she could make out — an old-fashioned record player, and framed pictures taken throughout his life.

She saw Kane as an awkward teenager, then with his military squad in different parts of the globe. Those latter pictures his eyes seemed the different, haunted by the horrors he had been forced to witness. She tore her gaze away from them, uncomfortable by how they made her feel, to examine the photographs of Bud, which took up an entire shelf of their own.

Tellingly, she couldn't see any which held family or a love interest.

She wondered why that part of his life was so empty... even emptier than hers. At least she had her parents, but where were his family?

A guitar stood propped up against the corner with a strange padded handle screwed onto it, but other than a large plasma television screen, there wasn't much else. The bedroom was likely to have had the same sparse treatment, though she stopped herself from prying any further: a man's bedroom wasn't a place one should visit without an invitation.

Kane fed Bud, then grabbed plates, cutlery, and plastic tumblers from the kitchen.

"Any objection to eating outside?"

If she said yes, he wouldn't know what to do. This place was too small to provide any kind of distance.

"No, that sounds great. Do you need help with anything?"

He inclined his head at a throw hanging over the back of the booths that formed the dining area. "Can you bring that?"

Lexi grabbed the brown throw that was made out a hard-wearing and treated fabric. There was a simple blue criss-cross pattern on it that seemed too feminine a design for his tastes. Had this come from a previous love interest?

He dished up a plate and took it out to Johnny asking, "Are you sure you wouldn't prefer the lovely sea view and our good company?"

He was sounding pretty desperate now but he didn't care.

Johnny took the plate from him. "Perfectly sure. Don't keep the lady waiting, Boss."

Kane wasn't sure, but was that a smile Johnny was trying to hide?

He rejoined Lexi, who was crawling around the throw, trying to smooth it out under Bud's watchful eye. She'd already taken off her sneakers, setting them neatly to one side. It was possible that hers were the prettiest feet he'd ever seen, and he wasn't even a foot guy.

He opened the containers of food, setting them down in a row. Heavenly smells wafted into her nose, causing her stomach to flip-flop. She was really hungry and by the looks of the spread before her she need not have worried: he'd done a fine job of ordering.

"I went for their most popular dishes. For starters we have Ahi Tuna Tartar, Octopus Seaweed Salad, Lobster Egg Rolls and Crab Cakes. For the mains, there's Scallop Risotto, Grilled Swordfish, and Duck Two Ways. I thought we could pick and mix, have a taste of each but if that doesn't work for you, choose whatever you want and I'll just have the rest."

Her eyes were as wide as saucers. "It all looks divine. I think sharing is the way to go."

Kane let out a long, relieved breath. "Good. I was

afraid I'd have to choose between the Tuna Tartar and Egg Rolls."

Lexi laughed at the serious expression on his face. "If you were so attached to those dishes, why didn't you just take them for yourself?"

"Because I'm a gentleman."

He meant it, too. Taking a fork from him, she speared a piece of tuna and ate it. The delicately marinaded fish melted in her mouth, filling it with deliciousness.

"This is so good."

"I know," he responded. This kind of smugness would normally irritate her but the man did know his way around food.

With the waves caressing the shore and gulls soaring over their heads, they ate their feast as the sun began its descent across the sky.

They made small talk. Lexi asked about his early life, but when he briefly explained about his childhood, she found it difficult to fathom.

"So you don't have any contact with your family at all?"

"Some families are not worth staying in contact with."

After that, she didn't ask him anything more about them.

They chatted about her school and growing up with a movie star for a mother. She glossed over the unhappier moments in her life, mostly the long absences that took her mother away, and the friends who had betrayed her trust. If he hadn't read about those things, he wouldn't know about them now.

"What about your job, are you working your way up to be Stonewall's successor?"

She laughed, horrified. "I would never want his job. It's so time-consuming and takes so much out of him. You have to eat and breathe the industry to do what he does. I'm just doing the script coverage job until I can figure out what it is I want to do."

She ate a forkful of salad before continuing.

"It's funny, all the way through college, I thought I wanted to be a writer. I've always loved reading, and I love getting to know people and what makes them tick, but writing requires the kind of willpower that I don't have. And it's too isolated. Besides, with my parents' contacts, there must be something more helpful I can do. With everything I've been given, I feel like I should pay it forward, somehow."

It wasn't long before it hit him: she didn't seem to be like most of his clientele: not only did she understand how privileged and blessed she was, she came across as grateful and keen to spread the wealth to those who needed it.

He asked the question that had been preying on his mind. "What about personal life? Are you seeing anyone?"

She blinked at his question, unsure where it was coming from.

"There wasn't anything in your file, but I need to know. I have to know about all of my clients personal relationships no matter how embarrassing that might be for us all."

Technically, it was only half true — Kane wasn't sure

where his sudden interest had come from, only that he did want to know.

"I have a *file*?" She swallowed the mouthful of food she'd been chewing.

"Of course."

"Then you already know much of what there is to know about me."

"I don't think that's true. I don't know your shoe size for one."

"My *shoe* size?" The comment was so random, she didn't know what to make of it.

"That wasn't in the file, so you see, we don't know everything about you after all."

He flashed a sudden grin at her that took all the hardness out of his face. For that moment, he looked relaxed, without his usual edge and dare she say it, sexy as all heck.

"No, to answer your question, I'm not currently seeing anyone. Haven't actually since my jerk-off ex cheated on me with a close friend."

"Nice."

"I thought so. And the stupid thing was, I knew he wasn't right for me: we were too different."

She'd captured his interest now. "In what way?"

"He was all about the partying, getting his face shown everywhere. The first thing he did every day was to see how much his Instagram had grown. Imagine living your life concerned with an arbitrary number. So ridiculous."

"And you didn't know that about him?"

She shook her head. "He was so sweet in the beginning, incredibly attentive. It wasn't until I'd been in a relationship with him for a while that I realized we never stayed in. He was always making me go out where we'd be seen. Once I finally saw the writing on the wall, he decided he'd have a more publicized relationship with Angel and took off with her."

She shut her mouth suddenly, shocked by how much she was revealing. How had they gone from their prickly interaction this morning to confiding matters of the heart like this?

She blamed it on the food and the romantic setting.

When their stomachs were full, Kane lit a small fire. As they were warming their feet on it, Bud went into the trailer, emerging moments later with the guitar gripped by that handle she'd noticed earlier.

He carried the guitar to Kane, who shook his head. "Ah, no. Not tonight."

Bud tilted his head at him, a look of confusion in those soulful brown eyes. He set down the guitar before Kane, laid his chin onto it and stared up at him beseechingly.

"Maybe later, Buddy." Kane tried again.

Bud huffed and shoved his nose at the strings, looking for all the world like he was trying to play it himself. When that didn't work, he draped a paw over it, managing to pluck the odd string, creating a not very pleasant soundtrack.

"What's he doing?" Lexi asked, fascinated and amused by whatever his dog was trying to do.

"Nothing," Kane tried to take the guitar from him, but Bud was doing his best to stop him. "Give it here!"

And now the mutt thought it was a game, ducking

and weaving and dragging the guitar with him. Kane faked Bud out with a step away from him, then lunged for the guitar, wrestling it from him.

Triumphant, he sat back down with it in his lap. At Lexi's bemused expression, he reluctantly explained, "I usually play the guitar after dinner each night. He likes to listen. It's a thing we do."

If he had admitted to being an alien, she wouldn't have been more shocked. She tried to picture the two of them, Kane serenading his dog each night on this beach, and the image made her feel warm inside.

It was uncharacteristically adorable of him.

Feeling wicked despite seeing how the admission had embarrassed him, she replied, "I don't mind listening to you play. In fact, I'd like that a lot. Besides, look at him." She pointed at Bud. "You'll break his little heart if you don't."

Kane looked at his dog, then at Lexi, and he knew he'd been played. Even so, he couldn't risk disappointing Bud.

It was what they did after all.

He began to play, his fingers skillfully plucking the strings in an acoustic version of an Adele song — which just happened to be one of her favorites — but it was when he started to sing with a strong baritone that her insides turned to jelly. Men who could sing was a particular weakness of hers.

Had he learned that in her file too?

There, with his dog's head resting on his bare feet, Kane sang as if nothing else existed. His dark, broody eyes stared out into the blue-black horizon. The rich smoothness of his voice captured her soul while the longing in them toyed with her heart.

When he was finished, the air between them crackled with electricity.

He looked at her with eyes that had grown hooded. Instinctively, she licked her lips. His gaze flicked down to them. As if they were magnetically pulled together, she felt herself drifting dreamily toward him.

Kane had never sung to a woman before and wasn't sure what had possessed him to do so tonight. But there was something about Lexi that confused him. On the surface she was everything he abhorred about this city, yet when he scratched below that surface, there was much to be admired and liked.

The flickering light danced through her hair, giving her a mane of fire that only made her more spectacular.

Maybe it was the effect of the great food they'd just eaten, or the impossible romance of the shimmering stars above, but he couldn't stop himself from drawing close.

Bowing his head, he took her lips into his own. They were every bit as sweet as they looked. A current shot through him as the kiss deepened. Lexi's arms rose up to wrap around his neck.

It felt like every nerve in her body was reacting to him. She wanted to get closer to him, to connect to him deeply and understand everything about him.

Through his lips she could taste his life and she wanted more, craved it in fact. When her arms went around his neck, it felt so natural that she hadn't even noticed she had moved.

The world swam and her skin felt hot as his lips

pressed onto hers more urgently. Her pulse raced, blood rushing through her veins. She felt more alive than she could ever remember.

When he pulled so abruptly away, she felt as if she had been ripped apart.

"I'm sorry. I shouldn't have done that."

His words were an ice-cold wash to her heat. She drew in a sharp breath, hating the tremble in her voice.

"Last I checked we were both complicit."

He tore his eyes from her, fixing them on a point far away, away from her, apparently unable to look her in the face.

"But I know better than to get involved with one of my clients. That was a mistake. It won't happen again."

He got up and took the guitar inside, locked up the trailer and put out the fire before Lexi managed to rise to her feet.

She barely had time to pick up the shoes she had discarded before Kane was already heading toward the car, apparently eager to get away from her.

Her heart seized painfully.

What on earth had just happened?

14

———

The midnight sky was a cloud of ash and dust that rained down around him, choking his airwaves.

Everywhere he looked, there was agony and chaos.

Where the buildings had stood, there was now only rubble. His military squad so jovially singing the theme tune to Armageddon only moments before, had been flung from the jeep, and now lay in crumpled heaps among the dirt and debris.

Flashlights combed the area, civilians and soldiers alike, fighting to locate survivors of the bomb that had violently exploded, though their beams had to compete with the thick wall of dust that littered the air, cloying their throats.

He struggled to see through the devastation, knowing that time was of the essence. Any survivors had to be found so that aid could be administered. The longer it took, the smaller their chance of survival...

Among the hazy beige dust, he spotted a burst of red.

He moved closer only to discover it was the end of a detached limb. Bile rose at the back of his throat, but he forced it back down.

There was a ringing in his ears that sent the world spinning, making his reactions seem so slow as to be underwater.

"Help..."

The weak call had come from his left.

Kane spun, eyes scanning the area, inwardly cursing the darkness that had made spotting the bomb impossible and which was now heavily affecting his rescue attempt.

"I'm here!" Kane shouted, hoping his call would rise above the commotion. His voice sounded tinny to his own ears, that ringing distorting everything he could hear.

He wasn't convinced he had heard anything at all... It could very well have been a hopeful illusion, his mind refusing to accept the idea that none of his squad had made it.

Surely, some of them were alive?

"Turner? Is that... you?"

It was one of his men! Hope surged anew, and with it came a burst of energy. "I'm coming! Where are you?"

"Here... Over here..."

He spotted a pile of bricks that suddenly moved. It was a second before he realized his mistake. His man was right in front of him, though only a fraction of his face could be seen.

He started for him when a flash of pain erupted in his

chest. His hand moved up to investigate but came away sticky with blood.

He was hurt though he took comfort that he could still move, but he couldn't say the same for his brother-in-arms who was buried beneath those rocks.

His eyes slid upward, quickly assessing the scene. What remained of the buildings were stacked precariously above him. At any moment they could collapse on them.

Forcing aside his own pain, he started hauling broken bits of brick and rock, tossing them away until they formed their own pile. On and on he dug, listening for any signs of the building shifting, ignoring the cuts on his fingers and the wounds on his hands until finally, the face of Ricky Dickins appeared.

Kane inhaled a sharp breath. Ricky was the youngest of the group, the one they all considered their kid brother.

He'd been with Kane for two months now, learning everything he could from the experienced marine. The kid was like a sponge, eager to absorb anything Kane would feed him.

He knew he came from a big family who didn't much care for him, but when he joined the marines, he'd finally found the close-knit bond he'd been searching for. It was such a close parallel of his own past that the two had become inseparable.

Now Ricky's life lay in his hands.

Tears of desperation stung his eyes as he dug out the rubble, shouting for help though none came. Maybe they couldn't hear him. Maybe they were all dead.

Whatever it was, Kane was alone with Ricky when the ground suddenly shifted beneath his feet.

He knew without looking that the surrounding buildings had started to crumble once more.

Ricky's eyes were pinned on him. The world slowed to a crawl as an unspoken thought came between them. Both knew it immediately, but neither could find it in them to say the words.

They had run out of time.

"Go," Ricky cried weakly, wheezing, refusing to allow Kane to suffer the same fate.

But Kane could not move his feet.

He couldn't leave his brother to die, not when he was so close to saving him. He'd gotten one of Ricky's arms free now. It was crushed in several places and sat there limply, but it was free. He only needed a little more time. A few more minutes and he would have him out.

With a frenzied war cry, he made a Herculean effort to continue his efforts when with a rumble that made the ground move, the top of the building started coming down toward them.

"You can't save me, Kane. You've got to go! GO!"

Kane froze, his mind desperate to find a solution, but there were none. His eyes filled with guilt and anguish.

"It's been an honor, Brother."

Ricky shot him a resigned smile as Kane backed away. When the building came down onto Ricky, he bolted, moving as fast as his legs could carry him.

He could barely see, blinded by the tears that streaked his face. His heart was numb, his mind destroyed. It was too much.

It was all too much.

He was still running when he had cleared the village, their screams and devastated cries an indelible soundtrack that would haunt him for the rest of his life.

He fell to the ground, so exhausted that he couldn't move. He was at mercy to this hostile world, but he didn't care anymore. Nothing mattered. Nothing would ever matter again.

But then a great weight came over him.

A pressure that covered him from head to toe. Rather than induce further panic, the weight seemed to comfort him. It was soft and warm.

It was familiar.

Kane opened his eyes to see neon stars blinking down at him. It took a moment to realize that they weren't real: these stars didn't rest in the midnight sky. These stars he had stuck onto the ceiling of the trailer for the very nights he would wake in a blind panic like this.

They were a visible reminder that the past was just that: he was safe and there was nothing to fear.

Bud's breath blew into his face, providing yet more comfort as his tongue snaked out to lick the tears that had escaped from his eyes.

His heart still pounded in his chest, his body unable to discern the difference between the nightmare flashback he regularly suffered from and the reality that he was safe, far away from the terrors of war.

He stared at his dog, letting the love he felt for him calm the turmoil inside.

He didn't know when this had started.

Soon after he had brought Bud home, he had woken

in the middle of another of his night terrors to find his new dog lying on top of him. Somehow, Bud had sensed that he needed him, that his very presence was able to calm him through the ordeal. Like the weighted blankets used by the Autistic community, Bud would lie on top of him until he eventually fell asleep again.

"Thanks, Boy. I'm good now."

Bud chuffed as if to say "no problem" when a loud klaxon sounded from his phone, forcing the sleep away.

"Down," he commanded. Bud jumped off immediately as Kane sat up. Grabbing his phone, he checked the screen.

One of his new alarms on the Rockefellers' property had been tripped.

This wasn't of immediate concern. Sensors had been placed all around the estate, which could easily have been tripped by one of the coyotes that roamed the hills at night. His men would check the alarm and let him know if there was more to it.

But this did mean that it was time to get up in case he had to head over there. Tossing off the covers, he padded to the small shower room: there was nothing like a cold shower to really wake a man up.

Ten minutes later, he was dressed, his Keurig going when he received a message from Stan, his second-in-command that simply said: *Sorry to wake you Kane, but you need to get over here. Everyone is safe, but there has been an incident.*

Stan was very capable of handling things on his own, so the very fact that he was requesting his presence meant only one thing: their threat was back.

Grabbing a meal he'd already prepared for Bud, the two tore out of the trailer. He gunned it toward the estate, getting there in record time thanks to the late hour. At almost 3am, most of the city was asleep. Picking up on his concern, Bud sat quietly beside him, yawning occasionally as he waited for his command.

As the streets blurred past, images of Lexi snuck into his mind. He saw her as he'd first met her frightened yet brave. His mind flashed back to the dog shelter, to the care and patience she'd shown to the dogs — even the one who had attacked her. He saw her staring dreamily at him as they had kissed on the beach... and the devastated look she had given when he'd pulled away.

He couldn't have handled things worse if he'd tried.

The last thing he wanted was to hurt her yet how could he explain what the problem was?

There were a million reasons he shouldn't have kissed her, not least because he had crossed a professional line. What had he been thinking?

He hadn't been, that was the problem.

She wasn't the kind of woman he could sleep with then leave when things inevitably turned sour. She was his client. Hell, technically, she was his boss. What a bad example to set for Johnny.

But that kiss...

For those few seconds the rest of the world had faded away, leaving only the two of them. He had forgotten himself and more importantly, the mental scars that always flitted on the edges of his mind. They squatted there, waiting for any moment where he'd forget himself and then they would strike.

But for that blissful moment, he had been whole.

He shook off the thought, took a sip from the travel mug of coffee he'd brought with him and focused on the drive. Less than an hour later, when he screeched up to the front door, one of his men was already waiting for him.

Stan had been with the company since its inception and was one of Wilson's best. At fifty, he still had the athletic build of a man half his age which he attributed to the healthy LA lifestyle he had adopted.

Stan drank a green protein shake for breakfast and ate a Keto diet the rest of the time. When he wasn't running marathons, he was pushing weights and sparring in a ring. The man was as solid as they came and not prone to drama, so the concerned look that furrowed his brow was worrisome.

"They're all fine," Stan began before he could even ask. "A sensor was tripped on the property."

"Where?" Kane's eyes took in everything, looking for suspicious activity.

"Nowhere near the house. Along the perimeter, at the spot you found before."

"So, our perp is back?"

Stan nodded. "Though something must have tipped them off, as by the time I'd gotten out there, they had gone. But that's not all. They'd left a bunch of climbing gear. Things you could pick up at any Walmart."

"They're cheap then. Don't have much money. I'm not happy that he or she seems to be advancing whatever their plan is."

"We've already combed the footage recorded tonight. They're not on any of the cameras."

"At least they didn't make it onto the grounds. I need to do a quick check on the clients then I'll be back with you."

He entered the house, hurrying to Lexi's room. Bud's nails clipped on the Spanish tiles that decorated the floor. He knew he should speak to her parents first, but his instincts insisted that she be seen first.

The door to her room was wide open. Through it, he could see both of her parents were with her. They wore matching embroidered silk robes and slippers while Lexi was dressed in a black tank and shorts.

Despite just being woken in the middle of the night, she looked every bit as beautiful as she always did, maybe even more. Various strands of hair had escaped the loose side braid she had fashioned for sleeping somehow making her seem younger than her years. He felt a protective instinct kick in.

At his arrival, her face registered surprise, then confusion. Stonewall's was a blank, however, with no discernible expression other than annoyance at being disturbed this late hour.

Seeing Lexi, Bud trotted straight to her, greeting her with a solemn lick of her hand. Her fingers curled around his head.

"Hey, Fella." Kane couldn't help noticing how, despite how strange it must be to have them all in her room like this, she still had time to welcome his dog.

"I'm assuming there must be a reason for us to have been gathered together at his ungodly hour?"

It was remarkable how Stonewall made it seem like this was Kane's fault, given the circumstances.

"One of the new alarms we installed this afternoon was tripped."

"Faulty wiring?" Stonewall questioned, one bushy brow raised.

"There's nothing wrong with my men's work, as I'm sure you'll discover. It looks as if someone was attempting to get onto the grounds — my team found climbing gear left by the location of the alert."

Mandy inhaled a sharp breath and shot a piercing look at her husband. Stonewall issued the briefest shake of his head. Whatever Mandy might have said next died a fast death on her lips.

"This is the same person, isn't it, the one who took the pictures of me?" Lexi asked.

She still thought it was regular paparazzi though Kane doubted pictures was all they were after not — this was a lot of effort and risk.

"I'm following up a lead on those pictures. I'll let you know as soon as I hear back but it would be negligent to dismiss the threat, not when we've had two in such close succession."

He looked pointedly at Stonewall, silently urging the man to come clean to his daughter. It was madness not to. Catching the look, Stonewall retaliated with a glower of his own. He shifted the weight on his feet, somehow managing to make the gesture look menacing.

"But you're sure whoever it is never made it to the house?"

"Yes. The cameras would have picked them up. Bud

and I still need to check ourselves but for now, it looks like whoever it was, is gone."

Hearing his name mentioned, Bud's ears swiveled around to him.

"If it's just another pap trying to sneak shots, couldn't your men have handled it?" Lexi asked.

"Yes, of course," Kane replied without thinking, his brain not quite firing on all cylinders yet.

"Then why are you here in the middle of the night?" She stared at him as if something wasn't sitting right with her. He waited for her parents to make this easier for him, but when they stayed silent, he knew he had to lie, however much he disliked himself for it.

"I was already awake when the alert came. It wasn't an issue for me to come."

His answer seemed plausible, but Lexi was picking up a great deal of weariness around him. She knew it had more to do with what had happened between them than this late-night alert.

She understood that it might not be a great idea to be involved with a client, though his reaction had still hurt. Until the moment he had pulled away, there was a real connection between them. They hadn't seemed so different then, just two lonely people finding an attraction to one another...

And that was before he had sung to her with a voice that she could still feel in her bones even now. Losing herself, she had leaned into that kiss and felt the electricity surge between them...

And then nothing.

On that long drive home, he'd barely said a word.

Picking up on the vibe, Johnny had turned on the radio to drown out the awkwardness. He'd thanked Kane for the meal — the best he'd ever had — but Kane hadn't engaged in much of a conversation other than to say he was welcome.

All the closeness she had felt with him, the playfulness and joking around as they'd worked side-by-side earlier in the day had vanished. A wall had come up between them.

Her heart ached as she once again felt that stinging rejection that always seemed to follow her. What was it about her that stopped people wanting to be close? Why could they never see her as who she actually was?

What was so wrong with her that even Kane felt he had to pull away?

Lost in her thoughts, she jolted when her father spoke again.

"It's been a long day. Why don't we leave my daughter so she can get some rest? If there's anything else, we can discuss it in my office."

"I'll take my leave too if you don't mind, early call in the morning," Mandy yawned, looking suddenly exhausted. Stonewall planted a kiss on Lexi's head as the trio left the room.

"Get some sleep," Stonewall told his daughter, shutting her door. Mandy kissed him on the cheek, tossed Kane a small wave then padded off to sleep leaving the two men alone. As soon as she was out of earshot, Kane spoke up.

"We've had two incidents in two days. The perp is

obviously not quitting. We need to tell Lexi about the threats. It's ridiculous not to."

Stonewall's expression turned hard.

"Let me make this clear to you. Lexi stays out of this. She is not to be told anything. She has enough on her plate worrying about the State going up in flames and feeling as if she has to personally save everyone affected by the fires. You've just spent the day with her, can't you see that she's a sensitive girl? She takes things to heart. I am not going to give her more to worry about, so we are not going to have this conversation again. If this is a problem for you, maybe I should speak with your superior?"

This was one of those moments he would have told his client where he could shove his demands, but for the promise he had made to Wilson. He couldn't drag his buddy's good name through the mud, which would be exactly what happened if he said what was on his mind. Instead, he swallowed his retort and took one for the team.

Bud made a sound that showed how unimpressed he was with Stonewall's treatment of him. Picking up on the antagonism in the air, he'd planted himself between the two, ready to defend his master should anything kick off.

"I'll keep our deal... for now," he made it seem as if he had a choice in the matter.

Stonewall fixed him with steely eyes which probably intimidated lesser men, but Kane had been down the pits of hell and clawed his way out on a nightly basis.

He stared right back at him.

Stonewall's gaze went past Kane to Lexi's door. As if

he could picture his daughter on the other side of it, his expression suddenly softened.

For the briefest moment, Kane caught a glimpse of the anguish any caring father would feel in the same situation... but it was gone in a flash.

"See that you do." With that remark, Stonewall spun on his heel and left.

15

T he crisp night air was a welcome to the fog inside his brain.

Driving to that same spot he had investigated before, Kane welcomed the fresh air pouring through the open windows, knowing it would keep his mind alert and his body awake. There was also the added bonus that Bud might be able to pick up on a clue left behind.

He breathed in a deep breath that cleared his head, though it did nothing to erase the look Lexi had given him when he'd first arrived.

He recognized the look, had felt it keenly himself at times. A part of him thought he should apologize, but the fact of the matter was, it was better for her to be angry at him. If she was angry at him, she would stay away.

And they wouldn't have the chance to cross that line again.

If they kept their distance, kept their relationship

professional, he was sure the two of them would be able to co-exist without issue.

There was sure to be some iciness tossed his way: he had no doubt about that, after all, egos were such fragile little things, but they were both adults and from what he'd learned of her so far, she wasn't the petty type.

He nodded to himself, happy with his decision.

All he had to do was to ignore what had happened between them until she eventually grew bored with the lack of drama and moved on.

Arriving at the spot, he parked nearby and got out. His men had set up a couple of floodlights in the area. Stan greeted him with a nod. "We left the climbing gear for Bud, haven't touched it so it won't be tainted with our scent."

"Thanks," Kane replied.

A quick examination and Kane could see that they weren't just cheap but brand new. There were several ropes that looked as if they were in the process of being turned into a homemade rope ladder, a box of carabiners (light but strong metal rings with spring-loaded gates), a harness and other odd bits and pieces — none of which made much sense. Try as he might, Kane couldn't quite see what it was their porp was attempting to do.

One thing was becoming clear, however: their intruder was likely working on their own and wasn't part of a wider network. Networks were usually financed productions, and this looked like a very confused one-man band.

Even so, the thought of this didn't bring much relief.

Individuals had a habit of being unpredictable.

When push came to shove, it was usually the unknown who behaved in a manner that would prove detrimental to all. It was why, if faced with a big angry man and a panicked teenager, a person needed to be more weary of the unpredictable teenager as they were more likely to do something stupid out of fear.

Turning to Bud, he held out an end of rope to him. "Find. Find where they are."

Bud moved to him and investigated the gear with his nose. While he took in the scents, Kane thought about how amazing his sense of smell was. During their early training together, he had learned how they can smell one hundred thousand times better than humans and how each nostril can also smell separately giving the dog a 3D picture of where something might be in an environment.

All dogs have this amazing sense of smell, but German Shepherds have one of the best. That with their calm-under-pressure natures, their intelligence and how they loved to work were some of the main reasons why they made such great police dogs. It had been a no-brainer for him to train Bud for his line of work, though he'd underestimated just how useful his dog could be.

Bud alerted, having caught a scent.

He took off at a light pace as Kane jogged after him. Following him in the car would have been too noisy plus the fumes from the exhaust wouldn't have done Bud's health any favors while also masking the trail he had found.

He stayed close to his dog as they ran down the grassy path beside the road. It wasn't quite light yet, though the sky had lost its deep shade of black. Kane didn't expect much traffic to come this way this time of the night, but he kept two eyes fixed on the road ahead for any unwelcome surprises.

Bud took him on a weaving path, navigating the edge of the property until eventually looping back to the Rockefellers' house.

When he finally stopped outside one of the property's back doors, he barked a sharp, short bark to let Kane know that he needed assistance with the door which led directly into the kitchen. Kane couldn't hide his surprise that the trail would lead here, particularly as no one had broken into the house.

He opened the door with a master key that he'd been given. Bud's only response was a quick wag of his tail before he moved past.

Once inside the kitchen, however, he stopped as if confused. Turning, he spun to the left, then right, before turning in a full circle, not knowing which direction to go. He was still looking confused when the housekeeper entered the room.

"Oh, hi there! I wasn't expecting company this early in the morning," Ruth cooed, bending to fuss him. Bud danced around her, enjoying the sudden attention as Kane felt a surge of disappointment move through him.

Bud had lost the trail, which seemed to have stopped right outside that door.

He looked up at the door. His movements had caused the camera to turn on. A small blue LED light indicated that it was currently recording. The camera was working exactly as it should.

None of which made any kind of sense.

If their perp had come up to the house, to this door, and gone through into the kitchen, the camera would have caught them and his men would already have been in touch about it.

But if their scent stopped here… did that indicate that whoever it was had business at the house?

"Who uses this door Ruth?"

She stopped stroking Bud, considering his question. "Some of the household staff use it instead of the staff entrance."

"Why's that?"

"If they come through here, I'm usually around. I tend to offer food and drink, which people like. Speaking of which, can I feed him something?" She offered, gesturing at Bud, having no idea of the turmoil in his mind. "I've got some roast chicken in the fridge?"

"He's on a raw diet, I'm afraid."

"I've got just the thing." She took out a tub of beef bones that she presented to Bud. "I keep this for making bone broth. Mrs. Gray, she swears it's what keeps her young." Bud whined, his body quivering at the unexpected delight.

At the hopeful expression on his face, Kane felt any objection fade. "Go on then."

His thoughts went back to the door. "Other than the staff, would anyone else use it?"

She nodded, wiping her hands on her apron. "Yes. All of our deliveries go through there."

Her eyes went wide suddenly. With the questions and

his early appearance, things were falling into place. "Why? Has something happened?"

"I'll let you know if it's of any concern." His cryptic answer wasn't lost on her. It wasn't her place to know of these things, and she must have realized that. Her face turned pink. She reached for a mug.

"Can I get you something? I've got coffee on the brew, though it'll take a few more minutes. I wasn't expecting company."

Kane nodded his thanks. "Thank you. Are you normally here this early?"

His tone had become conversational now but Ruth knew it wasn't an idle question. Her shoulders stiffened.

"My shift doesn't start until later but when you get to my age, sleep doesn't always come easily. I find the worst thing to do is to lie there getting anxious about how much rest you aren't getting. On those occasions when I know it's fruitless to try, I come in and get things started. I like to keep myself busy."

He sat by the marble island and watched as Ruth went to work preparing for the day ahead.

"You've worked for the Rockefellers a long time?" Although he already knew the answer, it was still interesting to hear people's responses: nuance wasn't something that came across in a file.

"Oh, yes. Since my boy was little. We moved from North Carolina when he was only seven. My husband — he was killed in an accident at work when some scaffolding fell down on him." Her voice quivered and she stopped to take a breath.

"I'm sorry," Kane replied. There wasn't much else he

could say to soften the terrible blow life had dealt, nothing that wouldn't sound like an empty platitude. "What made you decide to come here?"

This he didn't already know. Most people moved to LA with a dream of working in the film industry, though this seemed highly unlikely of Ruth, given what he'd just learned of her.

"Emilio — my husband — his family are here. Initially, they put us up in their home so I could find my feet, but as time went by, I guess they felt they had done enough in his memory. When the job came up for the Rockefellers, I took it because it offered a self-contained cottage on the grounds. We lived there until Hank — my son — was older and then we moved out as they wanted to renovate the cottage, change it into a guest house for visitors. Of course, they've never used it — the Rockefellers don't usually entertain at home. This party they are throwing is very out the norm for them."

The coffee maker, a futuristic chrome monstrosity hummed, ready for use. Ruth spooned a cup of ground coffee beans into the machine, hit a metal lever and slotted an espresso cup beneath the spout. Hot water passed into the beans, filling the air with the rich aroma of fresh coffee, making Kane's mouth water. Next to good food, great coffee was his other vice.

"Will the party be a nightmare for you?" She seemed to have her hands full just keeping things running around here; he couldn't imagine having to staff a large event on top.

Ruth looked startled, handing him the espresso on a saucer. "Goodness, I won't be doing much for it other than to take in the deliveries. Lexi has hired a catering company to take care of all that. I wouldn't know where to begin a job that big, and thankfully, she has not asked me to. She's a very good girl, you know. Never seems to have many friends though. Maybe you can be her friend?"

The older woman winked suddenly, apparently having decided to not take offence by his questions. Ridiculously, Kane could feel himself getting hot.

"Mind if I take this with me?" He gestured at the coffee, eager to get away. She turned to focus on peeling mushrooms for the breakfast she'd be serving later.

"Of course. You can leave the cup in your office. One of the staff will collect it when they do their rounds."

He left, Bud carrying that bone between his teeth as if it were the most precious thing in the world. When he took a sip of his espresso, his mouth rejoiced.

It was quite possibly the best coffee he'd ever tasted.

He knew immediately that he'd be paying many more visits to Ruth and that kitchen, even if it meant having to sidestep her personal questions.

16

The florist couldn't stop staring at Kane, something Lexi was only too aware of.

The woman was in her late forties and reeked of desperation if the too-tight, revealing jumpsuit that she was wearing was anything to go by. Strong perfume poured off of her, stinging the back of her throat, making it itch.

Why did people feel the need to douse themselves in toxic chemicals, particularly when scent was such a personal thing? What appealed to one person might — and often was - - off-putting to another.

Then there were the asthma sufferers and those with chemical sensitivities where inhaling any kind of fragrance could be the difference between life or death.

Lexi coughed and waved her hand under her nose pointedly. But Elise — the florist who owned the store — didn't seem to take the hint. Tapping a long red talon against pouty lips that had obviously been enhanced, she cast an eye over the list Lexi presented. "Yes, that should be fine. I'll have this delivered to your home on Thursday as planned."

With the party only two days away now, Lexi was feeling the heat. Everything had to work out as planned. She wasn't going to be the reason that funds weren't coming in.

By the wreaths, Bud sat by Kane's side, nose twitching a mile a minute as he took in the floral-scented room. Kane's attention was on the call that had just come through. Lexi snuck a sideways look at him.

He wore his usual outfit of cargo pants and a simple, light-colored shirt that barely fit his biceps. While his men all wore dark suits to work, the same rule didn't seem to apply to him. He was always neatly turned out, but he held a clear disdain for the constricting suits.

She couldn't discern the gist of his conversation, but whatever it was, it wasn't putting him into a good mood. The longer he spoke to the person, the more clipped his responses became. His body was as rigid and unyielding as a steel bar.

All morning, he had seemed tense, though she wasn't sure if it was their kiss or something else that was the cause of the tight line of his shoulders. He hadn't mentioned it, hadn't referred to anything remotely personal with her. In fact, he was giving her such a wide berth that they could have been on opposite sides of the Atlantic.

It was driving her insane.

She didn't know what to make of his withdrawal. He was as attentive as ever, doing his job to the best of his ability, but there was a definite distance between them now, a wall she couldn't penetrate. Only Bud was still the same adorable dog. He acted like a buffer between the two of them.

Truth be told, her early disappointment and puzzlement had turned quickly into anger: if he was going to ignore what happened, then so could she. She would be damned if she'd beg for any man's attention. If nothing else, her mother had taught her that.

"Cute dog," Elise commented, hoping for Kane to hear but he was too involved with his conversation. "They say the owners take after their dogs, that's definitely true in this situation."

Damned or not, however, Lexi wasn't quite ready for another woman to move in.

"Yes," Lexi replied before she could give much thought to what she was saying. "A shame that he's not into women. What a waste."

Elise blinked, startled. "*Him?* Really?"

"Oh yes," Lexi affected a conspiratorial tone. "I caught him in Mickey's down in West Hollywood. His heels were higher than mine had been."

All the wind seem to leave Elise, she deflated right before her eyes. "That is annoying."

Lexi looked over at Kane, sighed wistfully. "Still, we can look."

"Hell yes we can."

Lexi took her clipboard back. "Are we good here? I've emailed through this list but just wanted to make sure we were on track."

Elise nodded, tearing her eyes reluctantly from Kane.

Lexi slid the clipboard with the checklists into her oversized boho bag and they left, Elise staring sadly after Kane as her dreams and libido came dashing to the ground.

"Lexi..." Kane's tone was serious, underlined with a layer of disappointment. She was so surprised to hear him actually address her that she almost stumbled.

He looked her in the face, his expression troubled. "That was the lab calling. They pulled good prints off the soda can but unfortunately, they didn't match anything in the database."

She didn't know whether to be relieved or not. "So this is the first crime they've committed?"

"Or they haven't been caught before."

Neither thought was of comfort.

"What about the photographs? You mentioned the other day that you had someone making enquiries?"

He nodded. "I'm still waiting to hear back. Clara works for my boss. She has a few contacts that might be able to dig out some info on how the photographs were sent to the gossip sites."

He looked as if he wanted to say more, but something stopped him. Dropping his gaze from her, he proceeded to study the row of cars beside them.

"Was there anything else?"

Like an apology or explanation for what happened the other night?

The question popped out without her meaning it to. His eyes flicked back to her, concerned but still with that impenetrable wall.

"What do you mean?"

She'd given him an opening, but he wasn't going to take it. She had to fight to quell the wave of crushing disappointment.

"Nothing."

They continued with Lexi's tasks, working their way through her never-ending checklist.

After the florist, they visited the caterers, a family owned business in the valley that Lexi had initially met via PAWS when they had catered an event there. She performed a last-minute taste test of the delicacies — which Kane keenly noticed — she did not offer him, despite his knowledge and love of food.

He knew she was angry at him, could see it in the bristly way she answered his questions. She never quite met his eyes, unable to stare him in the face for fear that she would reveal her true emotions. At times he felt himself weaken, but there wasn't anything he could do about it.

He swallowed his own feelings on the matter, focused on keeping her safe. Bud knew something was up. He could tell by the way his dog kept leaning into him and sighing, almost as if he was trying to say that they should make up. Throughout the morning, he went between the two of them, checking that they were OK.

If only humans were as uncomplicated as dogs.

They'd been going for several hours and were stopped at Verve for a fast coffee break when Kane noticed a group of men staring at Lexi, openly watching as she stood by the counter studying the various options on display.

The men — who couldn't have been more than

twenty-five — jostled each other, running their eyes suggestively up and down her body in a way that raised his hackles.

She was dressed in shorts and a white tank today with a pair of strappy sandals on her feet. Her clothes weren't exactly revealing, though there was no outfit in the world that would be able to hide her dangerous curves. Still, their open leeriness made his blood pound.

He took several steps toward them, dropping down to focus on Bud's collar so he could hear their conversation.

"I'm telling you, it's her! I'd recognize that body anywhere." This was said from a lanky guy in skinny jeans. His blond hair couldn't successfully hide the bad acne scars that had left deep pockets on his skin.

"Because you printed out those pictures and plastered them all over your wall?" His friend, a hipster with a mohawk and cropped pink pants retorted. Kane never trusted a man who wore pink.

"Are you going to talk to her? What're you going to say?" Asked another. The smallest of the group, he seemed shyer and the most nervous of the bunch. He stole a glance at Lexi then flushed as if she had caught him staring. The guy couldn't have had any experience with the opposite sex in his entire life.

"Any girl willing to put herself out like that isn't interested in what I've got to say," Mohawk laughed, grabbing his groin. "She's only interested in two things: money and the D."

The group laughed, much louder this time. Lexi finally noticed them as she turned toward them.

"What's up, Babe? You wanna hang with us today?

I've got a pool you might like. Bikinis are optional which I figure will be fine seeing how you're quite the exhibitionist."

Lexi's reaction was stunning.

She went from looking normal to stricken in under a second flat.

Her mouth went slack, her eyes filled with shame. She didn't reply, stunned by this horrible intrusion into her life. She moved her oversized bag to cover as much of herself as she could, all thoughts of a drink now clear out of her mind. It took every inch of willpower not to just run out of there.

Kane cursed himself for waiting this long to deal with the situation. Striding to the group, he growled, "That's enough."

If they heard the threat in his voice, they didn't show it. Mohawk laughed louder.

"You don't have to defend her. Any girl who would sell pictures of herself in little more than underwear is desperate for the attention. I'm just giving her what she wants."

His friends laughed as Kane felt a rage so strong that it burned like fire. Eyes narrowing into slits, he spoke in a low but lethal tone.

"It's jerks like you who give guys a bad name. Those pictures were taken against her will while she was at home. And even if they weren't, it doesn't give you the right to talk to her like that."

The others backed down a step, not wanting to get into it with a man several times their size, but Mohawk's reputation was on the line now, as was his ego. Jutting out his chin, he glared back at Kane, defiance in his eyes.

"Who the hell are you, her boyfriend?"

"No. I'm her... friend."

"Well, *friend*," Mohawk sneered the word. "Good luck defending her honor to the masses. You'll need it since no one is buying that story."

Kane wanted to punch the arrogant punk's face. Reading into the tension, Bud bared his teeth, issuing a low growl that caused the group to take stock. Sparring verbally with Kane was one thing but an angry dog on the defense of his master was something else entirely.

Lifting both hands, Mohawk retreated. "Get your dog to calm down, man or you'll have my parents's lawyers to deal with."

Kane had had the punk's number before he'd even spoken a word. He was some poor rich kid whose parents had likely never paid him enough attention, so now he paraded around the world looking to make everyone as miserable as he was.

"He's reacting to the hostility you're throwing our way. He sees you as a threat... and he's been trained to take those out, so if you don't want to see a chunk taken out of that skinny ass of yours, you'd best be leaving now, *man*."

Mohawk glared at him, but he also knew the game was up. "Come on," he said to his friends. "The clientele sucks in here, anyway."

His remark didn't make any sense, but Kane chose to let it go. The faster Lexi's color came back to her, the better he'd feel. Bud, however, wasn't placated from the group's exit. Sniffing the air suddenly, he alerted, letting Kane know that something else was wrong.

The danger hadn't yet passed.

"What is it, Bud?"

Bud barked, then stared off into the distance. Kane crouched down to his level, trying to see what had drawn his dog's attention.

Traffic weaved alongside on this, another typically sweltering day. Shoppers went in and out of the row of stores that made up this particular strip of the street, some to incur major damage to their wallets while others only wanted respite from the relentless sun. There wasn't anything out of the ordinary that he could see.

Except for the stationary figure made hazy by the heat coming off the sidewalk.

The man was noticeable as not only was he not moving, he seemed to be staring directly at them. He was far too overdressed for the weather in the baseball cap that shaded his face beyond the dark sunglasses, long-sleeved shirt and jeans he wore. Barely an inch of him was left uncovered.

Something glinted in his hands, a metallic object that he held onto. It took a moment to register what it was.

A camera with a wide-zoom lens.

The hairs on the back of Kane's neck rose, apprehension flooded his spine sending his nerves shrieking.

It was him, the man making threats to the family.

Kane knew without a moment's hesitation. He started toward him, determined to catch the bastard who was the cause of Lexi's current distress.

"Where are you going?"

The puzzlement was clear in her question. He froze, torn between going after the guy, but it wasn't safe to leave Lexi alone. What if the perp wasn't working on his own as all the evidence had suggested? There could be one or more of them, and this could all be a trap.

He spoke into the radio receiver that was clipped to his shirt as he pulled out his phone.

"Johnny, I need you."

He didn't bother to mask the urgency of his request. Activating the camera on his phone, he snapped picture after picture of the man who had turned around and was now leaving at a brisk pace.

Lexi's eyes turned uneasy. Wrapping her arms around herself, she took a step closer to him. "What's going on?"

His mind worked through what explanation he could give when Johnny's worried voice came down the wire. "What's up?"

"I'm sending you some pictures now. I need you to head down Melrose, find and tail this guy."

"Got it, Boss," Johnny replied. "Swinging back onto Melrose now."

"Kane. Please. If something is wrong, I deserve to know."

He held up a hand to her, unable to answer her question just yet. He needed his full attention on the guy who was heading into another street.

"He's turned left onto Robertson Boulevard," he told Johnny. "I've lost eyes on him now."

Johnny's voice came over the line, "I see him. I'm moving up. You want me to just follow him?"

Kane stared at the junction their perp had turned off into, filled with a burning rage that he couldn't go after him. "No. I need you to detain him, but only if it's safe to do so."

"Got it," Johnny replied. "He's just ahead of me, maybe fifty feet or so... Wait... I think he made me... Dammit..."

"What's happening?" Kane demanded, shoulders stiff with tension.

There was no response from Johnny for several moments. When he came back on, he sounded out of breath.

"He's gone. Sorry, Kane. He ducked into an alley that's too small for me to get the car into. By the time I'd gotten out of the car, he'd vanished."

The crushing disappointment took his breath away.

They'd had the guy right there!

He felt a hand on his arm... Lexi. She stared at him with such a mixture of concern and fear that their issues faded away in an instant.

In that moment, he knew he couldn't keep his promise to the Rockefellers. He could never be in this situation again, one where he had to risk her safety in order to capture their guy.

He could not keep her safe if she didn't know what the threat was.

It was time to tell her the truth, but it wasn't something that could be discussed out in the open like this. They also couldn't go to her home, not without dealing with her parents. And his trailer wouldn't be able to protect anyone wide open as it was.

The fact that their perp had so brazenly followed them today meant Lexi was not safe out in the open like this. He needed to control the environment before any such discussion could begin.

"We need to have a discussion. Is there anywhere secure that we can go?"

Of all the things she had expected him to say, that wasn't it. Something was clearly going on, and she didn't appreciate being kept on the outside. A thousand questions whirled like a tornado in her mind.

"Why can't we just talk at home?"

"I'll explain after. Can you just trust me for now? It's important or I wouldn't be asking this of you."

His eyes exuded such sincerity that she felt the anger that had been with her since yesterday melting away.

"We can go to LoftHouse. The private club my parents are members of."

"Will there be a lot of people in the club?"

"It's called a club, but it's more like a hotel. I can call ahead and see if a room is available."

"And the place is secure?"

"Like Fort Knox. Only celebrities are allowed and there's a stringent application process."

Ordinarily, he would have stayed far, far away from such a place which sounded like his kind of personal hell. Instead, he found himself nodding.

"That should work."

"I'll make the call."

He flicked through the images he'd taken, staring at her new guarddog.

So this was the man they had hired to protect her?

He took in his height, the broad shoulders and the physique which spoke of regular workout sessions. His eyes roamed over the tattoo, the stance that conveyed his military past, and the fleabag he liked to call his partner.

And he could feel the hatred burning a path inside.

When he'd first been made aware of the new security the Rockefellers had contracted, he'd pictured the overweight, lazy bums that guarded his local mall. But this man, this Kane Turner wasn't anything like that.

He looked as lethal as any fighting machine, and that wasn't even counting the snarling beast by his side.

He'd never expected for the dog to pick up his scent today, not when he was so far away and there were crowds of people going about their business.

How had the dog found him amongst all of that?

Even in the pictures, the mutt was clearly looking for him, his nose sniffing in all directions, *hunting* him.

Sweat gathered at the base of his neck just remembering how close a call it had been. If he hadn't left when he had or disappeared into that alley where the car couldn't follow, possibly his plans might have all been foiled.

Luckily, he was far too smart for that.

Too smart for them.

He clicked through several pictures until he came to one of *her*. She was standing a few feet away from the man, her arms around herself, though he could still see much of that body she so loved to flaunt.

Earlier, when he'd been standing on the sidewalk, staring down the wide-zoom lens, he'd been able to see inside the coffee shop to how she'd drawn the attention of that group of men, all of them, lusting after her.

Oh, she'd acted coy and shy, but he knew what a great actress she was. After all, there was more than one of them in the family, and she was certainly making the most of the publicity he'd given her.

The anger roared through his blood, turning the tips of his ears hot.

He'd expected her to hide away, to be ashamed of having herself being exposed to the world like that. Instead, it seemed to have bought her even more positive attention.

Once again, he was reminded of how unfair the world was to one like him.

He glared at the bodyguard. At the face which women seemed to flock to. He'd seen that too, how the female servers at Verve had noticed him. They'd thrust out their breasts, seeking his attention in a way he had never experienced.

It all made him sick to his stomach.

He continued flicking through the shots on the digital screen, studying every facet of that face. He had memorized every plane, every angle, every freckle so well that he could probably draw her face from memory.

There she was looking alarmed. The dog had noticed him then and was trying to let Turner know. She had been asking him something, but he hadn't responded.

It gave him a small jolt of satisfaction to see that her

bodyguard wasn't so enamored with her. Maybe he wasn't all brawn and no sense.

It wasn't until he saw Turner speaking into his cuff that he'd realized they weren't alone — that someone else was with them. If it wasn't for that, he might not have noticed the Asian in the Mercedes coming after him in time.

Really, he had to thank Turner for giving the game away.

He scrolled through the many shots he had taken today, his hatred bubbling deep as a well.

It didn't matter how big Turner was or how smart the dog — it wasn't going to help her in the end.

Nothing would.

In the end, she would know just what it felt like to be truly alone, at the mercy of others.

17

Lexi sat in the backseat of the sleek Mercedes with the tinted windows, burning with questions yet not being able to ask any of them was an exercise in patience that she did not think she'd pass.

She stole a glance at Kane in the passenger seat. From his stoney profile, she had no idea what was on his mind or what it was he wanted to discuss.

What had gotten him so worked up?

At first, she'd thought those guys had come back to cause more trouble, but there had been no sign of them. When she'd tried to see what Kane had been taking pictures of outside the coffee shop, he'd been too quick for her, hiding his phone away, which only caused more anxiety.

She'd heard what he'd said to Johnny though, heard the instructions to follow a man. Who it was though, she didn't know. And it seemed an extraordinary overreaction for a member of the paparazzi.

Why didn't he trust her with the truth? Did he think

she wouldn't be able to handle it? Did he think that little
of her?

It bothered her more than she thought possible.

Towering palm trees rushed by, that iconic sight
always associated with this city. Despite how she was
feeling, she still took a moment to admire their majesty,
knowing that one could never take things for granted.
One day they could be here, and the next, they could turn
into a smoking pile of ashes.

Johnny drove as he did on each of their journeys —
with purpose. He only ever joined in with the conversation if it was directed at him, otherwise he kept his mind
and business on the job.

Since they'd gotten into the car, Kane had said very
little to Johnny. Their driver had asked if what the
problem was only to be met with a terse, "I'll brief you
later." Unlike Lexi, however, Johnny had seemed satisfied
with that non-answer.

They arrived at the member's club a little after four.

A discreet-looking building of five floors, ivy tumbled
from the roof deck where a glass swimming pool could be
occasionally glimpsed through tiny gaps in the greenery,
though only the water could be seen, certainly not
whoever might be using the pool.

The tall windows that covered the building were
tinted so no one could record the proceedings inside —
many of the rooms were hired out by the hour for
"meetings."

The front door was always flanked by two giant
bouncers and a devastatingly pretty girl who greeted the
guests while subtly checking their credentials. An

annual membership to the club reached an eye-watering six figures. Only the wealthiest people on the planet were invited after a rigorous vetting process.

Lexi had been a member since she was a child, although she barely came without her parents. There was one time she had made the mistake of bringing friends, but they had only been interested in celeb spotting.

When she wasn't looking, they ran up a huge tab behind the bar even though none of them were old enough to drink. After an uncomfortable conversation with her parents, Lexi had given the place a wide berth despite always liking it here. It was quiet with a home-like feel. And it felt safe: no-one tended to stare when everyone was *someone*.

They left the car as their host, a stunning blonde in a tight-fitting dress that left nothing to the imagination, flashed a smile at Kane that made Lexi uncomfortable. Her breasts jiggled as she moved — it was obvious the woman wasn't wearing a bra.

To his credit, Kane didn't seem to have noticed the goddess or her bouncing globes that she seemed deter-mined to thrust his way. He only took a cooler out of the car and nodded to Johnny that he could go.

She wondered if whatever was in the cooler had anything to do with why they were here.

"I'll call when I need you. We shouldn't be more than a few hours."

Johnny touched the tip of his cap. "Sure thing. See you later, Miss. Lexi" He flashed another one of his conta-gious smiles, then left.

"Can I have the guest name, please?" Asked their host, whose name was "Amber" as the necklace that was nestled in the valley of her breasts informed them helpfully.

"Alexia Gray-Rockefeller." Lexi made herself stand taller.

"I see you have the penthouse booked."

"I asked for a normal room." She corrected her.

Amber looked a little flustered she checked a digital screen hidden inside a stand.

"I see what's happened. All other rooms have been taken, unfortunately, and in the past, your parents have always requested the penthouse. Would you still like it or I can move the booking to another day? Of course we will not charge you extra since this is our mistake."

What Lexi needed was to know what Kane wanted to say, and all these delays were making her antsy. "It's fine. We'll take it."

She handed Lexi a key card, then flashed another smile that she mostly directed at Kane.

"Enjoy your stay and if there's anything I can do for you, you can reach me by dialing 0," Amber said breathlessly. Lexi had to clench her fists by her side.

What on Earth was she getting so riled up for?

Yes, the girl was flirting with him, but it could have just been for a bigger tip. This was how the world worked, after all.

Pretty girls gave men the illusion that they were interested, bolstering their ego and making them think that they had a chance. In return, men would pay more attention to the girls and be looser with their cash.

It wasn't something she had ever stooped to herself, but she had seen plenty of this kind of behavior all of her life. There was even a time at school when she had been invited into a clique of beautiful daughters of celebrities. The group loved to party around town but never paid for anything: there was always a rich man or two to cover their meals and drinks so long as the girls pretended to be interested in them.

The whole duplicitousness of it all had set her teeth on edge.

Not picking up on her vibe at all, Kane placed a hand on the small of Lexi's back, steering her into a waiting elevator. At his touch, all thoughts of the other girl disappeared from her mind.

His hand burned a path through her clothes and directly onto her skin.

As the numbers flashed up, Lexi grew more tense. She studied Kane, trying to find any clue as to what he was feeling, but the man had a great poker face. She could get nothing from him. And if he saw her looking, he was doing a great job of ignoring her.

She took comfort in the fact that Bud was acting normal — at least he didn't seem worried by his master's silence.

When the doors pinged open directly into the penthouse, Kane stepped onto plush white carpet and sucked in a sharp breath.

He was standing in the living room where a giant flat screen dominated an entire wall. Sunken sofas formed an L-shaped sitting area where a basket of artisan food sat waiting to be feasted upon. He could see cheese, grapes, bread and crackers and chocolate truffles. Inside a silver ice bucket, a bottle of Dom Perignon chilled.

It was almost a shame that they wouldn't be here long enough to enjoy any of it.

A wall of doors were opened onto the private rooftop terrace where sun loungers were artfully placed around that pool he had glimpsed earlier, making the most of the glorious view of the city and the Hollywood Hills beyond.

Having been here before, all Lexi noticed now was the Californian King-size bed that beckoned with its inviting luxury. Set on a raised platform, its presence loomed over the living area. It didn't help that dotted discreetly around it, scented candles perfumed the air, lending the room a spicy aroma that drew her toward it.

Without meaning to, a picture of them writhing on the bed flew into Lexi's mind. Her face became hot. Worried that she might be turning red, she found a seat on one of the sofas and fixed her eyes on the food basket instead.

Remember, you're here for answers. Focus on the nice and unsexy cheese.

Across from her, Kane was acutely aware of Bud's sweeping tail — and of the devastation it could wreak in a pristine room like this.

Everywhere he looked there was something expensive to smash. It was like it had been the decorator's sole intention when they had furnished the room.

"OK. We're here now. What have you got to tell me?"

Lexi sounded impatient and he couldn't really blame

her. Not wanting to get into it in the car, she'd had to wait all the way here, so he wasn't unsympathetic.

"I need a few minutes to check the place out."

Her eyes flitted away from the food basket to land on him, exasperated. "Who's going to be here when we only gave them thirty minutes notice?"

"I still have to check, Lexi. It's—."

"Let me guess," she interrupted. "It's not negotiable."

A sigh hissed out of her and she folded her arms across her chest.

Kane didn't know quite what to make of her response — was that something he said too often? Judging by the glower she sent his way, the answer was yes.

He kept a hand on Bud's neck, a silent reminder to be gentle as he set the cooler onto the counter then worked his way around, examining the place for safety while keeping an arm's length from anything and everything.

He couldn't imagine someone being getting here ahead of them, finding a way to bypass the security trio downstairs and the five cameras he'd already detected on the ride up, but he had to be sure.

When he was done, he lowered into the seat opposite Lexi, who seemed strangely fixated with the food hamper.

He signaled Bud. "You can relax, Boy."

Bud yawned and laid down beside him. Kane turned his focus to Lexi, whose eyes were still averted from his. She was either really irate at him or...

"If you're hungry, you can help yourself. You don't have to wait for me."

His comment caught her off-guard. "I'm fine."

"You're staring at that basket like you're trying to set it on fire with only the power of your mind."

She spread her hands wide, giving him a withering *look*. "I'm just wondering when you're actually getting to the point. This is a pretty outrageous — and costly — way of getting answers from someone."

She was right, and he was only drawing things out, not looking forward to the coming conversation at all.

"You're right."

He softened his voice, choosing his words carefully.

"Your parents haven't been entirely honest with you."

The change in her was immediate. Her eyes turned flinty as she interlocked her fingers on her knees. "About what exactly?"

"For the past month or so, they have been receiving notes... threats that have grown increasingly more frequent in nature."

The hardness in her eyes turned dark with worry.

"That can't be true. They would have told me."

Even as she said the words, Lexi felt the lie in the pit of her stomach.

When Mandy had first received news that she had been nominated for her second Oscar, the news didn't break for days. They'd kept it from her — the biggest news of her entire career — sure that Lexi would accidentally blurt it out at school. Then there was the time Stonewall had suffered a cancer scare. A mole on his chest had ended up benign, but they had hid the truth from her until they had gotten the opinion of three specialists.

Her parents kept things from her all the time.

"They didn't want to worry you unnecessarily, but I think the time has come for you to know. I'm going against their wishes telling you this, but your life is at stake and I am not willing to risk anything happening to you."

The world seemed to spin. She felt sluggish as she blinked at him, as if she hadn't heard him correctly.

"This is about... *me?*"

He nodded, lips pressed into a thin white line. "That's how it would appear."

For the next twenty minutes he went over everything, from the first threatening note to the appearance of the man outside Verve. Lexi stayed mostly silent, listening as he explained and only asking the odd question for clarification.

"But how do you know that the person who is sending the notes is the same one who took those pictures of me?"

"I don't have definitive proof, but it seems likely." Kane gestured at his phone. "Clara just emailed me back to let me know what her sources have told her. I had her check to see who sent them those photographs. I knew it was a long shot but I was hoping we'd be able to find out who and where the payments were made out to."

"And? What did she find out?"

"That the person never requested any form of payment."

Lexi felt the wind had been knocked out of her.

"They weren't paid for those pictures?"

"No. More importantly, they never *requested* any money either, even when those shots could easily have commanded a six-figure payout. There are a lot of people out there wanting to know what you look like now, and, given the nature of those photographs... they would have generated a hefty price tag."

Lexi tried to make sense of what he was saying, but there was a loud hornet-like hum in her head.

"I don't understand, why would someone do that? If they're not getting paid, what was it for?"

"They said they wanted to make you pay. I'm assuming they knew that the photographs would embarrass you."

Her face turned stricken as an unwelcome thought came to her.

"Do you think they might actually know me?"

"The possibility has crossed my mind," he revealed reluctantly. He didn't want to scare her further, but as he'd already seen for this relationship to work, there couldn't be any secrets between them.

"And keeping their identity secret is more important than money."

Her eyes darted to his as the horror of the truth came. "They mean to do more than just embarrass me don't they?"

"I can't say for sure..."

"But that's what you believe."

"Yes."

And now it made sense, why Kane kept refusing to let her out of his sight, how protective and careful he had been with her this whole time. It wasn't to placate her parents as she had thought.

Her eyes closed shut. She felt herself swaying in her seat. The ground had disappeared. There was nothing around her but darkness. She felt panic begin to take hold when a soft breath landed on her clasped hands. A concerned whine as Bud laid his head on her hands.

Opening her eyes, she smiled at him, taking comfort in his presence.

"I'm OK, Boy."

She was taking this better than Kane had expected her to. There was no shouting, no tears or drama, just sensible questions asked in a forthright manner. She was much tougher than he'd ever realized. He pressed on.

"Have you upset anyone that you can think of? These notes are personal. They sound like they know you though it could all be the mind of a sick personality."

She shook her head, eyes large and luminous. "I don't have any enemies. I don't have many friends either, but that's just how it's gone for me. It's difficult to form any real relationships when all people want is to get close to my parents."

Her breath quivered and she took a moment to compose herself. Her raw honesty and the pain he could read in her voice was like a knife in the heart. He was suddenly compelled to take her in his arms, but he forced the compulsion away.

"What about your ex? Could he have any residual issues with you?"

"Pete? It's been a few years now. I doubt he's given me a moment's thought. He's too busy swanning around the world with Angel. He has the life he has always wanted. He was never interested in me."

She continued, fighting to keep her voice from breaking.

"Even though he's a horrible person, I would never hurt him or do anything to anyone that would ever warrant such a reaction."

"Some individuals don't need much encouragement. Look what happened with that group of idiots today."

She hated that he was right.

Faces flew into her mind of all the people she had ever had a disagreement with. Former friends, her first boyfriend, general members of the public. Had she ever done something hurtful that she just hadn't realized?

Her memories crashed into one another. Coupled with the lack of sleep over the last few nights, it was all too much. She started shaking. The edges of her vision began to darken.

Someone out there wanted to hurt her.

"Lexi?"

She couldn't speak, not understanding what was happening. His voice sounded far away, like he was on the opposite side of the world instead of the few feet of distance that separated them.

And all the while, there was that terrible ice-cold numbness inside.

"Are you OK?"

She tried to answer him, but her tongue felt thick, her mouth as dry as the desert. She couldn't have spoken even if she'd wanted to. Blackness was taking over and there was nothing she could do to stop it.

She was sinking, sinking into oblivion when strong arms enveloped her. She sank against them like her life — her very soul — depended on it. Her heart raced a mile a minute, thumping in her chest as heat radiated from his body.

Kane's body.

She pressed so close to him that she could feel his heart beating against her own. Her hands reached out blindly to grab hold of him.

"Breathe, Lexi. You're suffering from a panic attack."

Was that true?

Was that all it was?

Then why did the darkness seem so inviting?

"Everything is OK. I'm here. I won't let anyone hurt you."

He sounded so protective and solid, like an impenetrable wall, that the darkness didn't seem quite as wonderful now.

His skin was hot to her touch, warming her fingers as they held onto him. He was her lifeline, her salvation, and she knew she couldn't let go.

"Come back, Lexi. Breathe. Please."

It was his broken plea that pulled her out of that dark place and back into the light. She blinked rapidly, her vision returning until she found herself cradled in his arms. He stared down at her, his face filled with such concern that it took her breath away.

"Are you alright?"

Suddenly, she saw everything as clear as day.

What a fool she had been to think that he didn't care for her, when right there in his eyes was all she had ever hoped for. Whatever his reasons for pulling away, it wasn't because she didn't mean anything to him — if anything, she meant too much.

She could see it all now in the way his eyes roamed so desperately over her, reassuring himself that she was well.

Her hand lifted of its own accord and cupped his face.

He tensed, shock juddering through him. He started to pull away, but when she stroked her thumb over his mouth, a tortured moan shot out of him that he couldn't control.

Lexi watched him, her beautiful hazel eyes wide in anticipation, silently begging for him to do what they both wanted.

What they both needed.

Her lips parted in expectation.

And Kane was lost.

Lowering his head, he sank his lips onto hers, kissing her with all the fire he felt for her. His tongue darted into her mouth, exploring the honey sweetness inside. When he took her lip in his and nibbled, she did the same back, driving him wild. Sparks flew as she opened up to him.

She saw the torture in his eyes, the pain in his life, yet she knew she could be there for him, that she could heal it all.

Kane couldn't have stopped kissing her even if the world's existence had depended on it. When she had looked at him as if he was her world, the last vestiges of his self-control had shattered.

Never had a woman caused such a reaction in him.

His mouth trailed a path down to her neck. She sat up, freeing his hands which now roamed her body, touching, exploring, caressing.

She quivered at his touch, arching her back, moving into him, pressing herself against him, eliciting a strangled moan from him in the process.

His hands found the hem of her tank top and moved beneath it. At the touch of her silky flesh, a jolt of heat coursed through him. She felt like heaven in his hands and he couldn't get enough.

He wanted to taste every inch of her, feel every part of her softness as she melted under his touch.

Tearing his mouth away, he stared into her face, his eyes dark with passion. Her own had lowered until they were almost closed, but what he could see of them was hazy with desire. Her lips were pink pillows waiting to be feasted on by him.

At his pause, a murmur of protest eased out of her. Her hands wove behind his neck, drawing him closer.

At the back of his mind came the thought that this was madness.

They came from two different worlds with nothing in common. She was a Hollywood princess while he was damaged goods, conflicted by the things he had done in his past and the loveless place he had come from. She was perfection while he was scarred, both physically and mentally. He was so broken that even something as simple as sleep did not come easily.

And there was the matter of their professional relationship: what they were doing broke all the rules. There would be significant repercussions.

Yet there was no denying the chemistry between them. It took — she took — his absolute breath away.

As if she could feel his hesitation, her lips parted beneath his as she stared up at him with a fiery desire.

"Please... don't... stop."

Who was he to deny her very wish?

Crushing her to him, he delved into her softness. She tasted sweet, yet there was a hint of mystery about her. She shrugged out of her tank top to reveal white lace lingerie beneath. He tried not to stare, but the sight of her half-naked was causing his brain to misfire.

He unbuckled her belt as she stepped out of her shorts. His body instantly responded, heat tearing through his loins.

By God, she was stunning!

His eyes ate up the sight of her, imprinting how she looked into his mind. He wanted to remember this moment forever.

Usually shy under his desire, Lexi found herself feeling bold and sexy. Seeing the reaction in him and how much he wanted her was such a turn-on that her inhibitions fell away.

She pushed against his body, digging her nails into his back. He gasped as she was rewarded by the shiver of his shoulders. She pulled off his shirt, almost tearing it in her haste, and was rewarded by his ripped torso and abs of steel. Scars criss-crossed his chest, physical signs of his tortured past. She studied each one, compassion pouring from her eyes as she traced a finger along the most vivid. When she reached the end of the scar, she lowered to kiss it.

A groan rumbled out of him.

She looked so sweet, yet her body was a wonderland

ripe for exploring. His hand landed on her thigh as he moved it across her until it fell into the gap between her legs. She arched her back.

Hands on her butt, he lifted her off her feet, wrapping her legs around him. Lexi gasped, startled, and quickly grabbed onto his shoulders as he walked toward the bed. When Bud raised his head, wondering if he should follow them, Kane stopped him with a gesture.

He lowered her onto the bed. Her hair fanned around her in a halo of chestnut. He ran his fingers over her face down to her neck and her collarbone, feeling goose pimples raise on her skin. He dragged a finger down lower, playing with the edge of her panties. She shuddered, tensing up, waiting in anticipation, but he only moved his hands back up, drawing out the torturous wait longer.

Impatient with the delicate fabric getting in his way, Kane tugged both breasts out of the bra. They tumbled out as Kane nestled his face between those soft cushions. His tongue snaked out while his hands teased and played with her. Lexi's eyes turned dark with desire as she watched him.

He sank his face into her, delving into her glory. Lexi moaned, pushing herself toward him, loving the wonderful sensations he was causing in her body. He removed her panties, tossing them carelessly to the carpet.

Lying there naked before him, she was quite possibly the most glorious woman in the world.

Her hands reached down and unbuttoned his cargo pants, pulled down his briefs. When he was naked, she drew in a breath, startled by the power he exuded. He was all man, yet in her hands, he trembled like a boy.

He moved on top of her. She writhed beneath him, a dangerous mix of sweetness and heat. His eyes feasted on her beauty that was for him alone before he slid his tongue into her mouth. She whimpered, threading her hand through his hair and squeezing his head tight, moving into him, desperate for more.

His mouth kissed a trail down her body until he found her special place. She gasped, head snaking back and forth across the pillow as he took her out of this world. And when she thought there was nowhere else to go, he moved into her. She met his hips with her own as their bodies rocked as one.

Lexi gasped at the feel of him. "Please, Kane..." she cried.

Lexi moaned as divine pleasure took over. Her gasps were so sexy, her body so exquisite, that the pressure started to build. He moved more urgently, drinking in her every reaction a man possessed.

The pressure built until it reached a crushing crescendo. They went soaring over, wave after wave of their passion juddering through their bodies. She gasped, then shuddered as he collapsed on top of her. She panted, great big breaths as the orgasm washed over her.

When they were done, he brushed her hair away so he could see her face. Her eyes were glazed over with a look of complete satisfaction. He took great pleasure in knowing that he was the cause.

"You are the most amazing woman I have ever known," he said.

The smile that lit up her face was brighter than a million suns.

He wrapped his arms around her, knowing that everything he cared about in the world was in this one room.

Whoever the person making the threats against her was, he'd better be a bigger man because Kane was going to see to it that he would suffer for daring to even threaten her.

He would see to his pain himself.

18

Lexi lay cradled in his arms, marveling at the passion that had exploded between them.

They lay on their sides facing each other. He twirled a strand of her hair around his finger, eager to keep in physical contact even though they were both spent. A sexy, satisfied smile played on his lips, those lips that had done such wonderful things to her body.

She ran her eyes over his naked chest, greedily taking him in as if each second might be her last. Five floors below, the sounds of the city and her troubles seemed so distant as to have been in another world.

Then again, maybe this was just how it felt with him.

He wasn't her first, but this one time with him had blown all the others — few as they had been — out of the water. In his eyes, something had connected them... and it wasn't only sex. She knew he felt the same way, could tell by the protective manner in which he held her.

"What're you thinking there?" He asked, hoping that it was when they would be going for round two.

"I was wondering what the hell we're going to tell my parents."

Kane pulled a face and turned onto his back. "Can we not talk about your parents when we're lying naked like this. It's a bit of a come-down after what just happened."

She laughed, a delicious tickle of a sound.

"I guess we could keep it secret, for now at least, since we've not discussed what this is." She propped herself up onto an elbow to peer at him.

Even with the satiated mood, he could sense the concern her statement brought. She wasn't a one-night stand type of girl, he was acutely aware of that. This was very much out of character. He needed to put her mind at ease.

"I should say that this can't happen again..."

"But...?" She took comfort his tone implied otherwise.

"I'm looking at you... and it seems I'm not that strong or honorable as it turns out."

He joked, his tone light, but his brow knotted, troubled by their predicament.

"I'm a big girl, Kane, contrary to what my parents seem to think. I can make up my own mind about my romantic entanglements: I certainly don't expect anyone to dictate who I can be with."

"I'm not saying you can't. This is just... a complication. My boss isn't going to be pleased."

She arched a brow at him, fixing him with her sea-blue eyes.

"He can add his objections to my parents. I'm sure they'll have a lot to talk about."

Kane laughed, liking this new fiery side his passion had drawn out. She fell quiet then, her eyes taking on a distant, sad look.

"I'm still shocked by how they kept all of this from me. What were they thinking?"

"I wouldn't be too hard on them," His answer surprised him given how he had been feeling about their decision. "They thought they were protecting you."

A sigh rolled out of Lexi, long and deep.

"That's what you don't understand. Despite what they might think, I've always taken care of myself. Sure they make the money and pay the bills, but it's always been very clear to me that they are their own entity. They love me, yes, but I've never quite made it inside their inside circle. It's never been the three of us. It has always been them *and* me. Does that make sense?"

It did. It suddenly occurred to him how damaging that could be to a child, to always know that they weren't number one.

"And Dad might seem big and powerful, but when she's off on location, he's completely lost without her and I've had to be the one to take care of him. Why on earth would they think I couldn't handle this?"

He turned back on to his side, took her hands in his.

"Because the threat is directed at you this time. It's different, Lexi. Trust me, I know what I'm talking about."

His mind went back to those dark times in the service. Flashes of his injured squad mates jumped into his mind, twisting his stomach. His expression became haunted and he turned away, not wanting her to see.

Giving him the space that he needed, her eyes flicked

down to the scars on his chest. She hoped one day, he would be able to open up about them. Until then, she was happy to wait. As long as they could be together, she would be patient about this side of him.

A loud rumble came from his stomach. Kane glanced at the clock made completely out of glass that sat on the beside table.

"I should feed Bud. We should try out some of that delicious-looking food too."

He sat up, pulling her up with him just as the sun burst through the open doorway beyond. The rays lit up around her, casting her in an ethereal light. She looked angelic and not of this world; she certainly didn't look like she would be with someone like him.

He'd lucked out, big time.

He fed Bud from the meals he'd prepared in the cooler and they dined on room service and the basket of delicacies washed down with some of that Dom Perignon (though not too much as he needed his wits about him). When they were full, they took a nap only for it to turn into more pleasant activities.

Later still, they swam on the private roof terrace pool with Bud frolicking around them as the sun set over the city. Under the light of the full moon with the starry sky above them, they made slow, luxurious love in the pool until both were unable to move.

It seemed the most natural thing in the world when they fell asleep cocooned in each other's arms.

Sometime in the middle of the night, Lexi woke.

She couldn't move, lost to the deliciousness that was the aftermath of Kane's lovemaking. Her body tingled from head to toe and she was feeling sensations she had never felt before. She felt like a new person experiencing the world through different eyes. She felt like a woman now and it was wonderful.

Almost as wonderful as the man beside her.

She was still lying with her head on the crook of his shoulder when he suddenly tensed in his sleep. Beads of sweat started to appear on his forehead. He cried out, his distress a sharp call in the otherwise silent night.

He was having a nightmare.

From the foot of the bed, Bud's head shot up. She laid a hand on Kane's shoulder, meaning to wake him when his fist flailed out. Startled, she ducked. His fist whooshed past, missing her face by inches.

She knew he hadn't meant to hurt her, but short of risking another punch to wake him, there wasn't too much she could do to help him and yet, his face looked so tortured that it tugged at her heart. She couldn't leave him like this. Surely there was something she could do?

Seeing Lexi watching his master, Bud whined a greeting at her and climbed onto the bed. Very deliberately, he crawled until he covered the lower half of Kane's body. He might well have covered more of him if she wasn't already taking up some of that space. Almost immediately, Kane's moans became quieter, although he was clearly still lost in the hell of his dreams.

Instinctively, she followed the dog's lead, moving her own body over until she covered his torso with her weight.

He became still.

His heart that had been beating rapidly beneath her began to slow into a more natural rhythm.

"Good boy, Bud," she whispered, once again amazed by the connection the two had with each other. Bud responded with a big sigh that he blew out of his nose as he settled back down.

Laying her face onto Kane's chest, she let the rise and fall of his breathing lull her back to sleep.

When Kane woke a little later, he was startled to see none of his usual neon stars blinking above him. Disoriented, it took a few moments to realize he wasn't in the battle ground he'd been dreaming about or his beach side home.

Flashes of his day with Lexi came to him then, a heady mix of skin, sex, and the kind of intimacy that turned two people into one. Opening his eyes, he smiled to see her lying on top of him, fast asleep, although it seemed a strange place for her to do so — not that he was averse to it. If that's what she found comfortable, he could get used to it.

Bud made a sound that caught his attention.

His dog lay across his lower half, one paw stretched up as if trying to touch him.

Kane knew immediately that she had witnessed one of his night terrors.

Instead of running away like other women before her, she had taken Bud's lead to comfort him. Instead of finding him weak and leaving, she had stayed and helped.

He knew it was over. In that moment, Kane had lost his heart.

He reached up to envelope her in his arms. Though deeply asleep, she snuggled into him. Kane shifted his head so that he could see Bud better.

"Sorry boy, but you're not the only one in my life now."

Luckily, his dog didn't seem too disappointed by that.

19

———

They woke the next day, still entangled in each other's arms.

Kane was staring at her in a way that caused her chest to constrict. There was such tenderness there that left her breathless. She smiled and stretched, dislodging Bud, who apparently had been sleeping with his chin resting on her thigh.

He yawned and rolled onto his back, four paws pointed to the ceiling exposing his stomach. She reached over to stroke it, enjoying the feel of his silky fur as she turned to Kane. "How long have you been awake?"

"How long have I been staring at you like a creep?"

"Well, yes, but I was going to wait until I was out of the bed and closer to the door before I asked. Now you've foiled my escape plan."

He glanced at that glass clock, amazed it was still standing after a night with both he and Bud in attendance. "Not long, maybe an hour."

She propped herself up onto an elbow, eyes round and surprised. "Why didn't you wake me?"

"Because you were asleep," he answered simply. "You looked as if you might have needed it." He wiggled an eyebrow suggestively as a blush crept along her cheeks, remembering what they had gotten up to yesterday. Though she'd like to think that the only cause of her tiredness, she hadn't been sleeping well for days, not since those photographs had exposed her to the world so rudely.

She shoved the thought of them from her mind, affirming to relish this moment.

There were much more important things at hand like this gorgeous man lying in bed next to her, tempting her with that smoldering look he was flashing her way. His eyes ran a lazy trail down her face to her chest. A grin appeared on his lips as he contemplated what he wanted for breakfast and realized that it wasn't food.

She sat bolt-upright in bed, a horrific thought having entered her mind.

"Today's Thursday isn't it?"

He thought for the slightest moment and nodded. "Yes, why?"

"It's the day of the party."

He blinked slowly, disappointment registering over his face.

"Are you sure?"

She grabbed a pillow and hit him with it. "Yes, I'm sure! I've got to get out of here. Staff will be arriving at the house at any second!"

She scrambled out of bed, grabbing wildly at her clothes that were strewn all over the floor. The sight of her completely naked distracted him. Instead of getting up, he simply took in the wonderful view.

"Where are my panties?!"

Her question threw him. Where indeed? He thought back to the moment he'd first undressed her, how her lips had tasted so sweet in his mouth, and how the sight of her body had made his own pound with heat... much as it was doing right now.

Thwack!

She'd hit him with the pillow again.

"Focus! Help me find them!"

He finally saw them lying across the top of a crystal lampshade. Leaning over the bed, he hooked them with his little finger.

"How did they get over here?"

She didn't answer him but snatched them up, sliding them on. She dressed quickly, hopping around the room until he issued a deep sigh. Bud flipped onto his stomach, a questioning look in his eyes.

"You're probably hungry again, aren't you?"

In reply, Bud padded over to the cooler and placed his paw on top of it.

"Yeah, yeah, yeah. I'm coming."

He fed Bud, one eye peering into the bathroom where he could see Lexi brushing her teeth. She hadn't put on her jeans yet and was dressed in her tank top and underwear only. The easy domesticity of this felt like a truck had slammed into him.

He hadn't known how *nice* a simple thing like this could feel.

Sure, he'd slept with many women in his time, but he'd never wanted to hang out with them much afterward. And maybe that was on him and his choice of women; he'd mostly been concerned with having a good time and nothing more than that, but with Lexi, it was different. She'd gotten under his skin.

And he wasn't sure how he felt about it.

She emerged from the bathroom and tugged on her jeans.

"Aren't you ready yet? What're you waiting for? Do you need help?"

She picked up his cargo pants and crossed over to him. He stopped her with a gesture of his hand.

"If you touch me, I will have your clothes off in one second STAT, I can promise you that."

It was no idle threat either.

Her expression turned interested. She chewed on the corner of her lip, contemplating whether that would be such a terrible thing...

She threw the pants at him.

"Dress. Now."

There was only one way to answer a command like that. He saluted her smartly.

"Yes, ma'am."

But he didn't move, staring at her with lust in his eyes. She looked exasperated, annoyed even. Then with a curse under her breath, she leaped into his arms, knocking him back onto the bed.

"Fine. But make this fast."

"As you command," he grinned, flashing white teeth at her.

In the end, their love-making took longer than either had planned, though neither would complain about it.

20

―――――

The night of the party loomed bright and clear. Lexi had planned the guests' arrival to coincide with the setting sun. The grounds were a stunning vista of orange and purple: everything had a magical sheen.

Round tables with crisp white linen were erected over the lawn facing a stage that had been built for both the auction that would be taking place and the guest performances.

All week long, celebrities had donated goods and services to be auctioned for the cause, from costumes worn on blockbuster movies, to a catered private dinner by their world-renowned chef, to a diamond Harry Winston wreath that had formed part of a bitter divorce settlement. The industry was turning up in spades and Lexi was grateful for each and every gift.

Lexi checked her appearance one last time in the full-length mirror situated in their grand hallway. Their guests would be arriving any minute now so if there was something that needed to be addressed, this was her last chance.

To match the elegant style of her white empire-cut dress, her hair was loose with a waterfall braid to one side. Eyes were dusted with a neutral powder that only hinted at purple while a creamy peach adorned her cheeks and lips.

The only jewelry she wore was a pair of pearl-drop earrings that were a family heirloom: she wanted to keep it simple to avoid any issues with the animals she was having adopted tonight — anything dangling might well get caught up with a panicked animal.

The few personal items she needed for the night, including that panic button Kane had given, she carried in a diamond-encrusted vintage Dior clutch.

She was regal and effortlessly beautiful, yet there was also something different about her, a glow that she could pinpoint to Kane's influence. Her body still thrummed from his touch. Even now, only several hours after they'd first arrived back, she ached to feel his lips on her again.

"You look absolutely stunning, Sweetheart."

She jumped at the voice.

Her mother had somehow glided up behind her without her knowing. She wiped the dreamy look from her face, not prepared for the questions it might bring.

For the festivities tonight, Amanda Gray had decided to go all out.

She wore a sultry platinum dress of liquid silk that skimmed every curve of her body and left nothing to the imagination. There was no room for a bra or quite possibly any underwear, yet her mother managed to pull off the entire look in her usual classy manner.

Her long chestnut hair — darker than Lexi's by several shades — spilled down one shoulder in a glossy, twenties inspired flapper Marcel wave. Diamond bracelets, the exact same shade of platinum as her dress dangled around both wrists. She finished the outfit with a pair of strappy LV's that flashed their red soles whenever she walked.

They were two of the most stunning women to have ever graced this earth, yet Lexi could barely see her above the angry hum that was beginning to sound in her head.

It was on the tip of her tongue to confront her mother about the threats, but she knew that would break Kane's confidence. It would only take her smart mother seconds to guess where she had learned of them. As much as she'd like to hash it out with her folks, the matter would have to wait until her work was done.

Swallowing her feelings, she smiled at her.

"You too, mom. You never look anything less than perfect."

Mandy's smile grew wider by the compliment. She spun, turning so Lexi could get the full effect.

"My ass is almost as pert as yours. I've still got it." She slapped her own butt wickedly. At Lexi's smile, Mandy peered into her daughter's face.

"Something is different about you tonight. You're practically glowing. You seem unusually... happy."

At that precise moment, Kane rounded the corner with Bud, as the two went about their work patrolling the property. Without meaning to, her eyes slid over to him and held him in their gaze.

He had changed into a tuxedo tonight out of respect for the guests. She'd had to cajole him excessively — who knew that a man could be *that* attached to cargo pants? — but it was only the promise of more fun things to come that had sealed the deal.

Sending a courier to his home to pick it up, the tux — which he'd explained had only been worn one other time at Wilson's wedding — fitted him like a glove, emphasizing the broadness of his shoulders while tapering down to reveal his trim waist. As much as she loved his normal casual image, he looked so dashing in the suit, she found it difficult to concentrate.

He must have noticed her staring as he turned. The moment he saw her, a slow, sexy smile formed on his lips that only changed when he finally noticed Mandy, half hidden behind her. Abruptly, the smile dropped, replaced by a curt nod of greeting.

Mandy, who had followed the small interaction with an interested expression, tapped the corner of her mouth with a polished fingernail.

"Hmmm," was the only comment she made.

"What was that?" Lexi had to tear her eyes away from him. Even in that suit, his glorious physique was obvious. Her mouth went dry as a picture of him lying on top of her flashed into her mind.

"Nothing," Mandy replied archly as the bell sounded and their first guests arrived. Slipping an arm through Lexi's, they went to greet the newcomers, a ridiculously famous couple with the largest social media network of all. The wife, Coco, was an Instagram star who had shot to fame with the videos she'd posted of herself doing yoga in tiny outfits against spectacular backdrops, while her husband was one of the world's most successful rap producers.

Lexi had met both on several occasions prior but had found them rather superficial. Their money was as good as anyone though, and their social feed would do wonders for advertising the cause.

Ignoring her own feelings about the couple, she welcomed both with a warm smile. "So great to see you again. Thank you for coming."

They air-kissed, never allowing their faces to touch.

"I'm so thrilled you invited us." Coco cooed breathlessly, holding her cell in front of them, angling it into the house where staff could be seen scurrying to and fro as they performed their duties. "Smile for the camera, my fans are desperate to get a good look at us together."

Lexi found it hard to believe that her fans would be interested in her, but she smiled politely, posing for the picture. If her face must be exposed to the world, better she be the one to control it.

Coco posted the image onto her Instagram feed only to crow with delight almost instantly. "Ooh, look, my fans are responding already!"

After the couple headed inside, Lexi was stuck greeting guests for the next hour. She smiled until her cheeks hurt, air kissed and posed for publicity shots until her eyes were blinded by flashlights. Her feet were already beginning to suffer from the heels she'd wish she'd had time to break in and she was dreaming of the moment she'd be able to take them off.

When most of the guests had arrived, she moved into the grounds of their estate and started working on getting their guests to commit to a donation or possibly adopting one of the needy animals that waited to be seen in a quiet wing of the house, away from the festivities.

While she worked, Kane kept watch close by.

He wasn't comfortable by the mass of strangers flooding the property, even with his team working hard to keep the family safe. They had been fully briefed and knew what to look out for. Any commotions, distractions, personnel who didn't have the required security clearance or ID, even someone who simply sent their spidey senses tingling was warrant enough for pulling aside.

Kane was not willing to take any risks, not when it came to Lexi's wellbeing.

He followed her at a short distance, always watchful, listening out for any cause of alarm. Bud matched him step-for-step, ears pricked and alert. He could sense the tension in him and was dealing with it by being even more responsive than usual.

As Lexi drifted from guest to guest, he saw how well she fitted into this world, despite what she might think of it herself. Nothing fazed her. Not the super rich tech giant, the ex US president and his popular wife, or movie star Logan Steel and his girlfriend, the equally famous TV star Ellie Godwin.

Logan was popular for his suave good looks and blockbuster action films that had taken the world by storm. Men wanted to be him while woman wanted to be with him. His star — which had been on the rise ever since his breakout role in one of Stonewall's highest grossing movies — soared into an all-time high once he began dating Ellie, the most successful television actress on the planet. Kane had seen his movie, enjoyed it as fun entertainment even if he thought the scenes where he played a military man on the run were not very accurate.

With her girl-next-door charm and devastatingly pretty looks, outside of work, Ellie was known for being a good girl who never kissed and tell. For the past five years, the tabloids had sent themselves into a tizzy, wondering if she was romantically involved with a man. When she finally stepped out publicly with Logan — known to be a bit of a womanizer — the world had gone wild for their union.

It was Brangelina all over again.

People just couldn't get enough of them. Even Mandy had to take a backseat, much to her annoyance. She liked Logan though, adored him in fact. Something Kane could clearly see as Lexi's mother batted her eyelashes at him, hanging on to his every word.

When Stonewall joined the group, it was as if all the flashlights in the universe had gone off. The invited paparazzi went to town, shooting picture after picture while even the guests pointed phones their way, eager to record the star wattage currently on display.

Throughout the mayhem that followed, Lexi chatted with them, seemingly oblivious to the reaction around them. She smiled a genuine smile as she conversed with Logan.

"So, I hear you don't have any pets?"

He laughed, shaking his head. "I'm not sure I'm a pet kind of guy."

Lexi scoffed refusing to accept his reply. "You don't know until you've tried. Maybe you'll turn out to be a fantastic pet-dad?"

"I'm known for not being able to keep even a plant alive. I wouldn't trust myself with anything like a dog."

"A cat then? They don't take much looking after. Wouldn't it be nice to come home from a long day on set and cuddle up to one?"

Logan gave a small shake of his head. "You're very persuasive Lexi, but I know how rubbish I am at being responsible. You should ask Ellie, I'm sure she'd be interested."

Lexi turned her attention to his girlfriend, who was looking into a compact, powdering her already perfect nose. It seemed to him that she was using the mirror to see behind her, possibly searching for other, more useful conversationalists.

For the briefest of moments, Kane thought he caught a glimpse of annoyance on her face before it was masked with a beatific smile.

"Oh, I would love to," she responded. "But what with such the hectic schedule NBC has me on, I couldn't, possibly."

Kane didn't buy it for a second.

She had enough money and help that they could do pretty much anything. No time for pets? She could simply hire someone to walk and train them, besides which dogs could be with their owners while they were on set working. It was much more likely that she just couldn't be bothered to accept the responsibility.

Lexi too was finding that she wasn't taking to Ellie as much as she did Logan. He seemed straight forward and easy going enough, but Ellie... there was something about the way her eyes never stared directly at her that made her seem not very genuine.

"I love what you've done to the place," Ellie said now, interrupting her thoughts.

"You've been here before?" Lexi didn't think she had but she didn't keep tabs on the comings and goings of her home, big as it was.

"Oh no," Ellie laughed as if she'd said something funny. "I just meant that it looks lovely. Well done." She added — rather lamely, Lexi thought.

"Thank you. I had help, obviously."

Ellie stared over the top of Lexi's head at her father, clearly looking for someone more influential to talk to. Stonewall was laughing with Logan, one arm around Mandy as the two went over a shared experience.

"So auditions were a bust," Stonewall explained. "We'd been going for six maybe seven hours, each of the actors growing preceding worse than the one that had come before when right as I was packing up to leave, in walks Logan with the kind of swagger and attitude that commanded the room."

Logan laughed, explaining, "I was in character but he wasn't to know that."

"Beth, the casting director asked him if he was ready to run the lines when Logan flew into a rage at being questioned. His indignation was so believable that we almost called for security until we realized that he'd segued into the lines of the script. I hired him on the spot."

"And the rest is history," Mandy supplied.

"How about you, Ellie? When are you ready to make your big screen appearance?" Stonewall asked of the TV starlet. Ellie stepped forward immediately, effectively cutting Lexi out of the conversation, but she didn't notice, too eager to answer him.

"Why, are you offering me a role?" Stonewall looked momentarily stumped, this not being his intention at all.

Galant as ever, Logan swooped in.

"Maybe we could play something together, as a couple?"

Stonewall could almost see the profits roll in. "I believe I could find something that would accommodate that. Leave it with me."

Talk turned to vacation spots next as they each name-dropped islands so exclusive that Kane had never heard of them. Lexi fell silent, this part of the conversation not interesting to her when she caught Kane's eye.

She smiled at him, causing Ellie to notice him. She crossed the few steps to him. Laying a hand on his arm, she purred up at him. "I would love a glass of champagne."

Lexi froze, horrified by her assumption. The smile that had been in his eyes only moments ago faded. Keeping his voice calm but firm, he replied, "I'm not part of the wait staff."

Ellie laughed, shaking off his objection with a wave of her hand. "Oh Darling, you do work here though don't you?" She looked his outfit up and down, clearly insinu-ating that it wasn't off the standard of the guests.

At the look on his face, Lexi's heart plummeted to her stomach.

She wanted to elbow the bitch out of the way and throw her arms around him. How dare she insult her man? She was embarrassed, wishing that she'd never invited her to the party — money or not. But before she could respond, Mandy defused the situation by grabbing the said drink from a passing waiter.

"Here," she pressed the drink firmly into Ellie's hands. "Kane is our head of security and he's far too busy to see to our every silly whim."

She had graciously offered him a way out which he took, but Lexi could see from his stiff posture that he wasn't overly pleased. Bud knew it too, in the way he kept looking up at him.

She made a move toward him, but was stopped by a hand on her wrist.

"Isn't the show about to start, Dear?"

Her mom inclined her head at the stage where singing sensation Stella Speed waited to be announced. Long white curtains hid her from view, and they wouldn't be lifted until Lexi had made her introduction.

Every nerve in her body wanted to stay to talk to him, but there wasn't time for this right now. Kane would have to wait until her work was done.

Then she would fix the damage the stupid Ellie had wrought.

21

Blood pounded in his ears.

All around him came the sounds of merriment, but he could barely hear it above the fury that raged within.

That actress had taken no small amount of pleasure at belittling him. Worse than that, Lexi had been there to hear it. Until she had spoken, Lexi had been smiling at him like the sun shone out of him. At her words, her smile had dimmed until it had vanished completely.

She'd looked horrified, but it was her embarrassment that had cut him to the quick.

He glanced down at himself, trying to see what the woman had seen so quickly: that he was a fraud.

He wasn't one of them, not worthy of the air they breathed.

His fingers curled into claws by his side.

For some reason he couldn't fathom, he recalled an image of him as a child, hiding beneath the kitchen table as his drunk parents argued with the authorities who had been called out by the neighbors, concerned with the racket they could hear. By the time he was yanked out from under there by his father, Kane had heard plenty about how their "kind" was a stain on the rest of the community.

He was feeling like that small little kid again, the one he'd thought he'd long gotten rid of. Stalking through the grounds, staying close to Lexi, the image of Ellie's smug, upturned face refused to go away.

Having worked in this industry for several years now, Kane knew what he was feeling had everything to do with his relationship with Lexi. Although it had only been a short time since they'd been together — since they'd even known each other really — but she'd gotten under his skin in a way no woman ever had.

Yet they came from two different worlds, which had been made so clear by this recent interaction. Much as he'd wanted to, he hadn't been able to defend himself or put Ellie in her place, not without risking the job and therefore his protection of Lexi. This also wasn't the place to do this, not when he knew how much she had invested in the night.

His phone buzzed against his leg.

One of the sensors had been tripped again, but it was one on a side of the property that was off limits to the guests.

With a mansion as big as this, it would be almost impossible to guard every area without bringing on an army to patrol. Kane had compromised by keeping several parts of the property off limits, including the wings the Rockefellers slept in.

The alarm that had been tripped was by Mandy and Stonewall's quarters.

His mind went back to Lexi, to the times she had admitted that nothing was ever about her. It was always about her parents.

A shocking thought suddenly came to him.

What if Lexi wasn't the target, but Mandy?

It made sense, after all. She was the famous movie star, the one in the public limelight. He had become so infatuated with Lexi that it seemed obvious to him that she was the one at threat. But suddenly, he wasn't so sure.

What if it was all a ploy to detract from the real target?

Stan appeared a few feet away, having received the same alert on his phone. He spoke to him through the earpiece. "You want me to check it out?"

Kane looked across at the steps to the stage where Lexi was climbing up. She was in full view and he felt safe in knowing that nothing was likely to happen to her out here in front of all the guests.

"No. I'll go. You stay with Lexi. Don't let her out of your sight."

"I won't," Stan promised.

Turning away from Lexi, he disappeared into the crowd and made his way toward the site of the alarm.

When he arrived at the Rockefellers' suite, he saw immediately that something was wrong.

The door was ajar even though his team had made sure to keep all of them shut. He could hear a rustling inside, though it was some distance from the door.

"Stay back. Quiet," he whispered to Bud, not wanting his dog to go charging blindly in there.

Bud didn't make a sound, though his expression made it clear that he'd understood. He stayed close to Kane, but let him take the lead.

Kane opened the door as gently as he could. It swung open with barely a sound. The first thing he noticed were the bedside drawers that had been pulled open and rifled through.

The sheets on the bed had been thrown hastily onto it, as if someone had been searching beneath it for something. The windows were secure, there was no sign of whoever it was.

Several clicks sounded from the walk-in closet, then the sound of someone stubbing a toe and cursing.

Bud strained beside him, wanting to go on ahead but obeying his command to hang back. Sliding his gun from his shoulder holster, Kane pointed it in front of him.

"This is security. I know you're in there. I have a gun aimed right at you so if you don't want to be shot, put your hands up, come out and let me see you."

There was silence in the closet as the person hesitated. He could almost hear their mind ticking over, wondering what they should do.

"I'm not going to ask again. If you make me go in there, you'll have to take on me and my dog."

At the mention of the word "dog", Bud started to bark ferociously.

Suddenly a woman stumbled out. Dolled up to the nines, some would think her beautiful though she had the kind of plastic and overtly sexual look that Kane abhorred.

Instead of the bag of jewels he was expecting her to have stolen in her hands, she held only her phone.

"Don't shoot, please! I'm not a thief."

She sounded very demanding for a woman under house arrest. She laughed suddenly, a laugh as fake as the rest of her.

"I was only trying to take some pictures of their room. They never invite people into their home after all."

"Don't you think they have a reason for that?" He wasn't surprised by her lack of apology. She didn't seem to think she'd done anything wrong.

"But my fans are so curious and I didn't want to disappoint them."

Fans? The woman must be someone, though who, he had no idea.

"I'm Coco," she introduced herself, seeming shocked that he didn't know. "I have like, twenty million subscribers on Instagram."

"Let's hope they'll enjoy the sight of you in handcuffs," Kane retorted thinking only of arresting her. Of course, she took that to mean something entirely different from what he'd intended.

"Is that what you like?" She purred, batting her lashes at him. "I guess I'm game so long as you don't tell my husband. He tends to get angry at these things."

Kane didn't bother to hide his disgust.

Escorting her out of the room, he led her to the security office where his men could have the pleasure of dealing with her.

Lexi introduced the singer to a cheer of approval from the audience.

This was a big win, to have Stella Speed performing a private concert, but Lexi couldn't hear a word of the chart-topping song she was singing.

As soon as the curtain had risen, she'd dropped her mike and went in search of Kane, though that was no easy feat. While he was practically anonymous, she couldn't move a step without someone stopping her to wish her a happy birthday — in all the excitement leading up to today, she'd actually forgotten that it was indeed, her birthday. She'd had to suffer through their well-wishes, excusing herself as she hurried after him.

But the man had simply vanished.

She was acutely aware of the absence he had caused and was startled by how much that affected her. She wasn't the clingy type, had never considered herself so. This was a whole new sensation for her and one she wasn't particularly enjoying.

She tried him in the security office — the first place she went to — but his men hadn't seen him. She stopped by the kitchen, hoping that maybe he'd been tempted by the food on display only for Ruth to reveal that she hadn't seen him for a while now, but didn't he look wonderful in a tuxedo?

Stella's powerful voice soared over the grounds via the network of speakers her stage team had carefully erected. Even here, inside the private wing of their house, her talent could be enjoyed.

Lexi had made sure that everyone — even the staff who worked in the house — could enjoy the festivities tonight.

What a shame, then, that it gave her not one iota of joy.

A wave of exhaustion came over her suddenly, brought on by the lack of sleep last night. Her shoes were pinching and she wanted them off her feet. Slipping out of her heels, she carried them in one hand, her clutch in the other. She was entering her wing of the house when a voice stopped her.

"Miss. Lexi, I'm afraid this part of the house is meant to be off limits right now."

It was Stan Kane's right-hand man.

"I know, but I just need a few minutes alone."

His eyes crinkled with apology. "I'm not sure I can allow that."

"I know, you've got orders to have eyes on me all times, correct?"

He nodded, but didn't say anything else.

"This entire wing is has been sectioned off, so no one could have gotten here. I will literally be only a few feet from you."

"I understand," Stan began, "but—"

Horrifically, Lexi's eyes started glistening with tears. "Please. I just need a few minutes."

The tears were his undoing. With three twenty-some-thing daughters of his own, Stan could never say no to a crying woman.

"Alright. But I will be right here." He gestured at the wing's entrance.

"Thank you."

She hurried past him, escaping into her bedroom, shutting the door behind her where she let out a relieved sigh.

It was only when she'd gotten halfway across the room that she noticed a figure by the chest of drawers. His face and figure were hidden in the half light, but she could tell it was a man. Her heart did a relieved flip flop.

Of course he'd be here.

This was the only place they could guarantee some privacy.

"Kane... I'm so sorry about what happened out there—"

The rest of the apology died on her lips as the lights that illuminated the stage flashed, illuminating where he stood.

And she saw that it wasn't Kane in her room at all.

But someone else.

Terror spiked in her throat, but she fought to keep her expression stoic and her voice calm.

"What are you doing here?"

22

———

The man shifted, startled by her appearance.

Lexi saw that her underwear drawers were open, having been rifled through. Panties and bras had been shoved to one side in a messy heap, presumably to search for valuables.

Anything else was unthinkable.

She froze, not knowing what to immediately do. He took the opportunity to maneuver himself around, circling her until he was almost behind her.

Too late she realized he had effectively blocked the door of her exit.

A million thoughts crashed through her mind, all vying for urgency.

You need to get out of there!

Scream, Lexi, alert Stan to help you! He's only down the corridor!

No, don't scream. That would only alarm him further, and God knows what he would do if he was pushed into it. Maybe you can talk him down.

She chose the latter option.

She reminded herself that with security crawling all over the house, he was unlikely to be able to do anything to her. Even so, her blood turned to ice. Would he stop at just her underwear now that she was here?

Think, Lexi! There must be something you can do.

The panic button!

Her eyes must have betrayed her intention as he followed her gaze down to the clutch. In the split second that it took to register what it was, he dove for her. Faster than it seemed possible, he grabbed her around the waist. Despite his thinner than average appearance, he was surprisingly strong.

"NO!" He cried out, looking hurt that she would even consider going for it.

She swung the heels that were still in her hand at him, the only weapon she had. The sharp points struck him in the back, which only made him more upset.

"Stop it!" It was more of a desperate plea than a command, but Lexi was reacting on pure fear now. His sour body odor stung her nose. The arm around her waist was slippery with sweat. She couldn't think what to do, only that she had to get away.

"You aren't supposed to be in here," he babbled. There was a manic gleam in his eye that she could see perfectly reflected in her vanity mirror.

She twisted, bucking wildly, the heels dropping to the carpet. Her mind raced with thoughts of escape when one hand went around her neck and squeezed. There was a flash of pain, a closing of her lungs. The air whooshed out of her.

She froze, terror turning her body numb. She was rewarded by a release of the pressure. She gulped in air greedily, knowing instinctively what she had to do.

As long as she didn't struggle, he wouldn't hurt her.

All she had now were her words. What could she say that would buy her time?

"Was it you? You sent those pictures of me to the press?"

His expression turned frantic, and she sensed she had guessed the truth.

"Why? What do you want?"

His head shook back and forth. He muttered under his breath. Lexi couldn't hear a lot of what he was saying, only picking up the odd word here and there, none of which made a blessed bit of difference: he wasn't answering and seemed to be in a near state of panic of his own.

"You should have been nicer to me."

This she did hear, though it made as much sense as everything else. As far as she knew, she *had* always been nice to him. He was obviously disturbed.

She had to keep him talking.

Surely Stan would hear their struggle?

"I'm sorry if I upset you. Can you tell me when I was mean to you?"

"Shut up!" He snapped abruptly. "Must... think..."

While he was preoccupied, she pried open the clutch slowly and slipped a hand inside. Her fingers felt around the contents of the bag, searching for the panic button that she knew was in there somewhere. They brushed against the metal tube of lipstick, the small pot of Kiehl's lip balm and her waterproof mascara, but couldn't locate the panic button.

Why didn't she have a special pocket sewn into her dress for it?! How could she have been so stupid when she knew she was at risk?

Stretching, she reached in further, digging in deeper until her fingers grazed the metal ring that it was attached to. Just a little more and she'd be able to hook it up with a finger.

Adrenaline caused her heart to beat like a drum.

She managed to leverage the tip of the ring around her index finger when the bag was suddenly knocked away from her. The contents spilled over the floor, the panic button bounced then skidded a few feet away until it landed beneath the dresser.

"What're you doing?!" He snapped, alert to her actions. His voice had risen higher, the tension causing a vein to pop on his head.

He was getting more desperate. Lexi knew she was running out of time, could feel it in her bones. She tried talking to him again, grasping at straws, hoping this time, maybe a threat would cause him to rethink his plan.

"There's security patrolling the house everywhere. There's even a guard right down the hall. You won't be able to get out without them seeing. If you just let me go, you won't get into any trouble. I promise you."

A sound outside on the terrace interrupted her plea — an amorous couple, arms around each other, looking for a dark corner to fool around in. Seeing her opportunity to raise the alarm, Lexi screamed.

But Stella had just reached the bridge of her song, which happened to be the loudest moment of it.

Her scream disappeared into the music to fall on deaf ears except for one pair.

He had heard it.

And he knew that she was trying to escape.

Face twisted in fury, he covered her mouth and nose with his hand. She knew instantly that she had made a terrible mistake. Giving up all pretence, she tried to pry his hand away from her mouth. Fueled by a desperate rage and anger, he was much stronger than her.

All the while, her airways were emptying.

She was thinking of her loved ones. Picturing her parents's beloved faces when he suddenly threw her to the floor. She gulped in the air greedily.

"Get changed."

"What?" The request was so bizarre, she thought she'd heard wrong.

He pointed at some clothes she'd left tossed over a chair. A pair of jeans and a thin sweater. "Put that on."

"No." Her reply was shaky, but she wasn't going to do whatever this was. He lunged toward her pulling a knife out of his pocket that he held at her throat. Its razor-sharp end nicked her neck, drawing blood.

"Get changed... or I will do it for you."

The threat turned her blood to ice. She got off the floor and tugged the jeans on. Slipping a T-shirt over her dress, she managed to change without letting him see any of her body.

She took small comfort in that.

A knock sounded on her door. Before she could even think to respond, he had that knife back to her throat.

"Get rid of him," he hissed. The white of his eyes flashing wildly. The hand that gripped the knife trembled. He must have seen the hesitation in her eyes as he continued, "I will kill you, then I will kill him."

She had no doubt that the slightest more panic and he would end her life.

"Yes?" She called out, hoping her voice didn't relay her fear.

"It's Stan. Are you alright? The camera outside picked up some movement."

Stan's three faceless daughters flicked through her mind, and she knew then that she couldn't risk either of their lives. Her best chance was to keep him calm and find a way to escape when there wasn't a knife held against her throat.

"It's... a couple from the party. I think they're looking for privacy."

"Well, they shouldn't be here. I'll move them along."

"OK."

She held her breath waiting for him to leave, but she could still see the shadow of his shoes through the one-inch gap under the door.

"I'll only be a moment. You have your panic button?"

"Yes," Lexi lied, terror rattling her ribcage. Her life was one thing, she couldn't be responsible for another's death.

"Do not leave the room. I'll be right back."

The shadow moved away as Stan retreated down the hall.

She felt some of *his* tension lessen. He pressed something scratchy and voluminous into her hand.

"Put this on too."

It was the blonde fancy-dress wig she'd worn at a function they'd thrown at PAWS last Halloween. She'd kept it as a reminder of how much fun she'd had that night, but she was now regretting not having thrown it away.

She pulled it on. The cheap synthetic fibers scratched at her face, but she resisted the urge to brush them away, worried that any extra movement from her might startle him further.

Forcing her to the door, he nodded at the handle.

"Open it. Make sure he's not out there."

She did as he commanded. The hallway was clear at both ends.

"It's empty."

He prodded her with a finger. "Walk."

"I don't have any shoes on." She didn't really care about her lack of footwear and was only hoping to buy herself more time but it seemed his patience and nerves were out.

"I don't care!" He hissed. "Go. Hurry up."

He took her by the elbow, holding the knife low by her side. She hurried down the hall as he called out instructions.

"Left here, then right... don't look up! Keep your eyes on the floor."

So that the cameras won't capture your face, he all but said.

She followed his instructions all while her mind

searched frantically for a way to escape, but that knife was too close to her ribs and she was too scared to think coherently.

Kane, where are you?

They reached Lexi's workout room, where she kept her body in shape with Pilates and the hot yoga her mom swore by. Instead of heading to the French doors that led outside — and where she knew a camera would be — he steered her to a window.

Opening it, he leaned in close to her ear. "Don't try to do anything or I'll come back and hurt your parents."

The threat didn't make much sense. Then again, this whole time he seemed to swing from rational to disorderly. Climbing out of the window, she prayed that someone outside would see them.

But the grounds on this side of the property were empty — as he knew they would be.

She took a step away from him, ready to bolt when she was yanked backward by her hair. The nerves on her head screamed a protest. She gasped from the shock of it. Before she could recover, that knife was pushed against her ribs again, and they were walking.

He took her to the area that had been set up for staff cars, to a white van parked at the end. She knew there were cameras set up out here which gave her a sense of hope. Surely, they would be captured in at least one of them?

It wasn't until he opened the van's rear door that she suddenly realized that no help was coming... and if she allowed him to take her away from here, her chances of survival were exponentially less.

She had to fight.

If he was going to kill her, she'd rather it be here.

"Get in," he hissed, tossing a nervous look over his shoulder.

Adrenaline pumping through her veins, she shoved at him with all of her might. Since he was already looking backward, he lost some of his balance, stumbling backward.

Then she ran back toward the house, toward the safety that she knew waited there.

"HELP!" She screamed at the top of her lungs, though it barely made a dent over Stella, apparently giving an encore to her rapturous audience. "SOMEONE! I'M BEING KID—"

She never got to finish her sentence.

He tackled her with a flying leap that knocked her to the ground. The breath hissed out of her. She bucked, twisting until she was on her back, but then he swung the handle of his whittling knife at her head.

And all became black.

23

K ane had left Coco with his team and was now making his way back to Lexi.

The concert erupted in an explosion of fireworks and neon lights as Stella took her bow.

She waved at the jubilant crowd, knowing that she had them in the palm of her hand. After thanking them for their time, she followed up the announcement of her new tour dates with a donation of fifty thousand dollars to Lexi's foundation.

Several of the guests who walked past reached out automatically to pet Bud. He recognized their faces, but couldn't place how he knew them. When he politely asked if they could refrain from petting him — he was on duty and working — instead of the usual apology that came from typical people whenever this happened, he received curt remarks and dirty looks.

He noticed they had failed to *ask* if they could touch his dog too, something he would never understand. It was not only respectful but sensible — some dogs hated or were frightened of strangers, and the very notion could cause them to bolt... at times straight into heavy traffic.

It was just another reason to add to his growing list why he didn't belong.

He studied the faces in the crowd, unsure why that tingle in the back of his neck hadn't gone away, but chalked it up to his own discomfort at being here. He reached up a hand to massage the tense muscle, tugged at the collar of his monkey suit, mentally counting the hours until he could get out of it.

On the stage, Stella had finished her routine but was looking a little perplexed at what she should do next. Holding the mic away from her face, she conversed with someone offstage, but whatever their reply had been, it apparently hadn't been very helpful.

She raised the mic back to her mouth, shrugging apologetically. "Apparently, the auction is due to start, but we're waiting for our host to get here. I don't suppose any of you have seen Lexi and can give her a gentle nudge? I mean, I'm happy to help but I'm likely to make too many demands... if the press are to be believed."

The crowd roared with laughter, though that tingle had turned into a full-blown jolt. Kane spoke into his cuff.

"It's Turner. Where's Mace?" Mace was their code-name for Lexi in the event their airwaves were hacked from someone on the outside, something that could occasionally happen.

"She's in her room. Stan over."

He should have felt relieved by that, but something

wasn't right. Why would she be in her room when she was supposed to be announcing the next event?

"Do you have eyes on her Stan?"

"No, but I'm right here. I'll check," Stan began then cursed, sounding gravely concerned. "Her room's empty. It looks like there's been a struggle."

The instant panic his words caused made him breathless. He started for her wing of the house, but his way was blocked by a sea of people.

"Move!" He demanded, but either they hadn't heard him or simply didn't think it applied to them. He snapped out a command. "Bud, bark!"

His dog began barking at the top of his lungs. While the crowd hadn't been concerned with his demands, they were certainly listening to his dog. They separated. He barreled through the path they created for him, bolting to Lexi's room to find Stan waiting. His face was ashen.

"There was a disturbance on the terrace. I went to check it. I only left her alone for a few seconds, Kane. One, two minutes, tops."

Kane didn't want to think about it. He couldn't. He went into her room, assessing the area fast.

The chair by the vanity table was upturned and the clutch lay open on the carpet a few feet beside the heels she had worn. Pulse racing, he sprinted to her clutch to find most of its contents had spilled around it.

But no panic button.

Hope flared in his chest, but then he noticed the spread of the cosmetics. They looked to have fallen out of the clutch by force, sending the items scattering across the floor toward a dresser in the corner.

On a hunch, he got down to floor level to look beneath the gap of the dresser.

There it was, the one thing he was hoping not to find.

Reading his stiff body language, Stan asked, "What is it?"

Kane didn't reply. He picked up the panic button, showed it to him.

Stan's face turned a paler shade of gray.

The room swam as terror clawed its way into Kane's throat.

Each of the things taken in isolation wasn't a cause for alarm, but all of them put together painted a harrowing picture. Bud whined, sensing his distress.

"Who was on the terrace?" His mind kicked into automatic work gear. If he focused on the facts, the pieces of the puzzle, he could keep that desperate fear that wanted to take over at bay.

Maybe.

"Just a couple wanting a corner to fool around in." Stan paused, the full realization of what had happened hitting him. "She said she was fine. She said she wanted a few minutes alone. I even checked she had her panic button."

Kane couldn't lay into him, not when he himself was to blame. He shouldn't have left her safety to anyone else — not even Stan — even when he thought Mandy was the one at risk.

This was his fault.

Desperate to make amends, to find Lexi, Stan jumped into rescue mode.

"I'll check the cameras, notify our men. Do we tell the parents yet?"

"No." Kane's voice was a hoarse whisper. "Let Bud have a go at finding her first."

It was possible that Lexi was still on the property, and if that was the case, his dog was their best bet. There was no point in frightening her parents before they had performed a search.

He held one of her heels under Bud's nose. "Find her. Find Lexi!"

Bud barely had to sniff the shoe to get her scent since he was already so familiar with her. He barked, letting him know he was ready, then took off at a lightening fast pace.

Bud tore through the house, guided by his nose, taking the hallways so surely that Kane felt hope in his chest. With Bud hot on the trail, surely they would find her?

He led him into the gym, then skidded to a stop by an open window that proceeded into the grounds beyond. He barked three sharp barks — Bud, for "hurry up" — until Kane caught up to him.

It was clear that Lexi had gone out of the window, bypassing the cameras by the doors.

Together they went outside as Bud led him around the back path until they reached the area on the side of the house that was currently being used as the staff parking lot.

Bud reached one of the empty spaces, ran around in a circle, alerted and whined.

This was where the trail ended. Knowing what this meant, his heart hammered like a drum.

She'd been taken off the property.

He knew it without any doubt.

Lexi had been forced into a waiting vehicle and driven away. His eyes squeezed closed as an image of her, terrified and struggling, forced its way into his mind. The thought morphed into a memory next of the acrid heat of the Afghan desert where when women were taken, they never returned whole again — if they were returned at all.

He choked at the sudden dryness in his mouth.

He forced himself to focus. He couldn't let the fear get in his way, not when she was counting on him. Whenever a kidnapping occurred, time was of the essence. The sooner she was found, the better her life expectancy.

With this fact coldly etched in his mind, he hurried to the security office where Stan was already examining the footage that had been recorded throughout the night.

The CCTV footage didn't show much out of the ordinary. Other than the guests who came in through the front door but then were led directly through to the back gardens, all the faces they could see were staff that they knew. All were people who should be there.

They looked through the footage of the camera that covered the staff parking area. Saw the white van in the spot that Bud had led him, too. But mud covered the license plate — they wouldn't be able to ID it through the usual means. All they could see were a man and a woman heading to the rear of the vehicle. The woman didn't even look like Lexi. She was dressed casually and had blonde hair.

Kane studied the footage, fighting to keep his panic down. Unhelpful thoughts came into his head, blaming him for this. If he hadn't gotten involved with her, if he had just been professional and kept her at arm's length, he wouldn't have gotten upset when that actress had embarrassed him; he wouldn't have made a stupid mistake.

And Lexi's life would not be at risk.

It was his own insecurity that had brought them here.

His entire life he'd been trying to run away from his history, from his background. Worried at repeating his parents's loveless marriage, he'd swung too far the other way, not letting anyone in. But just as he'd come to understand how much she meant to him, it was all coming too little, too late.

Something in the footage on-screen caught his attention, pulling him from his pity party.

"Rewind that back a few seconds."

Stan turned the wheel on the player, shifting time back. When the action played, Kane studied the screen with the intensity of the desperate.

Something wasn't right with the picture, but what was it?

And then he saw it: the woman wasn't wearing any shoes.

His mind flitted back to Lexi's room, to the heels that she had dropped onto the carpet.

"That's her," he cried out. "That's Lexi."

He explained his reasoning to Stan, cursing the angle of the camera that didn't show much beyond that. Seconds after the Lexi apparently got into the van, the van left. He wasn't able to ID the driver as he'd kept far away from the camera.

Kane's fingers dug into his palms.

"Where's our list of staff vehicles? Crosscheck that with who's on shift today. Who's not here anymore? I want to know what vehicle was parked in that space and who it belonged to."

"What about the other cameras? Inside the house?" Stan offered.

They scanned through that footage too.

Among the household staff that had been captured, he caught a glimpse of a man who seemed to be very aware where the cameras were. To the point that his face and not much of his body were ever recorded.

"You see him?" Kane asked, those hairs on the back of his neck sending a prickling sensation that went all the way down to the base of his spine.

"Yeah," Stan replied, just as grimly. "It's like he knows where the cameras are."

"He must've been gotten inside before, scouted their locations."

"How did he do that without tripping the alarms? Without any of us noticing?" Stan was a picture of confusion.

Kane had his suspicions. While he trusted Stan, he'd rather keep what would be an unpopular opinion to himself for now. He needed more proof before he'd openly reveal his thoughts. He started for the door.

"What are you going to do?"

"What I didn't want to. I'm going to break the news to her parents."

Stan nodded. "I'll call LAPD, let them know what's happened."

The Rockerfellers took it about as well as could be expected.

Mandy went as white as a sheet and would have fainted if her husband hadn't caught her. He lowered her onto a couch then went through a whole gamut of emotions striding back and forth across the room; first shock, then horror, then rage against the man and his team who were paid to keep her safe but had failed so spectacularly. After he had let them know exactly what he thought of that, there was only a terrified father left.

Kane could have dealt with all but that last.

"Is there a ransom demand?" Stonewall croaked out the question without any of his usual commanding presence.

"Not yet."

"Isn't that unusual?" The fact that he seemed to have some understanding about these matters didn't surprise Kane in the least. To be the head of a successful movie studio, he would have had been briefed about such matters, not least in case any staff were taken while a production was in progress. He probably never imaged this happening to one of his loved ones, however.

"It depends on the type of kidnapping and where it has taken place. In high-risk areas of the world, kidnappings are almost conducted as a business with the ransom taken care of by K&R insurance. In our case, I would expect a demand to come through within a few hours."

"Why?" Mandy asked. Her voice had none of her usual animation and verve. Her skin was pasty beneath the glamorous makeup.

"Firstly, to confirm that she has indeed been kidnapped, that she hasn't just gone off on her own accord. Second, to induce fear and impress the need for the ransom to be paid — and quickly. Third, the longer the kidnapper has to hold onto the victim, the likelier they are to be discovered."

He answered automatically, an info-dump that he tried to distance himself from. He certainly couldn't keep picturing Lexi as the terrified victim he spoke of — not if he wanted to be of any use to her.

"Whatever they want, we'll pay it." Mandy said, looking to her husband for confirmation.

He nodded.

"Have the police been informed?"

"My man is on it now."

"Good. We need all the help we can get." This wasn't directed at him, though Kane still flinched. There was no one who could blame him as much as he already blamed himself.

"I need to stop the party, question the guests." He needed the place on lockdown while both they and the LAPD investigated the property.

Stonewall joined his wife on the sofa, wrapping her in

his bear-like arms. She sank into him, fragile as a leaf, shoulders shaking with grief.

There was nothing more he could say to them. Nothing his presence would do other than to cause further misery.

"Come, Bud."

They left the Rockefellers to their despair as his own threatened to overwhelm him.

24

Lexi woke to find her head thumping and a tight pressure around her neck that swallowing did nothing to assuage.

Something coarse and thin scratched at her face, making her itch, and there was another thing covering both her head and mouth.

Her mind was foggy, as if she'd woken up after several days of sleeping. She felt disoriented and out of sorts. Her dry lips protested at whatever it was that covered them so tightly. Her body was deeply uncomfortable on the hard wooden chair that she sat on.

Why would she fall asleep on a wooden chair and not her bed or even the chaise lounge?

She reached up to examine her neck, but found that she couldn't move. Her hands were caught on something. She tried to move them again. No... they weren't caught. They were tied.

Cable-tied to the back of the chair.

She gasped as her tongue felt the fabric that was tied tightly around her mouth, muffling any sound she might make. She came abruptly awake, mind no longer foggy as the cold realization hit like a bucket of ice-water and she found herself remembering everything.

He must have taken her after she'd blacked out!

The itch around her face intensified as panic built. Unable to scratch at it, she shook her head and the thing that was around it fell off.

The wig.

She had forgotten about it, but everything came crashing back now, sending a chill that spread its iciness down her body until she could feel it even in her bare toes.

Focus Lexi!

Where are you? If she could figure out where she was, maybe she'd be able to find a way to escape.

The room was dark with the only light coming from the green display of a cheap digital clock. Pictures were stuck all over the walls, ghost-like faces who appeared just out of focus, yet something about them seemed strangely familiar. A chill pervaded the air of the sort that might come from an outbuilding. Beneath her feet, the floor was concrete.

Possibly a basement?

She blinked, trying to get her eyes to see better in the dim half-light. Focusing on the wall of pictures, she tried to make sense of them, instinctively knowing that they were important to her plight. It took a few seconds, but the features of one finally became clear.

The dimples on the cheeks, the elegant nose that was identical to her famous mom's...

She drew in a horrified breath.

The faces plastered on the wall were all hers — except they were all crossed out with a thick red marker.

Fear blasted through her chest, leaving her shaken.

This wasn't just a game or even a normal kidnapping. Her kidnapper was a disturbed individual who held a deep hatred for her.

And she was bound to his every whim.

She had to get away, call for help.

By now, the alarm must have been raised. Her eyes darted to the clock again — almost eight in the evening. Stella would have finished her performance just before seven. The auction was to start right after — and Lexi was supposed to have announced it. So, she hadn't been missing for more than an hour.

A glimmer of hope sparked inside.

She hadn't been taken across state lines or even that far from home. Surely they'd be able to find her?

She wasn't willing to wait.

What could she do to help herself?

Tugging against her restraints, she pulled until her wrists were cut and bleeding, but the cable-ties held firm. She'd only do more damage by continuing to strain against them.

Well, if she couldn't break the ties, maybe she could break the chair?

Thankfully, he'd left her legs untied, so it wasn't too difficult to get onto her feet. The cold floor turned her feet numb. Hobbling at an awkward bent angle, she found where the closest wall was. What she could feel of it was as cold as the ground and made of concrete too.

God, was she in an underground bunker of some sort?

The thought of that brought a new surge of panic. If she was underground, what chance did she have of getting out and anyone finding her?

She gave herself a mental shake.

There was no point in jumping to worst-case scenarios. She needed her wits about her. She couldn't afford to lose it now.

Steeling herself, she moved a foot or so away from the wall. Taking a deep breath, she threw herself at it, tucking her fingers in as much as she could to protect them. The chair hit the wall, sending a judder of pain arcing through her. She gasped, tears stinging her eyes.

She sat back down to catch her breath and had to let the waves of pain subside. Shifting around on the seat, she used her weight to test for any sign of weakness.

But the chair held firm.

Once the pain had lessened to a tolerable rate, she tried again, throwing herself at the wall harder this time. The pain that hit was ten times worse than the first, but the chair made a cracking sound.

When she sat back on it there was a definite wobble that hadn't been there before. She tossed her weight from side to side, working away at the chair until it gave a final crack and the seat came away from the back.

Her hands were still tied to a piece of the backing, but at least she was free now. She bent over, bringing her bound hands forward as she stepped backward through the hoop of her arms, mentally thanking the yoga classes her mom had insisted she take since she was young that had given her enough flexibility to do so.

Tugging off the towel he had tied around her mouth, she opened her mouth to call for help but stopped herself just in time.

If she was in a basement of some sort, *he* might hear her cries and all this effort would be for nothing.

She couldn't cry out for help, no matter how much she wanted to. Her best chance of getting out of there was by being smart, by learning what she could about her surroundings.

She strained her ears, listening for any sounds.

Only silence greeted her. She couldn't even hear traffic or anything else that would give her a clue as to where she was.

She needed to get out and flag down help.

Letting the glow of the clock guide her, she worked her way from one wall to another, feeling for a way out. Progress was achingly slow until she came to a wooden door. Reaching down, she scrambled for the door handle and grabbed hold of it just as it turned in her hand!

The door flew open as fresh night air rushed in. Bright light from a flashlight blinded her. She raised her bound hands, trying to block it from her eyes as a smile of relief came over her.

"Oh Thank God! Help me, I've been kidnapped..."

The flashlight lowered until she could see the face of her rescuer.

Except it wasn't someone who would help her at all. The smile died on her face.

"Shut up!" her kidnapper demanded, swinging the flashlight at her head.

For the second time that night, the world faded into nothing.

25

The guests were being questioned and released though some who were close friends of the family and seemed genuinely concerned, remained. Huddled around Stonewall and Mandy in one of the family's many lounges, they offered what comfort they could at a time like this.

Kane had struggled with the idea of making Lexi's abduction popular knowledge, worried it could endanger her life, but after consultation with the LAPD, it was decided the best course of action.

She was a celebrity whose face had recently hit the tabloids. While she was still so much in the public eye, they should capitalize on her notoriety making life diffi-cult for the kidnapper and hopefully increasing the pres-sure to release her.

The other alternative he couldn't think about.

He was almost certain they were dealing with a one or two-man band. This entire thing was messy, but he was beginning to think that possibly the kidnapper had an accomplice in the house. It would certainly explain his ability to enter the home on more than one occasion, and the knowledge of their cameras.

But who could it be?

If he could only answer that, he'd be on the fast track to finding her.

Officers from the LAPD flooded the Rockefellers' home, investigating the crime scene, questioning witnesses and staff. Forensics had arrived and were sweeping her room as well as the rest of the property for prints and whatever other evidence they might deem useful.

Kane had just gone through his own interrogation, though he knew there would be more questions coming later.

The cop heading up the case, Detective Summers a mixed-race man with a calm almost friendly presence yet incredibly sharp eyes that didn't miss a thing seemed satisfied with his take on proceedings. He peered over the top of his leather-bound notebook, pen poised.

"Is there anything else you'd like to tell me, anything at all that might help us locate her?"

"I've given you everything I know."

Perhaps not everything.

He hadn't spilled the beans yet about his own relationship with Lexi.

He went over this in his mind, again and again, torn between telling the truth yet knowing it would only call his own motives into question.

He wasn't afraid of that, even if it meant being under

suspicion, but it wouldn't do Lexi any good if he was detained in a room under hours of questioning.

Knowing he needed the freedom to continue his own search for her, he omitted the fact from his statement. Of his men, only Johnny had an inkling that there might be more to his relationship with Lexi, but he would never betray his trust, not unless he thought Kane was guilty of causing her harm.

Summers scrutinized him with an open stare that seemed to convey he didn't believe him. Kane had to thank his years of training for being able to stand beneath the man's gaze and not give himself away.

After an uncomfortably long time, Summers snapped his notebook shut.

"If you think of anything, let me or any of my people know. No matter how small. Let us be the ones to determine how useful the information is."

"Of course."

"I guess we're done for now, Mr. Turner. But keep close, I might have more questions for you later."

"I'll be right here or in the security office. You can also reach me on the radio. I'm on channel eight."

Summers started away, attention already drawn to someone else as Kane let out a small sigh of relief.

He stood outside Lexi's bedroom, having an out-of-body experience as uniforms invaded every inch of that privacy she so cherished. With every drawer that was opened, every rifling of her wardrobes and tug down of the comforter on her bed, he flinched.

It was their job to do this, but somehow if felt as if

they were violating her. It took every inch of his willpower not to run in and demand that they leave.

He felt a warm breath on his wrist, followed by a nudge of his hand and the top of a silky head. Even Bud's presence couldn't lessen the empty hollow inside. He paced the hallway, Bud matching him step for step, mind going through the clues they had uncovered to date in the hope that something would pop out.

Their perp had come to the property three times that he'd known of.

Once, he'd stayed on the other side of the fence to take those photographs, and another with climbing gear, fully intending to cross inside... but why? Had he been hoping to take Lexi then?

No. Even if he had made it all the way to her room, how did he expect her to get over the fence? The idea was clumsy and unattainable.

He scrapped the thought.

What about the day he'd followed them to Verve, the coffee bar? He'd clearly had his camera then but no new pictures had been sent to the press. Had he been hoping to abduct her in broad daylight?

That seemed even more unlikely than taking her from home in the early hours of the night.

Then of course, there was tonight. With their added security measures, how had he waltzed inside as if he belonged here.

Unless, of course, he was known to them.

He was leaning more and more to that theory. But who could have done this? Stan had gotten back to him with the staff list — and it all checked out: all the people who were supposed to be here *were* still here.

No one had left.

Round and round his thoughts went, none of them able to reach a satisfactory resolution.

What was he missing?

There had to be something here, something so obvious that he'd not paid attention to it.

"Sir, I'm going to need you to leave," came a voice that interrupted his thoughts. One of the uniforms, a twitchy bean-pole thin man announced with an imperious tone. "This is an active crime scene."

"I've got clearance to be here," Kane began fishing for his ID. The cop didn't care to look at the badge he offered him, staring down his long nose at him instead.

"That's news to me. You need to leave, right now."

"I run the security in this house."

The cop gave him a look that clearly showed what he thought of *that*. He didn't like Kane's tone or that he wouldn't do as he was told.

"Perhaps, you'd like to look for another line of work, all things considered."

He might have had a foot over him, but Kane must have weighed fifty pounds more. He could knock out the fool without even trying. Subconsciously, his hands formed into fists when he caught a glimpse of Bud, who seemed fixated by something.

Not wanting to alert the cop, Kane shrugged, allowing his face to twist into apology. "You're right. I'll get out of your way. Let me get my dog."

Content that he had won the moment, the cop left him to it.

Hurrying to Bud's side, he saw what had captured his attention: round and red and half hidden beside a plant pot where it had been dumped. It was a soda can. Some of the dark, sugary drink had spilled out onto the white pebbles covering the soil, leaving a sticky stain.

The white lettering on the can said it was Cheerwine.

He tensed, a jolt of recognition shooting through him: he had seen this can before.

Finding a quiet corner away from any cops, he made a call to the lab he had used, got through to the tech who had lifted the prints of the soda can found on the property previously. After a quick greeting, he jumped right into it.

"I forgot to ask before, did you manage to get a look a what brand of drink that can was? It was so crushed that I couldn't make out what it was."

"One sec. I can't remember off the top of my head. It wasn't something I've seen before."

The tech tapped away on a keyboard, recalling the information.

"Here it is. Once we'd straightened it out, some of the lettering was gone, but we were able to match it to a brand called Cheerwine. It's some sort of cherry soda manufactured regionally."

"Where from?" Kane held his breath.

More tapping came down the line.

"North Carolina, looks like."

Kane's breath hissed out of him. "Thanks."

Disconnecting the call, he went to the kitchen where

having been unceremoniously removed from their work stations, Stan, Johnny and other members of his staff congregated around Ruth sipping from drinks she had made for them.

On his arrival, her pale face turned to his. As in the previous times he'd seen her, Bud bounded over and started pawing at her apron. Absently she patted him on the head, but he didn't move from her, choosing to sit by her feet.

"Any news?" She was as concerned as any family member. Reaching for a clean cup, she started to pour a coffee for him.

"Possibly." He set the empty soda can on the marble island his men sat around. "I found this outside Lexi's room."

"Cheerwine?" Stan queried, studying the can. He didn't look as if he was familiar with the brand either.

Ruth waved a hand in the air, dismissing it. "Oh, that's not anything. I keep telling him not to leave his trash around, but it's like talking to a brick wall. I'll get rid of it."

She went to take the can but Kane stopped her. His instincts had been right — and finally, he could now see what Bud had been trying to tell him all along. He needed her to say the words.

"*Who* do you keep telling?"

"My son, Hank. He loves that brand of soda, has since he was a little kid back in South Carolina. He drinks that stuff like it's water, orders it online. I tell him how bad it is for him, but he won't listen."

"He was here tonight?"

She nodded, not picking up on his tone yet. "He helps out occasionally, when I need a pair of extra hands."

"He wasn't on the list of staff?" Kane knew that very well, having checked it recently himself.

Ruth's smile started to fade. "I never put him on it. I mean, he's my son. He just helps me when I need it."

And is granted access to come and go as he pleased.

"Where is Hank now?"

She must have realized it wasn't an idle question. Her eyes turned dark with panic. The coffee pot trembled in her hand.

"Oh no, he won't have anything to do with this. He loves Lexi. He talks about her all the time."

"Where is he Ruth?!"

She blinked up at him unseeingly.

"He left a little while ago to pick up more ice for us. We were running a bit low." Her voice had turned to a whisper.

"When? When was the last time you saw him?" It was crucial for him to establish a timeline.

She looked at the Victorian clock hanging on the wall.

"About an hour ago."

Kane and Stan shared a tense look. "The same time she was first reported as missing."

A haunted look came into Ruth's eyes. The coffee pot dropped onto the island, spilling hot brown liquid onto the marble.

"No. He wouldn't. I know he's not like everyone else, but he wouldn't hurt her. He wouldn't have taken her..."

But Kane knew differently.

"What's his address, Ruth? I need his address!"

She blinked up at him, shell-shocked and shaken.

"He has the house next to mine. I bought it for him so he could have his own space."

By the time she sank into a chair, Kane had already left.

26

R uth wasn't much use after that.

In shock, her body had gone into total shutdown.

Kane hadn't even been able to get her address from her and had to rely on their staff files instead. Even if she had given it, he would have crosschecked it against their database in the unlikely event that she would lie to them to protect her only son.

By the time he'd scribbled down the details, Johnny had brought the car round to the front. They floored it to her house, risking life and limb to tear through the LA traffic.

All he could think about was getting to Lexi.

They screeched up to the simple one-story ranch style home with the neat flowerbed of Dutch tulips.

Johnny wasn't as trained in combat as Kane was so he made him stay by the car though he was still able to help by parking their own car strategically, blocking the white van — the van from the security footage mud covered plates and all — that sat in the drive.

If Hank made it out of the house, at least he wouldn't be able to drive away.

Kane ran next door. Bud stayed close to his side, ears pricked on high alert.

Though this house was identically made to Ruth's home, Hank's was a much less welcoming affair with more weeds than flowers, and the windows looked as if they hadn't been cleaned this side of a century. A pile of empty Cheerwine cans sat in a crate on the porch, ready for recycling.

He peered through the windows, hoping to catch a glimpse of Lexi but what he could see through the grime wasn't very promising. Worn furniture sat around in no particular order as if Hank had no idea what to do with it; a lamp bulb had obviously blown at some point and had been replaced with a new one but the light shade still sat on the dirty carpet beside the sofa gathering dust. Empty chip bags, candy wrappers and more of those Cheerwine cans were dotted all around.

Hank seemed to have the same diet and house-keeping skills as a teenage boy.

He moved to the next window that overlooked a dining room, though it was being used for storage. Opened boxes sat on the scratched mahogany table where packets of Ilford photographic paper spilled out from them. There was a space where one of the dining chairs should have been and marks on the carpet that inferred a chair had been dragged out of there.

Bud bristled by his side, growled a low warning that stopped Kane dead.

Silently padding on his paws, he moved toward the back of the house. Kane followed quietly, hoping to be able to get the jump on Hank.

Through the glass pane in the door, Kane could see a man on the other side. Around five ten, slim, he was slightly hunched over from a deformation of the upper spine that Kane could clearly see from his back view of him. Hank paced the room, clearly agitated.

A small, off-brand TV set — the kind usually given away as part of a promotion — was tuned into the ET channel. Hank kept glancing at it, at the breaking news where Lexi's smiling face stared out at the world.

Guilt covered his face, turning it twitchy, and Kane had no doubt in his mind: this was the man who had taken her.

He pressed the panic button he had retrieved from Lexi's purse.

Although he was confident he could handle the jerk, he wasn't prepared to risk Lexi or even Bud's life. Regardless of whatever happened next, his men would notify the authorities of his location.

He didn't bother to knock. He wasn't the police or FBI, so there was no legal requirement for him to announce himself.

Aiming his shoulder at the frame of the door, he slammed into it, using the full force of his anger and desperation to drive it forward. The weathered door that should have been replaced long ago burst open and almost fell off its hinges from his assault.

Hank spun around to be tackled by two-hundred pounds of one pissed off ex-marine as Bud barked loudly.

He fell to the floor with a thud, screaming. Kane rammed a knee under his neck. Any thought Hank had of fighting back faded with the pressure against his windpipe. His hands clawed at Kane's knee, gasping for the breath that wouldn't come while Bud bared his fangs. Lowering his snout so that he was only inches away from Hank's, he snarled at the man who dared to upset his master.

A whimper slid out of Hank as he tried vainly to move his head away from Bud.

"Where is she?" Kane hissed, about ready to crush the man's life. The rage inside was a furnace that wanted any excuse to extinguish him.

Hank squirmed beneath him, so pale that he looked nothing like the monster Kane had pictured him to be. He cried out pitifully.

"I didn't mean ... to take her... but she was being... difficult! She wanted to... tell... on me!"

That was his defense?

He sounded like a sniveling child.

"I don't care about your excuses. I just need to know where she is! Is she still alive?!"

Shockingly, Hank started to cry. Big, blubbering wails in between shuddering breaths. The idiot was going to give himself an anxiety attack. A desperate growl rumbled from Kane's chest.

"I don't have time for this!"

He yanked Hank onto his feet and shook him until

the other man's teeth rattled. Unexpectantly, Hank's foot flew out, catching him in the groin. Pain exploded in the region, causing Kane to see stars. Reflexively, he shoved Hank away. Hank stumbled back, tripped on his own feet and collided with a wall.

He bounced off the wall only to hit his head on the radiator. He slithered to the ground, eyes rolling into the back of his head. Out to the world.

Kane swore violently under his breath.

"LEXI! It's Kane! Make a noise if you can hear me!"

Nothing.

Fear wrapped its icy fingers around his heart. That tingle, his sixth sense — all of his senses — were alert and screaming at him.

She couldn't be dead...?

No. He would not let himself think that. Shaking away the growing fear that threatened to swallow him whole, he asked for Bud's help.

"Find Lexi. Find her, Boy."

His voice broke on the last word.

Bud licked his hand then, with his nose to the ground, he found her scent and barked. Hope mixed with dread as he followed behind him, silently urging his dog to hurry.

"Johnny!" He yelled out, knowing his man would hear him. "Cover the perp! He's knocked out in the kitchen."

"I'm on it!" Johnny called back.

Bud navigated the hallways through the house until he came to a door that lead to the basement. Kane threw it open to reveal a flight of stairs leading into the dark.

Taking them two at a time, he sprinted down to find himself stopped at yet *another* door.

Two steel bolts were drawn across this door. He could tell they were newly installed by the sawdust still coating the floor, created when Hank had drilled into the door.

Bud barked loudly and alerted, announcing that this was the place. He pawed at the door, eager to get through. Kane slid back the bolts and crashed into the basement.

Darkness greeted him, though he picked up the outline of a still figure slumped on the ground.

Lexi.

His heart about stopped in his chest.

Was she breathing?

He ran toward her, silently praying for a movement from her chest, something that would show that she was alive, but it was next to impossible to see if she was breathing. He took hold of her wrist, feeling for a pulse.

The next few seconds were the longest of his life.

When the pulse came, strong and regular, the breath hissed out of him. Bud couldn't stop licking her face as if he were trying to wake her up.

She was still fully dressed, thank God, although she was no longer in that white dress. She wore jeans and a T-shirt, and there was a cheap-looking wig on the floor beside her. Her feet were bare and there was a nasty looking bump on her head. A chain was wrapped around her ankle and looped over the metal pipes of an old-style gas furnace that must power the radiators upstairs.

Gently, he held her in his arms, cradling her head in case there was any damage he couldn't see.

"Lexi... Lexi. Wake up."

She murmured but didn't come to. He raised his voice, injecting a note of urgency into it.

"Lexi... It's me... Kane. Wake up for me, Sweetheart. Wake up now."

Her eyelids fluttered opened. She gazed up at him in a daze, filled with uncertainty.

"Am I dreaming?"

A smile burst out of him. He covered her with kisses.

"No baby. It's me. You're safe now. I've got you."

Her eyes turned bright with tears, though the smile she gave him could have lit up the darkest night.

"You found me?"

"Of course I did. I found you and I will never let you go again."

To prove he meant it, he claimed her lips with his own.

She welcomed him with her heart and soul, grabbing onto him as if she would never let go. Bud whined with excitement, picking up on their emotions and joining in with his own.

Holding her in his arms, the rest of the world faded away until there was only the three of them.

And, he realized, he had finally found his home.

27

Within the hour, the place was a zoo.

News crews and paparazzi littered the small property and were only held back by the strong presence of police that had since arrived. Stan and a few of his other men had come too, to give whatever backup he might need.

Standing to one side, Ruth was a mess of tears and confusion.

Her usually impeccable self was nowhere to be found. She dabbed at her eyes with a soaked tissue. Her nose, red from crying. In-between sobs, she tried to convince the two cops who were interviewing her of Hank's innocence.

"My son would never hurt Lexi. You must know that. He has social problems, but he isn't a monster. There must be a simple explanation for this."

Wrapped in a blanket, Lexi sat inside an ambulance while staff checked her vitals. She gripped onto Kane's hand, refusing to let go for even a second. Seeming to have understood the situation, Bud stayed glued to her side, perched before her like a brown and black guard dog, intimidating anyone who dared to come her way. Neither one of them would move, not even when requested by the emergency crew.

Once Detective Summers arrived on the scene, he took over the situation. One look at the officious cop and it didn't take long for Hank to blurt out his side of the story to him. Summers put the pieces of it together and explained the sorry tale to them now.

"Hank considered you all an extended family of his," he told Lexi. "He was a constant fixture at the property when he was young, when he and Ruth lived in your guest house. With his lack of social interaction and Ruth's chatty nature, he'd developed unrealistic expectations of how close you all actually were."

Lexi's eyes took on a faraway look as she recalled the past. "I do remember him of course, but he was at least ten years older than me and that seemed like a world of difference when I was a child. We never really spoke other than to say hi. I can't even think if we've ever had a real conversation."

"In his head, you've had plenty. He actually considered the two of you friends," Summers continued.

"Then why did any of this happen? How did he go from thinking they were friends to this?" Kane couldn't quite make the leap.

"A few months ago, a job came up in the house. Ruth had lobbied hard with your parents to give Hank the chance to prove himself to them."

"Right," Lexi confirmed, remembering. "But I told them I wasn't comfortable having him around us all the time."

"Had he done something to you?" Kane was quick to ask, wondering if it was something he should have caught earlier. He could already feel the shame starting to rear its ugly head.

"No. But it was the way he stared at me. I would always catch him watching me in this way that kind of spooked me. I don't know. I just didn't want to have to deal with that in my own home."

"I understand," Summers nodded. "Problem was, I don't think he meant to make you uncomfortable. In fact, he'd long harbored a crush on you."

Lexi fell silent for a moment, trying to picture this fact and how it slotted in with her view of events.

"I had no idea."

"Why would you? He probably came across awkward, maybe even creepy."

She nodded, confirming what he'd so astutely surmised.

"In order to spare both his and Ruth's feelings, they went ahead with the interview process, even though they had no intention of hiring him. Unfortunately, Hank learned the truth of it and in his simple way of thinking, decided to punish you all for your treachery..." Summers trailed off. Knowing where he had been going with it, she finished his sentence.

"But in particular, me."

"Yes."

"So had Ruth not been so desperate to protect her son

from the world, possibly this all could have been avoided?" Kane had to know, even if the truth was a bitter pill to swallow.

He didn't get an answer.

Loud sobbing drew their attention to the entrance of the property. Flanked by two officers, Hank was handcuffed and being led out of his home. His eyes were wild with terror and he seemed utterly aghast at the circus his actions had drawn. He struggled against the two cops who had to drag him toward a waiting squad car when a silver Rolls Royce pulled up.

The black-tinted windows hid its passengers from view, but the crowd still gave a collective gasp at its arrival. A hush descended as they waited for whoever it was to appear. The doors were flung open as first Stonewall then his frantic wife emerged. They gave no attention to the now cheering crowd, their eyes seeking only one cherished face.

When they saw her, they hurried over.

Kane released Lexi's hand, stepping away from her to give the family some respectful space. They embraced her, clinging onto her as if they would never let go.

"My Darling, thank God you are safe!"

Mandy's shoulders heaved with tears. Even Stonewall couldn't hide his.

"I'm fine," Lexi reassured them. "Thanks to Kane and Bud, I'm safe now."

They remained in their protective huddle until each were able to compose themselves.

Looking across at Hank, still struggling against the

police who held him, Stonewall's eyes narrowed into tiny slits. "I'll have him thrown in prison. He'll never see another day free if I have anything to do with it."

Lexi knew he would make good on the threat. Yet, despite how afraid she had been at the time, all she could see now was Ruth's distress — a mother's distress. She looked so frail and broken, her entire world shattering right before her eyes.

She had been through so much already, having lost her husband when her son was so young. She couldn't make her lose her son too, not when she loved the woman like a second mother.

She laid a hand on her father's shoulder.

"No. I don't want that."

Stonewall looked at her as if she wasn't thinking straight. His eyes began roaming her head, looking for signs of an injury the medical crew might have missed.

"He kidnapped you and would have done God knows what if he'd not been stopped."

"But he didn't mean to hurt me, Dad. He's not like us. He has... problems. He doesn't belong in a cell, he needs help. I'm happy to pay for it to make sure he gets the best."

Stonewall looked like he didn't know what had hit him. Kane, however, felt only pride and admiration. After everything she had just been through, not only did she not want revenge... she wanted to help him.

It was like he was suddenly seeing the world through new eyes. All of his previous objections, his excuses to why they couldn't be together, vanished in an instant.

She cared about his background, about as much as he cared for hers. He didn't want her money or fame, and she didn't care about his past or how he constantly relived it.

He had been so hung up on how different their worlds were when all that was important was how similar they were.

Nothing else was as important as the love he felt for her. Finally coming to this realization, a fire was lit beneath his feet.

He had to tell her... right now.

"We'll talk about this later—" Stonewall began, clearly not quite as forgiving or magnanimous as his daughter when Kane took Lexi's hands into his own.

Whatever Stonewall was going to say next died a death on his lips as he stared at the two of them, at his daughter who hadn't pulled away and was in fact, leaning into him with some astonishment and dare he think it... delight. He heard Mandy inhale a breath, but she seemed to have no other response which unnerved him.

"I've been a fool Lexi," Kane said, his eyes only for her. "I've been worried that I'm not good enough, that I'll never be able to provide for you in the manner which you're used to, when all the time, you were trying to tell me that you don't care about all of that."

"I don't," she answered, her heart racing with love for this man who had gone through so much and who had thought that he didn't deserve to have anyone in his life other than his dog. "I only care about you."

His heart swelled by the look in her eyes. His whole

life, whatever was in his future, it all lay with her. Smiling, he moved closer, lowering his head...

Stonewall's reaction was immediate. His expression turned thunderous.

"What in the hell is this now?!" he demanded. Mandy still hadn't responded other than the self-satisfied smile that was on her lips. Surprisingly, she didn't seem at all as outraged as her husband.

Kane wasn't able to hide his own surprise at their coming out, but Lexi just gave a small shrug of her shoulders and a sweet smile that he returned. Puffing up his chest, he stood a little taller and addressed Stonewall.

"I know this might come as a shock — God knows, I wasn't expecting this myself — but Lexi and I, we love each other."

"And we're going to be together," Lexi filled in with a firmness in her voice that held no room for disagreement.

"Like hell you are!" Stonewall cried. "She's my little girl... and you were supposed to be protecting her, not seducing her! I will kill you!" He lunged towards Kane, meaning to make good on his threat. Lexi squealed as Mandy shouted at him to stop. Kane simply stepped aside as Stonewall charged at him. The bigger man missed, stumbling into thin air.

The gathered news crews couldn't hear what the disturbance was about, but they were recording the whole show, broadcasting live to the nation as more of the drama unfolded.

"Mr. Rockefeller, there's no need for that—" Kane began only for Stonewall to go for him again.

He got closer this time, swinging a fist in Kane's direction. Kane's arm blocked the blow as easily as if he were swatting away a fly, which only served to make Stonewall angrier. He went for Kane again when Mandy suddenly called out in a stern and commanding voice that pierced through the madness.

"Oh, stop it, you fool. The man's a trained marine. Calm down and we can discuss this like civilized people."

Stonewall whirled on her. "Civilized? He is working for us! He is *staff*! How can you stand there and let this happen?"

"Because we raised our daughter to make her own decisions and she's usually pretty good at it. Why don't we go home and talk about this?" Mandy's reasonableness only seemed to set him off more.

"Are you forgetting that she was taken on his watch?!" He looked ready to explode.

"I doubt any of us will ever forget that," Mandy responded, seeing the stricken look that came over Kane's face. In that moment, she saw the love he felt for her daughter, and a peacefulness came over her.

"I'm going to destroy you until you've got nothing left!" Stonewall threatened until Lexi couldn't stand any more of it. She ran between the two men, protecting Kane with her own body.

"Stop it! Stop talking about him like we're better than him just because we have money! Anyone can make money, but there aren't many people in the world who has gone through what he has and still be a good person. Kane and I are happy and we are together. You just have to accept it," Lexi cried.

"Or else what?" Stonewall demanded.

"Or I will go away with him and you'll never see me again," Lexi said. Despite her love for Kane, just hearing herself say the words caused her eyes to mist up. She loved her parents and couldn't bear it if they made her choose between them.

Stonewall looked wounded. He'd never expected to hear those words coming from his daughter, but seeing how she meant them, the fight left him. He deflated completely, seeming to shrink several feet smaller.

Mandy rubbed his back with a circular motion and stepped forward.

"You really love our daughter?" she asked Kane.

Kane nodded. "As much as I never expected to, but yes."

Mandy's eyes turned misty of their own. "Well, OK then," she said simply.

Stonewall looked startled by her response. "OK, what?"

"OK, they have our blessing."

"No, they don't!" he began, but Mandy interrupted him.

"Honey, give it up," she said. "It's a lost cause. You only have to look at them to see how they feel about each other. And does it really matter what his job title is? You were only a junior exec earning less than eighty grand when I met you. Of all people, you really can't talk."

And with those words, Stonewall knew he had lost.

The ride home went past in a blur.

All Lexi could feel was the joy in her heart that Kane had put there. His love was filling a wound that she didn't know she'd had and for the first time in her life, she felt part of something special, something that was uniquely hers.

She was back in her bed in her room that had been carefully put back together after the police had turned it upside down. Propped up by a mountain of designer cushions and pillows, Mandy was seemingly taking root on the sofa as Stonewall fielded off calls from the media as well as friends and family. Kane moved around awkwardly, not sure where he should be or what he should do with them both side-eying his every move while Bud lay by Lexi's feet, his head across her ankles.

"Honestly, you don't have to be here. I'm perfectly safe now."

This was directed at her parents, but neither seemed inclined to leave. Mandy gave her a tender smile.

"You can't blame us for wanting to keep you close, Dear. You are our only child after all."

"But your only child needs rest and she's not going to get any with you both hovering around her."

As if to emphasize her point, Stonewall chose the moment to snap down the phone.

"If I see another shot of her on either your website or any printed publications, you'll be hit with a lawsuit so large you won't be able to count the zeroes!"

He hung up the call to Lexi's bemused expression. "What have I missed?"

"Lexi would like us to leave so she can recover,"

Mandy replied smoothly, standing up and brushing invisible lint off the Chanel sundress she wore.

"Of course, we'll all leave you alone." He reached out to Kane, clearly meaning to usher him out.

"Not Kane. I'd like him to stay."

Stonewall bristled. The muscles on his neck bulged as his hands turned to fists. An amused smiled started to appear on Mandy's lips and she had to look down to hide it, not wanting to upset her husband further.

Kane moved to Lexi's side, still awkward, like a colt just learning to walk. He went to sit on the bed, thought better of it and perched on an armchair beside her.

"For how long exactly?" Stonewall spat out the question.

Lexi tilted her head at Kane, a silent question in her eyes.

"I don't know. We haven't exactly had time to discuss any of this."

"I'll stay as long as you want me to," Kane began. "But not here. I don't think there's a house big enough for the two of us." He clearly meant Stonewall.

"But there's plenty of room. Dad will behave, I promise." She sent him a look that spoke volumes of what she'd do to him if he didn't.

"Lexi... Bud and I, we need our own space to retreat to." He left the sentence hanging, but she picked up on his message. Sleeping in someone else's home wouldn't feel safe for him, regardless if he was the one in charge of the security.

"Then I'll move into the trailer with you."

"I'm sorry, did you say 'trailer?'" Stonewall was

looking like he was ready to explode again. "Don't you have a house?"

"No. Never really felt the need for one before."

He might as well have said he was an alien. "This is the man? This is the one you've chosen?!"

Lexi chose to ignore his comment, not wanting to encourage more ranting. Clearly, her father would need a little more time to get used to the idea of the two of them being together.

Kane thought over Lexi's offer but knew it wasn't the right one for her. As much as he loved her, he couldn't see her living in that tiny cramped space.

"Why don't we compromise: I'll move my trailer onto your grounds here. I'll still be close by but with my own space."

Away from Stonewall.

He was too respectful to say it, but they all knew that's what he meant.

Lexi looked at Stonewall, waiting for his take on this. She didn't need his approval, but it would be nice to get it.

"I suppose that will do... for now."

"Come on, Handsome. Let's leave the kids alone." Mandy held out her hand, turning the full wattage of her charm on him.

The second the door closed behind them, Kane jumped onto the bed with such haste that Bud was jolted from his sleep. He barked, tail wagging in surprise at whatever game might be taking place.

"Sorry, Boy, but you'll have to wait. Lexi and I need a moment."

As if he knew exactly what he was saying, Bud chuffed and laid his head back onto his paws.

Alone finally, with the woman he loved safely in his arms, Kane sent a prayer of thanks to the heavens, his soul now complete.

28

————

S IX MONTHS LATER

Waves lapped on the shore, lulling Lexi awake.

She yawned, already smiling and ready for another blessed day with the ones she loved.

Her eyes flicked open to see the old oak beams that supported the ceilings of the house. White curtains billowed from the windows that were always open to welcome the outdoors in. It wasn't only for the ambience either; Lexi had discovered quite by chance that Kane slept a lot better when his subconscious could hear the ocean, when he could feel and breathe in the salty sea air.

The space beside her on the bed was empty but still warm from the heat of Kane's recent body. It was a Saturday morning — their favorite day of the week —

and he was likely off in the kitchen whipping up a feast for them.

That he could cook really well was just one of the many surprises she'd learned since they had bought her dream house on the beach and moved in.

She'd discovered an affinity for decoration while Kane had wowed with his manual skills around the home. He'd fixed up the ancient weatherbeaten shutters, replaced rotten floorboards, and even installed a new shower that they could both fit under at the same time.

Kane still had his trailer, which they'd parked up on the yard outside. In the event that he needed his own space, he could always retreat to his "man cave" though as of yet, he had to do so.

Life had changed in so many ways, though it made more sense now than it had ever did.

After her successful fund-raising on the night she was kidnapped — and perhaps, it was made even more so because of it — she was promoted to full-time staff as PAWS's Head of Fund-raising. She'd quit her studio job in a second, upsetting her father further.

Realizing that his heart wasn't in his job either, Kane had evolved his role within Wilson's company. He didn't work security detail anymore, but he headed up Diamond Security's new K-9 department, training both dogs (and their handlers) with dogs that had been rescued by PAWS, giving them a new lease on life.

Stonewall hadn't gotten used to Lexi moving out of the family home, much less to her living with a man. He was still uncomfortable with their relationship, though he couldn't deny that Kane was the best man for her —

mostly because he could and *would* kill anyone who dared to harm her again.

He took great comfort in that.

He also liked that the two had paid for their new home on their own. In fact, Kane had insisted on not taking any of her parents' money — it was important to him that he could provide for her, something which Stonewall knew only too well, having fought the same battles for his own wife.

Although no man would ever be good enough for his daughter, at least he had gotten over his urge to murder Kane with his own hands.

It was a step in the right direction.

Stretching, Lexi sat up and waited to be bombarded by the welcome party that she knew would be coming.

It happened almost immediately.

Hearing movement from her, a poodle hopped into the room on three legs.

"Morning, Elsa."

Elsa had been one of the shelter's longest residents, having lost one of her legs after she'd been caught in a trap. She was a sweet thing who adored Lexi and thought getting to greet her in the morning was the best thing ever.

Elsa was usually a little dirty — she could never stop diving into the ocean, then rolling around on the sand after — but this morning her fur was pristine. And there was a cute pink bow clipped onto her head.

"Who's an even prettier girl this morning?"

Elsa barked, she was!

There was movement by the door as another dog

came in, a mongrel who looked to be a mix between a shepherd and a corgi. Bagel — so named because he had been found in a bagel store feasting on their goods — was an old dog with renal failure.

He had such a nice nature despite having led a horrible life to date that Lexi took him home so he could live out the rest of his time with dignity and grace. And Bagel seemed to appreciate this too as he followed the two of them around like a lovesick puppy and cried if he couldn't be with at least one of them at all times.

Bagel padded in slowly, but with all the enthusiasm of a youngster. He wore a blue bow around his neck that he proudly displayed to her.

"What is this you guys?"

They answered her but of course, she didn't actually understand what they were saying.

Bonnie and Clyde, a pair of Chihuahua siblings that had terrible dental problems caused by years of malnutrition, appeared next, yapping with excitement, both newly shampooed and wearing bows too. Lexi giggled, not understanding what was happening but loving it, anyway.

Then Bud came into the room, his eyes bright and happy. He wore the biggest blue bow of all as he pranced over to her lifting each paw carefully, like a show horse. It was clearly practiced and something he took great pride in.

In his mouth, he carried a small Tiffany jewelry box so delicately that his teeth barely touched it.

"Oh." Lexi gasped. Butterflies danced in her stomach as a grin as big as Texas sprang onto her face.

And finally, Kane appeared in the door himself. He was topless, wearing the usual boxers that he slept in with a matching bow to Bud's. In his arms, he held onto the two cats they had also adopted: Spike and Einstein.

Spike was blind while Einstein suffered with Irritable Bowel Syndrome that could only be treated with a specialist diet. They, too, wore those bows.

Seeing all of his loved ones in the one room had set Kane's heart a flutter. Until now, he'd not known what it was to love this deeply.

Lexi opened her mouth to ask him a question, but he shushed her.

"Wait, please. One second. We've been working on this for days."

Setting the cats onto the bed, he turned to the dogs.

"OK. Guys, are you ready? Line up."

Bagel took front position straight away and sat smartly. Elsa quickly followed suit beside him. Bonnie and Clyde however were their usual over-excitable selves and bouncing around. Seeing Kane struggle to herd the two, Bud gently nudged Bonnie into place. He barked, ordering her to sit still. Obediently — she had a thing for Bud — her rump landed on the floor. With the others in position, Clyde followed suit until the five formed a row by the bed.

Lexi clapped her hands together, delighted with the effort but Kane wasn't done.

"Good... now bow."

Bud placed the jewelry box carefully onto the bed then went down first, lowering his head to the floor, stretching out his two front paws in front of him. The others quickly followed, though with nowhere near as much grace.

"Oh my gosh! You guys are amazing!"

Her excitement took the dogs over the edge. Immediately there was chaos as everyone scrambled onto the bed for their morning love fest.

Lexi spoke to Kane over the tops of their heads. "You must have spent so long getting them to do that."

Kane winked at Bud, who was sitting up now, pink tongue hanging out of his mouth.

"I had help."

He reached for the box and flipped it open. Inside sat a platinum diamond ring that took her breath away.

"Lexi, I have never felt this way about anyone before. Before you, I thought that I'd spend my life on my own with just Bud, and I thought I was happy with that. But you showed me what I was missing, and in this short space of time, look at this amazing family we've created."

He gestured at their fur-kids who, picking up on their excitement, could not keep still. Lexi laughed as a cat walked under her chin, rubbing his back along it until his tail tickled her face. Gently, she moved him out of the way, focusing on Kane again in this cherished moment that she wanted to sear into her head.

"You know that I don't come to decisions easily, especially life-altering ones. Hell, I couldn't even commit to where I'd live, but I know that I can't live without you. And Bud has decided that you're stuck with us."

She grinned at him, tilting her head in that adorable manner he loved.

"Bud, huh?"

"Yeah. He told me."

Bud backed him up with a bark, pawing the bed as his butt shook with excitement. He had no idea what was happening, only that it was important.

"So, I guess what we're trying to say is, will you marry me and make me the happiest man alive?"

A dimple appeared, followed by her even bigger smile.

"I can't very well let Bud down now, can I?"

"I was hoping you'd say that."

With a whoop that could be heard clear across the city, Kane swooped her into his arms and proceeded to kiss his fiancée until she forgot everything else in the world but him.

A NOTE FROM THE AUTHOR

If you've got this far then hopefully you've liked this book, maybe even loved it (yay!) in which case can you please take a few minutes to review this book and the series?

I'm an indie author which means I write on my little computer from my little rental home (London is expensive, y'all).

The websites, paperbacks, advertising, even the book covers... everything is done by me so if you love my books and would like to see me become successful as an indie author, and you know, maybe finally be able to have my own happily ever after by bringing my fella to the UK or by joining him in the US (we've been in a long distance relationship for six years now!), please help by leaving your reviews.

The more people that know about my books, the better they will do and the more time I will have to write you more books!

— Joanne

UNTIL THE SEA RUNS DRY
Silver Screen Secrets 2

*When she washes up with no memory of who she is, the last
thing she imagined was that she'd end up living with her
rescuer - a famous movie star - and his adorable puppy. But
someone out there knows her real identity and the more she
remembers of her past, the more her new life, and love, are in
danger...*

When no one comes forward to claim her, the now
named Jane Smith finds herself living in a dream house
with Logan Steel, the elusive movie star who saved her -
but it isn't the fairy tale the world thinks it is.

After his last few movies bombed due to his wildly
reported bad behavior and messy love life, Logan is
having a hell of a time trying to stay at the top. His
handlers give him an ultimatum: no more scandal and

absolutely no more women. So, the last thing he needs is another one to muddy the waters, but Jane reminds him of the one person in his life he has loved, and if he doesn't help her, no one else will.

Against his team's wishes, Logan takes Jane into his home, but from there, things only get messier. In a bid to make him more likable to the public again, his publicist has given him a puppy for all those candid photoshoots she'll be setting up, but Logan can barely cope with the dog - how on earth is he supposed to look after Jane too, without getting too close?

When an unfortunate incident threatens Logan's very livelihood, the only way to fix the damage is by contracting Jane as his new girlfriend. In the whirlwind of staged dates and events that follow, despite Jane not knowing who she is, she starts falling for him.

But can Logan really love an ordinary woman? And who is the sinister man who haunts her dreams?

Just when it seems they might survive their differences, Jane's past comes crashing into their lives, threatening to kill their happily ever after.

Forever.

Heat level: a hint of steam - nothing graphic.

This book also covers billionaire and rags-to-riches themes and contains a few scenes with violence, though nothing gratuitous.

This is a standalone book with no cliffhangers, though you'll get the best experience by reading the series in order!

Read the first chapters for free —>

CHAPTER 1

The sun shone, warming the bare shoulders of the woman as she wound the car down the familiar twisting lakeside road.

Gulls soared overhead as waves crashed against the surf below, a sound she had never heard as a child, but now fell asleep to every night.

It was a blessing, she knew, to live in this gorgeous place, with the means she now had — it was such a far cry from her humble upbringing in Oklahoma — but God seemed to give with one hand and take with the other.

It had been this way her entire life.

At just eighteen-years-old, she had known that there was more to life than what her sleepy hometown of Newcastle and devout Catholic parents could offer her.

Despite doing everything in her power to win their love, from attending church every Sunday, to the straight A's and saving her virginity until marriage, it seemed she could never please them.

It was only when she had overheard a passing conversation that she came to realize her parents had never wanted children and her presence in the world was an accident.

It would have been too shameful to have given their child away, and anything else was unthinkable. So, they kept and raised her, though she never experienced the love and warmth that was so prevalent among her friends and neighbors.

Her childhood was filled with isolation and indifference.

Though her parents were never horrible to her, she grew up questioning her value, and couldn't wait to leave this life — and town — behind.

When the job had come up to work in hospitality on a cruise ship, she had jumped at the chance. She would travel the world and get to experience all that life offered. Somewhere along the way, maybe, she would meet her handsome prince who would sweep her off her feet, and they would live happily ever after, surrounded by their many healthy children.

At least she had managed to accomplish one of those things.

Though the temperature in the car soared from the California heat, causing sweat to gather at the base of her neck, the woman kept the top of her sports car up and the AC off. She wanted nothing more than to feel the cool wind through her newly styled hair, but she couldn't afford to undo all of her stylist's good work, not after it had taken two long hours.

Today was an important day.

For what must have been the twentieth time since she had gotten into the car, the woman glanced at her reflection in the rearview mirror.

Though she would be considered a beauty by any of the people who tossed admiring glances her way, she couldn't see it herself and always reasoned away their reactions. It was the lighting, the angles, the professionals who spent hours getting her whipped into shape.

She stared critically in the mirror, analyzing every aspect of her heart-shaped face.

The plucked eyebrows artfully framed wide eyes that were a sapphire blue in color. Only the faintest dusky pink eyeshadow brushed the corners of the lids. Her lashes were coated in a natural brown mascara — never black — that would be too harsh for her pale coloring. Not for her was the heavy smoke-eye and fake-lash look of celebrities today, which her husband lamented as trashy.

He liked her understated, but classy.

Suitably, her cupid's bow lips were coated in a sheer peach lipstick that hinted at sexuality rather than exaggerated it.

It wasn't only makeup that was kept simple; the only jewelry she wore was a platinum band encrusted with diamonds on her wedding finger that she always found impractical, as the stones loved to catch on things.

There was no engagement ring as she had been young and impatient, too desperate to be whisked away.

Too stupid to have known better.

The traffic light changed to green. Behind her, a horn blared impatiently.

People were always in such a hurry in this city. It was one of the few things she missed from back home, the neighborly manners, strangers smiling at her in the street and saying hello. Out here, only the most ambitious survived: you were either born into the right family, worked extremely hard to make a success of yourself, or you married right.

She bit her lip as the thought flew into her mind that she might have failed on all three accounts.

Stepping on the gas, she turned the steering wheel a little too fast and felt a sharp pain shooting up her left arm.

She probably should have iced it today, but there hadn't been time. Trying not to flinch, she held her car steady as the vehicle behind overtook her Jaguar and sped off into the distance.

It was her fault, she knew, that her arm hurt at all.

She should not have angered him, but she couldn't seem to help herself. Over and over, she would mess up.

Take last night. She had spent several hours cooking one of his favorite meals, a simple lemon chicken and artichoke bake served with sauteed potatoes and steamed asparagus. Technically, it wasn't a difficult dish, but she had still managed to ruin it by leaving the lid on too long, causing the vegetables to turn into a soggy mess.

When he had come home from another hard day at work and sat down at the table to discover yet another meal had been wrecked, he had been rightfully upset.

She knew how stressful it was at work right now. Nothing was going the way it should, yet he was determined to see it through — for her.

Had he not given her everything she had ever wanted? Had she not traveled the world at his expense?

Look at the house they lived in, the designer clothes she wore. He provided everything, yet she couldn't make the effort to cook him a simple meal.

If she had been smarter, she would have apologized, and that would have been that. Instead, she'd tried to make excuses, even when she knew how much Marko hated it when she did.

Everything that had happened after that was on her. He hadn't even meant to twist her arm. If she hadn't tried to get away from him, she wouldn't have been injured.

After he'd calmed down, he'd held her, begging for forgiveness. He wasn't himself. Work was driving him crazy. He promised he'd do better by her, she just had to give him time. Time to get over this hump, and things would return to normal. Maybe they could plan a trip, visit somewhere exotic that they'd never been to?

In the morning she'd woken to a bouquet of beautiful roses, a lavish breakfast in bed, and to find that he'd booked her a day at his favorite spa as an apology.

She hadn't the heart to tell him that, when she was already injured, people working on her body was the last thing she needed.

Brooks was a boutique spa that served a VIP clientele. Only those who had deep pockets or were "someone" were allowed to become a member. She recalled how, the first time she had seen the price tag of its membership, she had choked on her cucumber water. It seemed ridiculous for a spa to not only charge a membership fee at all, but for it to be so exclusive.

But Marko had insisted she join.

She had been letting herself go lately and had put on at least two pounds — all on her hips, if he was to be believed. Needing as much help as she could get, she had reluctantly joined, and was grateful that the four-figure monthly price tag was something he took care of for her.

The day had passed by in a blur of appointments which began with a session in the sauna to clear her pores. This was followed by a seaweed mud wrap, a full body session which would cause any excess water to disappear out of her system. She was hoping she could lose enough liquid that it would get rid of those extra two pounds. To help it along, she had only drunk a protein shake all day.

After the seaweed mud wrap, she had tried their latest facial procedure, which involved hot rocks. She didn't really care for the details, had just let them decide what she needed and went along with it. Sensing that she wasn't one of their more talkative customers, the staff — though courteous — never bothered her with small talk. It was why they knew next to nothing about her other than she was polite and tipped well.

Her final appointment had been with the hairstylist. She didn't need her hair cut as she had a bi-weekly trim, and it had only been a few days since her last, but, wanting everything to be perfect, she had opted for a blowout of her long blonde hair. And since she was already there, she booked a make-up artist to work their magic too.

God knows she could never paint her face the way

they did. How they masked her many imperfections was truly something.

When they were done, the staff had exclaimed over how pretty she was, but she knew that only one person's opinion mattered.

And it wasn't theirs.

Driving towards his office now, she could smell the water as she approached. His office sat along the docks where the city skyline loomed pretty as a picture. She never enjoyed the city more than when she was at this particular dock. Something about the sound of water with that stunning view always calmed her. It made her feel as if she wasn't alone, that she was a part of this great universe.

Although she had always been a terrible swimmer and would never be able to utilize the ocean here, she was still able to enjoy it. Tapping French-manicured nails on the wheel, she glanced at the diamond encrusted Rolex on her wrist and let out a relieved breath.

Good, she had made it with twenty minutes to spare before his office closed.

She hadn't messaged him to tell him she would be coming. Wanting to surprise him for the thoughtful day he had planned, she had booked a reservation at Gino's, a local seafood restaurant he liked. She was going to prove that she too could do better, that the effort wasn't only his.

Killing the engine, she stepped out of the car on the Manolo heels she had bought a few weeks back, but hadn't yet broken in. They pinched at the front, but she gritted her teeth and tried to smile through the pain.

Marko *loved* her in heels. It would all be worth it when he saw her.

She smoothed down the black dress that clung to her body like a second skin. It was by Dior, his favorite designer, and he always complemented her whenever she wore his dresses. This particular one had been a gift for her last birthday.

He had presented it to her in a beautiful black box lined with red tissue paper. He had even bought matching lingerie to go with it. She was lucky he cared so much that he paid such attention to her wardrobe, when most men didn't even know their wife's size.

Locking her car, she shivered as a sudden gust of wind blew deep into her bones.

She glanced at the silk shawl lying in the back of the car, but refrained from reaching for it. She didn't want to spoil the effect by wearing it, even though it was always much colder here due to the proximity to the water.

If all went to plan, she wouldn't be here all that long. Once she was back in the car, she'd be warm again.

She started towards his office, situated in the back of this particular dock. She forced herself not to flinch as she balanced on her heels, wanting to appear calm and serene, hoping that it would rub off onto Marko.

As she turned the sharp corner, her husband's glass cubed office appeared. It was a modern design, sleek with minimalistic furniture, something which she had found at odds with the surroundings. She much preferred architecture that had identity behind it, and this glass modern cube seemed empty and soulless.

She could see straight inside and was surprised to

find that his assistant was already gone for the day: her computer was switched off from its usual screensaver of her two children playing with their spaniel puppy. This was unusual, as he liked to keep her there to close the office.

She passed by her husband's matching Jaguar (his was a blood red while hers, a metallic bronze) so she knew he was still here.

Moored beside the office was her husband's pride and joy, the AMELIA, an eighty-foot luxury yacht with not one, but two, VIP staterooms and a master suite that could rival any found at the nearby Hilton. He loved to spend weekends sailing down the coast where they would meet up with other yachters.

Truthfully, she found it boring, and often wished she could be back on solid ground, but as it was the only thing that seemed to take his mind off the stress of his work, she kept her feelings to herself.

The boat could accommodate up to eight guests overnight in five spacious cabins. Still, it would never be used in this way. While her husband was considered the life and soul of any party, he preferred to keep his colleagues and those he called "friend" at bay, even the fellow boaters — who he never invited onboard — though they would frequently visit theirs.

He didn't like anyone to get too close. He didn't like what they could find out about him if they were to penetrate his carefully orchestrated world.

Continuing to the Amelia, she heard raised voices. Amplified by the water, though the heat level was clear, the actual words that were being said, wasn't.

Standing on the deck of the boat, her husband argued with a shorter, squatter man in a suit, though it wasn't bespoke or half as well made as the ones her husband wore. The pant legs were an inch too short, while the sleeves reached well below his wrists. His well-worn leather shoes were in dire need of a polish.

The man's face was pale beneath several days of growth. His tie was askew, and he was explaining — no, pleading — with her husband about something, hands gesturing emphatically as Marko listened with an almost bored expression, those steely eyes of his fixed on his face.

She was still walking toward them when Marko reached inside his double-breasted jacket, took out a silenced gun and pointed it at the other man.

She froze, her heartbeat slammed through her chest. "No! Don't!"

This time, the man's words were crystal clear, soaring above his own panic and fear. The world slowed to a crawl as she sucked in a breath. Before she could think what to do, her husband pulled the trigger.

There was the tiniest whoosh of sound as the bullet shot out of the gun. Blood spurted from the man's back as the bullet tore through him. The man's eyes flew open in shock before the pain even had a chance to register.

His hands reached up to cover his heart but met only warm, sticky blood. It took a split second for what had just happened to sink in.

By the time he started falling to the ground, he was already dead.

His body hit the floor with a thud and never moved

again. Without any hesitation, her husband nudged his body with his gleaming Gucci shoes, rolling the man out of sight and into the yacht. He pulled out a handkerchief, wiped his fingerprints off the gun, and set it on top of the man's body.

Her initial shock had now turned into a stark, white terror.

She had to get away before her husband looked over and saw her. Holding her breath, desperate not to make any sound, she spun but stumbled on those damn new high heels.

"Honey... What are you doing here?"

Her husband called out to her softly, yet loudly enough that she heard him. She turned back around, willing her feet to run, but they had turned to blocks of ice.

"I... I was coming to surprise you. I finished at the spa and I'm wearing your favorite dress," she replied, unable to form a coherent sentence.

A million warnings screamed inside her mind, but she could only make sense of one of them. Even now, having witnessed Marko murder a man right in front of her, she heard her own voice berating her, telling her how stupid she was. How stupid she was for not running away.

She deserved everything that was going to happen to her.

"Come here," he said deceptively gently.

Though she wanted anything but to go to him, it was as if her feet had a life of their own.

She walked toward him, trembling with every step

until she made it to the boat. Scared out of her mind, she wasn't able to stop the tears that started falling down her face.

He reached out his hand, offering it to her as he had every time she had boarded the boat before.

She took it automatically.

His hand felt cold and heavy as stone as he pulled her up toward him. Seeing her tears, he brushed them away with a fingertip.

When he spoke, his voice was deeply regretful.

"I wish you hadn't seen that."

She swallowed, trying not to recoil at his touch.

"I'll never tell anyone. I can't tell them what I didn't see. No one has to know. Let's just go to dinner. I made reservations at Gino's. They have those clams you like back in stock."

She was babbling, her voice sounded shrill and alien, but she didn't care. As long as she could keep him talking, there was a chance she might get out of this alive.

Her husband studied her silently, his dark eyes boring into her soul. When he didn't respond, she thought maybe things would work out. If they could just go to dinner, she would make a plan to get the hell away from him. She didn't need his love or security.

She only needed her life.

She stared beyond him, hoping desperately for any witnesses that might be able to stop him.

But the dock was as empty as his eyes.

He placed a hand on each of her shoulders. "I wish I could believe that, but we all know how terrible you are at keeping a secret."

And as she started to plead with him, much as the other man had done only seconds before, Marko's hands slid across her shoulders until they reached her neck.

And he squeezed.

Blinded by the pain and gasping for air, she bucked, lashing out. The diamonds on her wedding ring caught him on the cheek, drawing blood, startling him.

She felt the pressure relax from her neck and greedily gulped in a lungful of air...

But then he swung at her with a blow so hard that she dropped to the ground, hitting her head.

And then the world went black.

CHAPTER 2

Warmth on her skin.

That's what she felt. Lying there, in the soft grittiness of the... sand?

She could feel the sun bathe her in its comforting glow. Waves lapped nearby.

She knew she was on a beach. Could smell the salt in the air tickling her nose. She must have fallen asleep while sunbathing.

That must be what it was.

She tried to open her eyes, but they felt like they were glued shut. Her tongue flicked out to lick her lips, only to feel how dry and cracked they were. She grimaced at the feel of them, which was the wrong thing to do as the skin tore.

Her tongue ran over her lip again. Tasted blood.

And then came the thirst.

The horrible, desperate thirst of someone who hadn't drunk in forever, it seemed.

She tried to gather the will to wake, though her body seemed sluggishly slow to respond, when something small and lively crashed into her, and preceded to cover her face with wet, slobbery kisses.

She recognized that strong — and not unpleasant — smell of doggy breath and felt immediately relieved.

She liked dogs. Loved them, in fact. And this little one was super friendly.

Her eyes fluttered opened.

The hazy black spots that clouded her vision took a moment to fade, but when they did, an adorable furry face peered down at her, head cocked cutely to one side in a wide-opened stare.

He had the same features as a German Shepherd, but with salt and pepper patches to go along with the usual black and brown. His eyes were an impossible ice-blue that matched the diamond studded collar around his neck. A small silver name tag hung from the collar with the word 'LOKI.'

He was only a puppy, possibly not more than a few months old, and at the stage where his paws seemed overly large compared to the rest of him.

Her lips curled into a small smile as she tried to ignore the flash of pain that the gesture brought. Loki didn't notice her discomfort, looking down at her adoringly as if they were the best of friends already. His tiny butt shook as he squirmed with happiness at their meeting.

"This is a private beach — didn't you see the sign?"

Not quite as friendly as the dog was the masculine

voice that had come from several feet away. The annoyance was unmistakable, as was the proprietary tone that had come with it.

She didn't recognize his voice, but something about the way he was talking to her was causing her heart to race.

And not in a pleasant way.

She looked past the puppy only to flinch at the sun that beat down on her. She noticed the sky next, so luminous in its brightness that it hurt to look at it.

Raising a hand to shield her eyes, she squinted towards the hazy figure of the man who was fast approaching, as Loki bounced between the two like this was a game.

The man pointed to a sign down the beach, but she couldn't see the words from her position on the ground.

What was so important that he needed her to see it?

She tried to sit up when crushing pain shot through her body. She yelped, sucking in her breath, and froze.

What was wrong with her?

"This is a private beach," came the voice again, this time with less of the annoyance that had preceded it.

She opened her mouth to answer, but the sound that came out was hoarse and unintelligible. She swallowed, but with seemingly no saliva in her mouth, all it did was make her throat feel even more scratched.

"Everything hurts," she finally managed.

As the words left her lips, she recognized how true they were.

The man kneeled down beside her, the sun against

his back making it difficult for her to see his face. All she could see of him were his startling green eyes with golden flecks that gave him a feline flair. He had sandy hair that framed his face in a perfect designer haircut. There was something so mesmerizing about his eyes that she found herself lost in his gaze, but the moment was soon broken as he stared down at her in concern.

He cursed under his breath.

"What happened to you? You're really hurt."

His quick change of mood filled her with an all encompassing fear.

Stomach churning sickeningly, she stared down at herself, at her bare legs, noticing how the short, tight dress she wore barely covered them. Ugly purple bruises covered her legs and there seemed to be hundreds of cuts criss-crossing them. Stunned, all she could do was stare down in horror as the pain from her injuries hit all at once.

The world spun.

Her balance fled, and her muscles turned to jelly.

She would have sank back down if he hadn't caught her. Strong arms held her close to his warm and solid chest as his face finally came into view.

And she found herself losing her breath all over again.

He had a chiseled jaw that framed an angular face which, combined with those eyes, made him seem even more animalistic. There was a magnetism about him that wasn't due only to the broad shoulders and muscular physique that didn't have an inch of fat on it. He hadn't shaved in a while, stubble covering the lower half of his face.

Then there was that sexy smell, like sandalwood mixed with the ocean.

She bit her lip. The pain cut through whatever confusion she was feeling until one emotion pushed through the rest.

Though he was clearly concerned, she couldn't help the flicker of fear she felt.

There was something untouchable about him, something that made him seem a world away even though she was close enough to feel his breath on her skin.

His eyes flicked up and down her body, assessing her wounds. Whatever conclusion he came to must have worried him greatly, as he softened his voice.

"I need to get you some help. What's your name?"

She opened her mouth to reply, but where her name should have been, her mind was a complete blank. She tried to shake the fog that had taken residence in her head. She was in shock. It would come to her in a minute.

But after several moments... there was nothing.

The world began to spin again. The blood pounding through her temple.

"I don't know. I can't remember."

And as she said the words, she knew with a stark, sudden terror that they were true.

She stared up at him, panic turning her blood to ice-water.

"Why can't I remember who I am?"

This is the end of your free preview of UNTIL THE SEA RUNS DRY, Silver Screen Secrets Book 2.

You can get it HERE now!

IF YOU LOVE THRILLERS AND DOGS, READ ON!

What would you do if you found an exceptionally intelligent dog only to discover he had valuable information inside his head that could change mankind forever?

**** Gold Medal Winner of a Readers' Favorite Book Award 2018****

"If you loved Dean Koontz's " Watchers," you're going to love this book." - Kindle Customer

The first time I saw him, I had no idea he had recently escaped from a mysterious lab. That he had been created there. I'd been living on the streets which was tough, but preferable to home. Then one day, I stumbled upon this mangy dog being attacked.

I saved him, but then he saved me, and I realized that Muttface wasn't a normal dog. He was crazy intelligent. I'm talking Mensa levels.

When we sought help from a grieving veterinarian

named Sully, his clinic was attacked and destroyed by mercenaries. So now here we are, the three of us. On the run across the country against a powerful enemy.

Who are they and what do they want with us?

Through the danger, terror, and pain, one thing was becoming clear to me: I have finally found the family I always wanted, and I will do anything to keep them safe...

Even if it means risking my own life.

With over 300 5-star reviews across retailers, Jo Ho's award-winning debut series is an action-packed thrill-ride that readers love, describing it as a "Must-Read" and "Unputdownable".

If you're a fan of heartwarming stories about dogs (and people) in desperate need of family and love, you will love *The Chase Ryder series*.

Read it NOW!

ALSO BY JOANNE HO

ROMANCE

Silver Screen Secrets Series

A heart-warming suspenseful romance series for dog lovers!

If you like Nora Roberts and our four-legged friends, then you will love this series!

Until The Stars Don't Shine, Book 1

Until The Sea Runs Dry, Book 2

Until The Last Leaf Falls, Book 3 (June 2020)

Until All Color Fades Away, Book 4 (Fall 2020)

YOUNG ADULT

The Chase Ryder Series

Read this heart-warming thriller trilogy to learn the story of a mysterious dog who has escaped from a sinister lab, a lonely homeless girl surviving on wits alone, and a grieving veterinarian still haunted by a past that he can't let go of.

Can they keep their new family together while fleeing from the army of a ruthless billionaire? Will they even survive?

Gold Medal Winner of a Readers Favourite International Book Award

Wanted, Book 1

Haunted, Book 2

Hunted, Book 3

Twisted Series

Between her bizarre roommate, standoffish new friends, and overbearing father who's followed her to campus, Marley's first year at Blackville University is off to a rocky start. But when a strange night out leaves her with magical powers, college starts to look a lot more exciting...

What Doesn't Kill You, Book 1

Beware The Signs (Book 2)

See No Evil (Book 3)

The Blood That Binds (Book 4)

When Trouble Comes (Book 5)

Bad Habits (Book 6)

Left Behind (Book 7)

Hell Hath No Fury (Book 8)

In Her Skin (Book 9)

First Date Jitters (Book 10)

Grave Matters (Book 11)

Plus more to come!

Standalone Books

Who is the boy next door? A thrilling mystery that will keep you guessing until the very last page!

The Boy Next Door

See them all including her special discounted boxset deals at:

www.johoscribe.com

ABOUT THE AUTHOR

A champion of complex protagonists, Joanne writes well-crafted, heartwarming suspenseful romance with characters that get under your skin. She writes romance books under Joanne Ho and YA books under Jo Ho - most of her books feature dogs!

A hopeless romantic, Joanne writes stories about lost and lonely people (and dogs!) who are in desperate need of love... even if they themselves don't know it. Weaving compassion, humor, and suspense, Joanne creates worlds filled with characters who will take you on an emotional journey that can be heartbreaking at times, but always end with a happily ever after.

Her debut novel WANTED, Book 1 of the Chase Ryder series - about a genetically engineered dog who has run away from the sinister lab who created him, and the homeless girl who saves him only for the two of them to find themselves on the run across the country against a powerful enemy - won a Gold Medal at the 2018 Readers' Favorite Book Awards.

Joanne lives in London with three adorable cats and hopes to move to the US to be with her fella once they can figure out a way around her MCS (Multiple Chemical Sensitivities), a debilitating condition she has developed over the last few years which has left her mostly house-bound. Unfortunately, it is still not officially recognized in the UK despite the World Health Organisation listing it as a physical disability. There is currently no help for sufferers of MCS in the UK. She writes about this in her newsletters.

Sign up to her mailing list for updates, book release details and offers at www.johoscribe.com

facebook.com/johowriter

bookbub.com/authors/jo-ho

twitter.com/johoscribe

instagram.com/johoscribe

DON'T MISS ANOTHER RELEASE!

SIGN UP

to Joanne's mailing list and be the first to her about her
news, book releases, gifts, competitions, and exclusive
offers at
www.johoscribe.com